Books by L.T. Shade

Single Titles

Under Her Authority

I0658898

Under Her Authority

ISBN # 978-1-78686-119-1

©Copyright L.T. Shade 2017

Cover Art by Posh Gosh ©Copyright 2017

Interior text design by Claire Siemaszkiewicz

Totally Bound Publishing

Published in 2017 by Totally Bound Publishing, Newland House, The Point, Weaver Road, Lincoln, LN6 3QN, United Kingdom.

Home of Erotic Romance

UNDER HER AUTHORITY

L.T. SHADE

Dedication

To my momma, who showed me what a strong and
independent woman looks like.

And to all the boss ladies out there, I admire you
endlessly.

Prologue

How do you grab the attention of a world-renowned millionaire?

With an under-the-breath curse, Rose turned the magazine over, hiding his photograph. She looked across the tarmac to Houston's airport terminal, wondering if someone behind the towering windows could see her face — hopeless, dejected and jailed by thick glass. *Jailed.* It was the most appropriate word she could muster, and it was exactly how she felt. Jailed. Imprisoned.

Royally screwed.

Raising her hand, she flexed her fingers against the warmth-glazed window. The purr of the plane's engine and sunlight caressed her open palm. This was the last time she'd feel the playful Houston sun, because even if her move was only temporary, she couldn't come back *here.*

Not after everything that had happened.

The plane's gigantic engine hummed, and its wings sprawled their full width as it began a steady glide down the runway from IAH. Rose was helpless, unable to do a thing as the freedom she'd spent eight years building was slowly dragged away from her.

'*Take life by the horns.*' That was what her mama had always told her, and that was what Rose had done. She'd broken the stereotypical mold of a Southern belle, and she was damn proud of herself for it. At nineteen, she'd graduated *summa cum laude* from Duke University. A year later, she'd moved to Austin to get her MBA from the University of Texas. Rose had become the youngest marketing manager at her firm, heading a team of six of Texas's most talented associates. She'd been engaged to the hottest cowboy in the Lone Star State and had a dream house on ten acres of pesticide-free land with a farm and horse ranch. Rose had had everything, except a bra that could double as two cereal bowls, hair redder than the devil's ass and legs a mile long.

She tugged her phone from her lap and began scrolling through the text messages she had neglected to read, if only for the fact that she'd never been one for saying goodbye, stopping when she caught Simon's name. The missing letters of his contact information that used to spell out *Simon My Future Hubby* were stark reminders of her new, single reality. It was just *Simon* now.

Tapping once, Rose opened the message thread.

There he was — *her* Prince Charming — locking lips with the supermodel lookalike, her co-worker Jessica Mayfield, the one with the legs and the hair and everything she'd never thought she needed to get his attention.

She clenched her fingers around the washed-out leather arm of her seat, muscles coiling with ice. Her head was spinning, the stale air mimicking the tightness in her throat as the plane shot forward and up. She thought if she viewed the picture often, the pain would ease and she'd come to accept her ex-fiancé's infidelity. So, she opened the picture at sixty-minute intervals, had been opening it for the past two months, like some sick form of conditioning.

The pain didn't get any better.

Sometimes it seemed worse.

Sometimes she'd go to breathe and her chest would physically ache from the inhale, as if her body was rejecting air that wasn't filled with his musky cologne or his contagious laugh.

Simon's cowboy hat was nestled on a crown of red, his calloused hands scrunched on the backside of Jessica's cropped blue-jean shorts. The photograph had everything Rose had always dreamed of — desire, intensity, *need.*

Furious wouldn't come close to describing how she felt. Five years in a relationship and she'd been traded in for a woman who looked like the reincarnation of sex.

Talk about a kick in the ass.

The couple leaning on the back of his rusty Ford pickup locked in a passionate display of intimacy looked like a cover photo for some sexy book about the Wild West. A wisp of jealousy fluttered through her chest as she imagined him murmuring to Jessica in his rugged Texas accent the types of sinful endearments Rose had only read about in erotic novels.

If she had any weakness, it was hearing the slow stirs of Southern twang slip past the charming grin of a low-pants-wearing, truck-driving, whiskey-chugging country boy.

Tension rained down her shoulders as she formulated the image in her head of a faceless man with a body like sin and an accent the exact way she liked her sex — rough, deep and drawn-out. Yeah, the last time Rose and Simon had had sex — over a year ago and her vagina was shriveled up from underuse *to this day* — he'd tried to feed her some dirty talk and, though she was never one to stop a man from spewing his white-hot desire, his declarations were an automatic mood killer. It was just so *unlike* him.

Never in his life had Simon spoken a dirty word to her, and all of a sudden, he'd been all *'fuck yes,' 'suck my dick,' 'pussy this'* and *'pussy that'*. In retrospect, she should've known something was wrong, but instead, she had stalled, telling herself that everything would fall into place.

If Simon accidentally slipping and falling penis-first inside a redhead's vagina counted as everything falling into place, Rose supposed she had been right. Not surprising. She usually was.

She thought she'd found her happily ever after, that she could stop worrying about success, success, success. She'd finally made up for the failures of her past. No more nightmares.

Rose had gotten her Prince Charming and her tower and she had been on her way to a promotion that would've given her the experience to pursue the position of her dreams as a chief marketing officer.

The perfect life.

Her five-year plan executed to precision.

Now she was wondering if happily ever after really existed.

She blamed the fairy tales she'd watched as a child. Those movies needed to come with a serious warning label, like cigarettes, but instead of *'General warning – this may cause cancer'* it would say something like *'Single lady warning – this may cause unrealistic expectations that could lead to divorce or your fiancé screwing your co-worker on your Egyptian cotton sheets'.*

She blew out a heavy breath that roused her bangs. Over a year ago, the greetings she and her fiancé had shared after coming home from a long day at work had turned into the echoing silence of an empty two-story house. She'd never cared to ask why he'd stayed at the range so late and left the house before the sun had broken through the horizon the next morning. It had taken two months to come to terms with what Simon had said as he'd handed over his twenty-four-karat gold band, which Rose had pawned for a measly hundred bucks, and she'd returned the Tiffany's engagement ring he had bought her three months prior.

'You're in love with your job. Not me.'

She had never been able to tell Simon the truth he'd come to see after years of shared lunch breaks and accompanying her to her seasonal work banquets. Her job was challenging, where he wasn't. It was an exciting contrast to his unbreakable routine. It offered Rose opportunity and growth for a family and community, where Simon had been more content being just two.

At the end of the day, no matter how much Rose wanted to curse him and call him names so dirty it'd make her momma want to wash out her mouth with soap, she couldn't hold his infidelity against him. If anything, she was more envious than betrayed.

Blinking to clear her eyes, the blurry image of her fiancé – *ex-fiancé* – came into view.

Rose *wanted* the passion motivating Simon and Jessica's kiss—passion that'd make her skin feel like fire and her insides liquid. But even when his attention had been narrowed in her direction, she'd never experienced the type of love emitting from the five-inch display.

Maybe that's what upset her most.

Simon had been a happily ever after in disguise.

During the darkest hours of the night, the bad dreams came back. They clawed at her subconscious, keeping her awake. A sliver of cold rose up her spine when she remembered how often. Wetness splashed against her phone screen as guilt and stubbornness clashed inside her. When she had tried to tell him about her nightmares, her throat had closed. All the oxygen had been sucked out of her lungs. She'd never been comfortable enough to share her deepest wounds.

Hell, her relationship had been a one-way ticket to Doomsland from the start.

"Ma'am. You'll have to power your phone off or put it on airplane mode."

Turning toward the gentle voice, Rose went hot with embarrassment.

She looked like a crazy woman, no doubt—eyes red-rimmed and wet, cheeks puffy, flushed. *Christ.* The last thing she needed to do was have a mental breakdown on a plane.

Unless…free liquor ensued?

"Sorry." Rose cleared her throat and switched off her phone. Before she could resume her work, Rose asked the stewardess, "Can I get a vodka on the rocks, please?" She lightly touched her throat. Her voice was scratchy with emotion. If she was going to keep up with these depressing thoughts, she at least needed a drink. She was a workaholic, not a masochist.

The woman's brown curls bounced as she nodded. "Right away."

Stowing away her cell phone, Rose exhaled. Her eardrums

tightened at the high altitude, and she pulled at her earlobes, shifting her jaw in an attempt to pop them, then settling back on the uncomfortable headrest. She pushed her fingers against her eyelids, hoping to massage away the tears that had been stuck there for months.

Overhead, the speaker blared. A North Carolina accent announced the Charlotte weather and the expected arrival time. Two p.m. EST.

After being rejected for jobs from Connecticut to California, she'd managed to land a position as the marketing director for a digital agency in the heart of Charlotte.

Having such a distinguished title like Marketing Director would normally be considered another check off her five-year plan, except the digital agency she was now the employee of was a start-up. Rose shuddered. Where was the stewardess with that liquor? She needed it in hand, pronto.

The term *start-up* was enough to give Rose shivers.

The issue with working for a start-up and why Rose didn't want to, was that most of them would hire college grads for management positions to cut their costs. Like her relationship with Simon, start-ups had a five-year life expectancy.

Lambda was on its third year, and, though it had been successful thus far, consumers were fickle and markets ever-changing. Still, what other choice did she have?

After the scene she'd made in Texas, no one had wanted to hire her.

Even *she* had been surprised when she'd gotten a call back from the office manager at Lambda—her only one—so, with a smile that had been as much hesitance as it had been unease, Rose had taken the pay cut and the sucker punch to her résumé and had gotten on the first flight to Charlotte.

In theory, becoming a marketing director, visiting her hometown after years and getting to see her family again sounded perfect.

Nodding a thank you to the stewardess, Rose took the

glass of vodka and placed it on the tray in front of her. Coolness spread below her fingertips as she traced its edge. To save herself from the sympathetic glances of her family, she hadn't told them her engagement with Simon was over, and she didn't know if she wanted to.

She'd barely gotten out of North Carolina's clutches the first time.

If they found out she'd lost her fiancé *and* her job, they might not let her leave a second, and that just wasn't an option.

She'd made a promise to herself to never move back to that place—the origin of her nightmares—but, then again, Simon had made a promise to fight for her.

How much are promises worth?

Brushing the moisture from her chin—tears she hadn't known were there until they'd hit her chest—she couldn't believe she was wasting her time crying when she *should* be focusing on Matthew Moreno, multimillionaire and president of Moreno & Blu Associates, the biggest event-planning business in the game. Philanthropist. The nation's most prominent advocate of LGBTQI.

Person of the Year—literally. Flipping through *TIME* magazine, Rose reviewed his profile again. She could smell his wealth through the gloss-coated pages, feel his regal authority. Never before had a man intimidated her, but she swallowed and her palms misted over with sweat as she absorbed his steely image. Enigmatic gray eyes above a pointed, attractive nose made for powerful features.

Determined to memorize each detail, she continued her study.

Mr. Moreno didn't know it yet, but he was going to save her career. For the first time in a decade, Moreno & Blu Associates was on the lookout for a new agency to represent their digital efforts—marketing campaigns, site optimization and content creation. A stunning opportunity for firms throughout the nation, this was the golden ticket. *Her* golden ticket. Again, Rose asked herself the all-important question.

How would she grab the attention of a world-renowned millionaire?

She smacked into a blank wall. A brick wall.

Rose had no clue.

Frustration formed behind her eyes in an ache she would need to get used to if things continued as they were. She had to think. Rose needed to formulate a plan to get to Matthew Moreno, to get her life back on track. No matter what, she had to fix this. For the sake of her career, her reputation…to make the nightmares go away.

But first—she tossed her head back and winced as the stinging liquid splashed her dry throat and came to settle low in her belly—Rose needed to get laid.

Chapter One

The scent of lemon oil that had been perpetually scrubbed into the wooden fixtures and peach cobbler so sweet cavities were forming in the back of Rose's mouth already, invaded her senses even before she could fully open the creaky screen door.

Her grandma's house, so old that it had its own soul and nestled in the dense woods fifty miles outside of Charlotte, had always smelled the same. Or it could have been that Rose's grandma had cooked her favorite dessert and got up from her rocking chair long enough to wipe down the wood only on those seldom occasions Rose came to visit.

The corners of her eyes beaded with tears as she took in the den's familiar layout.

Home.

She rejected the thought immediately. North Carolina had stopped being her home a long time ago. But, even as she resolved to this, Rose explored the den with a warm sense of nostalgia. Raising her nose toward the kitchen, she hunted for the source of the tooth-aching smell of baked peaches. Nobody made peach cobbler like her grandma.

"Well, I'll be! Is that little ole Rosemary I see?"

Rose half-grinned when her Aunt Helen came into view, throwing her arms out and shaking her bosom as if it were the 1990s and she was back on a late-night Las Vegas stage. She puckered her lips against Rose's cheek, encasing her in a smothering embrace.

For the briefest moment, Rose reverted to a little girl again, her cheeks burning the same shade as her auntie's cherry-painted mouth at the unwanted attention.

"Hey, Helen," she wheezed. It was hard to breathe when a pair of watermelon breasts were crushing her lungs. *Oh, Christ. Isn't this bad for them? What if they pop?*

A hint of laughter bubbled up Rose's throat as she imagined her auntie's boobies deflating like tires blown out. A consequence of moving back home, the friendly, if not a little unnecessary, reception would be practice for what was to come. Not bones crushed by bags of silicone, Rose *hoped* that wasn't in her future, but hugging, lots of hugging. Too acquainted with Houston's mind-your-own mentality, Rose preferred it over North Carolina's boisterous hospitality, so she was thankful when Helen loosened her arms.

"Oh, bless my heart! The last time I saw you, Rosey, you were about knee-high." Catching Rose's cheeks in a pinch, Helen squealed. "Aren't you as pretty as a peach?"

She nodded her reply, watching with horror as the room flooded with family members she'd not seen in forever, some whose names she didn't recall.

* * * *

Later that day, Rose sat on her grandma's back porch, taking in the outdoors. She was drunk on sweet tea, cobbler and compliments of how she'd changed into an attractive young woman.

The crickets, making their music, had her recalling the time she'd gone camping with Simon. Then Rose remembered why she was in Ellenboro to begin with. Her ego, ballooned from her family's praise, deflated. The reality check smacked into her. The scenic mountains changed from majestic to foreboding. The sky, spotted with fall colors like melted crayons, wasn't magnificent but melancholy. A leaf spinning loose from its dying branch was the same vibrant hue as the hair Simon had tangled his fingers in the day she came back early from her business trip to surprise him.

"How you figure Simon's gonna like being all by himself in that big ole house?"

Rose craned her neck. Her momma's arms were folded in their I-got-something-serious-to-say manner. This talk had been bound to come sooner or later. Her momma's favor of Simon was no secret. Rose sat up, wishing her sweet iced tea would evolve into something with a little more kick because her gut was churning with the kind of nervousness she couldn't will away. Rose despised lying to her family, especially her momma. The woman had a built-in lie detector that sniffed out untruths better than police dogs uncovered hidden drugs.

"Simon and I talked." Rose looked off into the woods, unable to face her mom as she spun the fabrication she'd practiced on the plane ride. "He'll be all right. He knows my move is temporary. This directorship is good for my career."

"Rosemary Louise Berkowitz."

She cringed, smart enough to know full names meant trouble.

"Why do I get the feeling that you're hiding something from me?"

"I think that's the peach cobbler you ate making your stomach feel funny." Rose gave her mother a look of sympathy. "I ate too much, too, but I swear Grandma has gotten better at making it. Is she using new sugar or something?"

"You wouldn't be tryin' to avoid your momma's question, now, would you?"

Sniff. Sniff.

"Did your accent get worse while I was away?" Rose asked.

Her momma's expression turned sour like she was sucking on a Warhead.

"I'm joking, Momma." Rose shuffled her way into her mother's arms, having missed the way they draped around her back. "I missed you and your accent," she said, chin wobbling and her eyes filling with watery affection. Rose had missed her momma in general, but never enough to come back to this place.

"Don't know why. All you have to do is speak and you'll hear it."

"Don't worry about me. Simon and I are fine."

She pulled away to give Rose a once-over. "Where's your engagement ring?"

Shit. "I left it in my luggage." It didn't even convince her. "You can't wear jewelry through TSA nowadays."

"Rosey!"

Rose exhaled, relieved when she heard the saving bell of her best friend's voice.

"Rose the Queen has arrived. Where are you?" the familiar voice called.

She clapped her hands together, rejoicing. "Olive is here."

Leaving her mother's inquisitive eyes behind, Rose raced indoors.

The second Olive's and her gazes connected, she nudged her head toward the front entrance, praying her best friend could decipher the plea.

Holton's voice permeated the kitchen. "Well, ain't that just a sight for sore eyes? Ms. Olive Wayward has found her way to my doorstep."

Before Rose could question where her brother's voice had come from, he zoomed past her in a gust of wind. Two strides later, Olive's feet were off the ground and her chest was mashing to Holton's. Olive giggled and slapped his shoulders, asking to be put down, but she wasn't *asking* that hard.

Rose rested her hand on her hipbone, her suspicions rising like the Holy Ghost himself.

It was no secret that Holton had harbored a crush on Olive for about as long as their friendship had been, but she'd never thought he'd act on it. Rose and Holton had had *that* talk — the talk in which she'd told her brother it was a bad idea for him to pursue Olive because if anything went wrong between them, an almost life-long friendship might be ruined.

He kept his word, right?

The enthusiastic squeeze he smothered her best friend with made Rose reconsider.

He was hugging Olive like he wanted to seal their bodies together permanently, and she seemed cozier than normal. Setting her back on her feet, Holton smiled all shy-like. Rose scoffed. She didn't know what he was acting timid for. That boy didn't have a shy bone in his body.

"Sorry. I got carried away, but it's hard not to when you're the sexiest thing I've seen on this side of town since—"

She cut off her brother's flirtatious talk. "Can I have my best friend back now?"

On cue, Olive ducked past Holton and found Rose, looping an arm with hers. "Let's get our happy asses to Charlotte. We've got plans tonight. Drunk plans." Olive always knew what to say.

"You have no clue how good that sounds," Rose said.

Everyone hugged and waved their goodbyes, and afterward, the three of them walked down the driveway to Olive's red Mini Cooper—bright red, *like Jessica's hair*. Rose's stomach flip-flopped as the images of Simon and her co-worker slammed into her.

Holton's voice pulled her out of her Houston bedroom. "See you later, Olive."

Did he just wink at her friend? Holton nodded and smiled Rose's way, answering her question. It was a weird twin-telepathy thing they had. He almost always knew what she was thinking and vice versa. She didn't like what was on his mind one bit as he mapped out her best friend's tank top like the pervert had never seen breasts in his life.

"How about, 'See you later, sister, who I haven't seen in forever, and whom I've missed more than anything in the world'?"

Holton smiled and encircled her in his Hulk arms, nudging Rose against his chest. Grinning, she sniffed Old Spice. He still used the same wash that he had since he'd been a boy. Some things never changed.

"Bye to you, too, Cookie Monster. I'm glad you're back. 'Bout damn time. Remember, I'm coming to visit you tomorrow to help set up your furniture. Eight a.m., sharp."

Rose groaned, a brooding and irritated sound. "Why so early?"

Tomorrow was Saturday. She started work Monday. Rose wanted all the leisure time she could get. She was still tired from traveling, for crying out loud.

"No can do. I got work at eleven."

How her brother had become a law-abiding policeman was beyond her comprehension. This was the same guy who'd smoked a joint before every final during his senior year of high school.

"Love you, Holt."

"Love you, too, Rosey. Have fun tonight, ladies." He straddled his police motorbike. "No drinking and driving, ya' hear? Don't wanna have to handcuff you."

"Yes, Officer Berkowitz," Olive yelled back.

Rose rolled her eyes but grinned.

She didn't realize how much she had missed her brother until he'd cranked up his motorcycle and pulled away, leaving nothing but dust and dirt at his tail.

"Since when did you start flirting with my brother?" She yanked the seat belt over her body, eyeing Olive as her friend did the same.

"Since when did he become hotter than Hades? Did you see those muscles? Had me sweating like a whore in church." She wiggled her eyebrows.

"Olive!"

Her friend's smile was too generous for her to be angry with. "I'm kidding. You know, Holton is... He..." Olive raised her chin, concentrating on swerving out of her parking space. Clearing her throat, she changed the conversation. "Wanna talk about Simon?"

The sound of his name sent pain zigzagging down her front. She'd forgotten Olive was the only one who knew the truth about her abrupt relocation.

As they began to drive, Rose stared out of the window, mesmerized by the giant trees smearing into one as the car flew past them. At this speed, the forest had no definition. It was nothing but a dark, never-ending shadow at Rose's side.

Houston didn't have this type of nature, at least not where she used to live, smack dab in the middle of a flat-bedded ranch. The air, filtered with pine cones and acorns, smelled fresher and somehow crisper as she inhaled. This was it, the beginning of her new life. Did she want to start it by reminiscing about her past?

"Let's not spoil the night," Rose said, her tone as resigned as the final look Simon had given her before pulling off his ring. "But, just in case... Until we get to Charlotte, can you talk about everything that has happened since I saw you last?"

Sometimes Rose's mouth had a mind of its own.

"I can do that." Olive reached over to Rose, offering her fingers a hug. "What do you want to hear about first? How my bomb-ass sex with Firefighter Dan ended and I've been going through withdrawal for over a month or how Kate got knocked up by her ex-boyfriend and asked me to plan her baby shower, even though she's only like three weeks in? I don't know how she is going to raise a baby when she can't even subtract. I'm telling you, Rosey, there needs to be some psychological tests or somethin' people have to ace before getting permission to bring *life* in the world."

It went like that for about an hour, her friend going on about things Rose would have found interesting if she weren't so focused on how badly her heart ached, before Olive pulled her Mini Cooper into a complex named Green Oaks Townhomes.

Gathering some luggage, Olive helped Rose haul her bags to the apartment.

"Time to get ready. I bought you something cute." Olive smiled, a sly twinkle nestling in her eyes, giving Rose the impression that she wouldn't like what was coming.

* * * *

"I can't wear this!"

This couldn't be *her* in the mirror. The person staring back at Rose looked twenty-five, not twenty-eight, in a little black dress, tight as flesh, and cut in a sleeveless V-neck at the top. Red-bottom Louboutin heels adorned her feet. Olive said the outfit was an early birthday gift. If Olive was going to spend a few hundred bucks on a birthday present for Rose, she wondered what the hell she would be buying Olive for *her* birthday.

After getting dressed, Olive had used what was for sure voodoo magic in the form of a curling iron on Rose's hair—curling irons had never responded to Rose *that* well—turning its normal flatness into subtle waves the color of fresh hay bales. Olive had done her makeup with professional accuracy, murmuring while she'd painted how all those years as a MAC associate were finally paying off. Olive had given Rose dark gray eyes that were smoldering and made her look so much more confident than she felt.

Her best friend had decorated every inch of her.

Even underneath the dress, Olive's influence was displayed in the form of lacy lingerie shoved so far up Rose's butt it was as if it were seeking refuge there. The thong was the result of another present from Olive—a Victoria's Secret bag spilling over with gifts her friend insisted would get her back on the market in no time. What Olive must have meant to say was that the scanty items would get her a one-way ticket to Satan's doorstep in no time. The clothes made her feel like a sinner, and when Rose told that to her friend, Olive smiled as if to say her task had been accomplished.

"I can't wear this," Rose repeated, mouth agape, not sure if she meant the makeup or the dress or, hell, both. "I look..." Turning in Olive's direction, her mouth fell to a frown. "Isn't all this makeup deceiving? I don't look like myself. I look like—"

"A badass bitch? Hotter than the Lord is holy?"

20

"I was going to say 'desperate'. Like seriously, Olive..." Rose returned to her smoky-eyed reflection. *Watch out, beer goggles. You have some competition named L'Oreal True Match.*

"I think there is a compliment somewhere in there."

Rose scowled at the sprawling figure on her bed.

"Listen, babe..." Olive bounced over to Rose, ruffling the sheets as she jumped up. Her friend placed her hands at Rose's shoulders, and together they stared into the full-length mirror, Olive's bright eyes at odds with the pale green of hers.

"You're so hot I could get preggo from looking at you."

Covering her chest, Rose shirked away from Olive's laugh.

"No worries, Rosey. No knock ups for me." She snatched a round pill holder from her purse, wiggling it like they were playing a game of show-and-tell. "I'm on the pill. I think I need to find a baby daddy soon, though. I'm getting old as hell, and I've always wanted a little girl. I gotta get a bun in my oven before it's out of service."

Rose relaxed her posture, taking on a solemn expression as she said, "With the move and everything, I just... Honey, I can't afford a child right now. I know, I promised you this year, but we gotta make do any way we can. Unfortunately, a child isn't in our budget."

"Be glad I'm a loving wife, or I'd have divorced your ass years ago."

Their conversations were always like this, uninhibited with a dash of crazy.

That was how Rose knew Olive was her best friend. Rose could say the craziest thing in the world to her, and instead of pointing out her insanity, Olive went along with it.

Twirling toward Olive, she narrowed her eyes. "Wait just one second, Olivia Wayward. If you're old, what does that make me? You're a year younger."

"I didn't say that. Why are you putting words in my mouth?"

"Look at you, trying to get out of trouble." Rose was

shaking her head, but she was smiling. It was hard not to around her best friend.

"On a more serious note, I need you to answer one important question."

"What is it?" Rose asked, trying not to sound too anxious, but really, she was somewhere between terrified and kid-in-a-candy-shop excited to see where the night would take her.

Sweeping her hair behind her shoulder, Olive's grin suggested foul play. "Do you want to get laid tonight?"

Just the word *laid* had Rose tingling all over. "Yes, yes and triple yes with a cherry on top—and a banana, preferably over six inches. The penis, not the banana."

Sure, she and Simon had broken off their relationship only two months ago, but Rose had disconnected from him long before that.

Emotionally, she wasn't in any condition to start a relationship, but sex?

The only word that came to her mind when she thought about sex was *frustrated*.

Wound tighter than the clothing on her body, Rose hadn't lost herself to a romantic touch except her own in over a year. It would be an injustice to use the term *romantic* to portray the last time she and Simon had had sex. He'd barely been able to stay hard after Rose had told him his unusual dirty talk was making her uncomfortable. That moment had been a red flag and a testament to their lack of chemistry.

Independent to her core, Rose didn't need a man to satisfy her, but she was sick of pleasuring herself. At the rate she was going, she'd have carpal tunnel by the time she hit thirty. Like hitting thirty wasn't bad enough already.

Olive interrupted her thoughts. "Then trust me. Wear the damn dress. You're gonna have boys sticking to you like pimples on a middle schooler."

"Not great imagery, but I'll take whatever I can get." Despite her low-spirited reply, she was happier around

Olive than she had in a long time.

Deciding she deserved a simple one-night stand—every woman needed at least one night of hot sex with a gorgeous stranger—Rose took the leap. "Let's do this. Let's get—"

"Bananas?" Olive giggled.

"If by 'bananas' you mean 'penis', then yes, let's get bananas." *A nice, long and juicy banana.* Thighs tingling, she salivated. *Jesus, maybe I needed this more than I thought.*

* * * *

The blaring nightclub music crammed into Rose's ears. Too loud. Her eardrums were going to erupt. Olive pounded the empty shot glass on the bar top just before she picked up another and threw it back. Rose leaned into Olive's side. "This is never going to work!"

"You're doing fine. It's still early." Olive unhooked herself from the delicious male she'd found about two seconds after walking into the club.

"You need to mingle. You keep getting tense when someone talks to you. Loosen up. Have fun. Dancing is good. Smiling"—Olive lifted the sides of Rose's lips, nodding sympathetically when they fell as she released them—"would also be really helpful."

Loosen up? That was easy for Olive to say. Rose never socialized outside of work. Like Simon, Olive was the outgoing and gorgeous, yet down-to-earth one in their relationship. The reminder of her ex-fiancé made Rose wonder what he was doing at that moment. What were her old co-workers doing? Were any of them thinking about her?

What was she saying? Of course they were.

Rose wasn't narcissistic but it was a sure thing, paved in stone and written in the stars, that after the mess she had caused, she would be the topic of conversation for months to come.

It had started with the #teamjessica and #teamrose texts

floating around the office once word had gotten out about her fiancé's new plaything. Christ, she'd sounded bitter.

The Wild West photo had gotten out, too. It had spread like wildfire, burning up every smartphone in Harris County. When she'd found out her co-worker had been one the perpetrators of the text games and leaked photo, years of professionalism had gone out of the window. She'd always heard she ruled the office with an iron fist. Apparently, she punched with one, too.

For the first time in her life, the phrase 'tunnel vision' made sense.

Frenzied with anger, Rose had given her employee, Michael — the country-club, khaki-wearing dirt bag — something to really text about. A black eye.

Luckily, Simon had gotten him to drop the charges in exchange for a hefty settlement — his final gift before kicking her to the curb.

The company hadn't been so lucky. They'd gotten a lawsuit for workplace violence, and she'd gotten a *sayonara*. Needless to say, she'd screwed up big — Empire State Building big.

Stop it, Rose.

She curled her fingers to the clutch pressed against her chest.

"I'm going to the bathroom. I'll be back." Upset for thinking of Simon when she should have been thinking about her under-used vagina, Rose stormed through the club, fire under her heels. Somewhere quiet would do. She needed a place she could pep talk herself into being a social butterfly. Veering away from the restrooms — pep talks and rank toilet smells didn't mesh well in her book — she flashed her wrist to the bouncer.

Weaving her way through a pitch-black hallway, Rose was glad Olive had spoiled her tonight, giving her an all-access bracelet that allowed her entrance to the VIP room. She entered the purple-lit lounge where there were less people and the music was low and hypnotic.

Following the sound of glasses clinking, Rose arrived at the bar.

She pressed her elbows into the sleek countertop, readying to order her favorite Martini — wet, with a twist — when her phone rang. She tensed as Simon's name appeared on the screen.

Her heart fluttered angrily, and she smashed the decline button as if Simon would disappear with the call. She needed to get control over her emotions. *Why am I even upset with him?*

It wasn't like she wanted to be with him. She didn't. Rose was glad it was over, glad she could focus on herself and her career without feeling guilty. Keeping that in mind, though, didn't take away the hurt she didn't know if she was allowed to feel.

"Hey." The greeting pulled her attention away from Simon and guilt and anything in between.

Rose faltered a little as she turned to address a man who couldn't have been much older than herself. Well, wrap her up in a box and call it Christmas, because Rose had finally found the guy she wanted to unravel her from head to toe.

"Hello." She smiled.

His lips raised in return. "My name's Devon. What are you drinking? I'll buy."

Among the flashy club scenery, he was out of place in washed-out jeans and a plain shirt with classic cowboy boots. Her type to a T, he had the country-boy style Rose was used to liking, but a small part of her protested. Simon had that look. Simon wore cowboy boots and blue jeans and smiled like this one was smiling, like all of life's pleasures could be summed up in a single Sunday — church, home-cooked meal with the family and at night, a college football game and a six-pack of beer. A tinge of disappointment fluttered up her chest.

Before they got carried away, Rose put a lid on her negative thoughts. This wasn't Simon. This was a man who wanted her attention, and if the saying about shoe sizes and sex was right, she sure as heck wanted his. Phone jingling, she ignored it. For one night, she wanted to stop thinking. She wanted passion she could lose herself in. *What if this is it?*

"Devon. Sorry," she said. "I'm Rose. I would —"

Her phone rang a third time. Simon's name dominated the screen once more. Why was he calling her so much? Worry gripped her stomach. What if something was wrong with him?

"I'd love that. Can you give me a second, though? I've got to answer this." *A dimpled smile, too?*

"As long as you're here, I'm not going anywhere," he said.

Rose's cheeks flushed.

Maybe tonight wouldn't be so bad after all.

Stepping away, she dialed the only number she'd ever memorized by heart. Simon and she may not have been a couple anymore, but she couldn't take it if something bad happened to him. Five years of caring about someone couldn't be erased overnight, no matter how much Rose wished it were possible. The ringing in her ear gave way to incoherent mumbling.

"Simon? You there?" she asked.

"Rosey!"

She winced. He wasn't allowed to call her that anymore.

"It's good to hear your voice, Rosey. How did your plane ride go?"

She balled her hands.

She walked through the lounge, attempting to calm her galloping heart, as if things like that were easily controllable. Good for her, there was an area marked 'private' without a bouncer preventing her from trespassing. She needed silence and no onlookers. The last thing she wanted to do was raise her voice in public. She was preparing to raise her voice, too.

Simon is drunk-calling me?

"Rosey?" There was a pause before he sputtered, "You

there? Talk to me."

After pushing her way past the rope barrier, she went into the first shut-off room she could find. "Listen, Simon"—she ground her teeth, allowing her voice to take on the dangerous tone he'd always disliked—"you can't call me whenever you're drunk."

"What'd you say? Rosey, I can't hear you."

Rose plugged her ear with her thumb. The music in here was way more deafening than anything she'd heard tonight. Screeching vocals and the angry rift of an electric guitar splintered the air. Turning to see where the heck she'd ended up, Rose sucked up every ounce of oxygen in her vicinity when her eyes connected with the unbelievable scene playing out in front of her.

On the other end of the line, Simon slurred, "Rosey, we didn't end things right—"

Her phone slipped from her hand, bounced on the couch beside her then flopped to the floor. Blaring with heat, Rose's cheeks were on fire. Her body followed suit.

She wobbled, backing into the same door she'd entered. Fate was teasing her. That had to have been it. How else could she have happened into *this* room out of all the others?

A half-naked woman was on her knees.

Rose couldn't see anything but the makeshift bondage cuffing the woman's wrists so that they gathered helplessly on her back and the blindfold that stole her sight.

No. Not a blindfold, a tie. A tie that Rose assumed belonged to the man she was kneeling in front of—the man who had his cock in her mouth. The room was empty save the three of them. She couldn't believe this was happening. She had to be dreaming.

With his head reclined against the wall, the man had his eyes—thankfully—sealed. Both of his hands spread atop her skull, as if to feel her move each time her lips worked in a seductive rhythm down his solid, so very solid, erection.

Oh, Christ... This is actually happening!

His shirt was open wide, exposing the most lickable chest

Rose had ever seen outside of her Internet search history. How often did he work out to get such a flawless pack of abs? There were four sets, hard and defined — not bulky enough to be scary but still intimidating.

A tattoo, whose detail Rose couldn't see in the dark red overcast, painted his entire left torso. She had never liked tattoos, but she wanted to touch his, to touch *him*.

He was striking, clenching and unclenching his jaw the farther she moved. A straight nose paired with thick, furrowed eyebrows and lips that even in the dimness had Rose boneless, made him look sexy beyond words.

The woman struggled to absorb his length, bringing all she could fit down her throat until her choking noises sounded through the music. With his fingers clutching at her roots, he held her there long enough to guarantee she'd come up gasping for air.

Letting out a sigh, Rose placed her palm on her climbing heartbeat. Her nipples hardened against her dress, tingling and alert, reminding her that she was *still* watching the two strangers going at it. *What in the actual hell am I doing?*

Never in her life had she crossed such a line before. Voyeurism wasn't her thing. It was so wrong. *Filthy.* Sizzling desire poured through her bones. Growling. Hungry. Her inner walls clenched with need. Rose wanted *so wrong* right now. She wanted his intensity — his gritting teeth, his clawing fingers. The man parted his lips as if to moan then shot his hips off the wall as he began thrusting harder, his knuckles curling tightly in the woman's hair.

She'd never seen oral sex like this. He fed his cock to her, assaulting her mouth with full, angry helpings. She pictured herself taking in every inch of the handsome stranger. The weight of her panties increased with the flood of images. *What am I thinking?*

She had to get out of here, now! She couldn't watch —

Her phone rang again, and his eyes, colorless in the dark, opened. Embarrassment washed through Rose like a summer downpour, so heavy that she became drenched.

Literally. Unable to move, she stared at him, her heart — at least to herself — now much louder than the music. A blizzard of emotions stormed through Rose as his unreadable gaze bore into her, some of them being horror, humiliation, guilt and others that curled in her belly and lower.

"Shane?"

The woman had released his shaft, giving Rose the full view, and what a marvelous view it was. Her breath caught. *Wow*, was the first thing she thought. He was hard and large, but he wasn't *scary* big. His size was intimidating, certainly, but fascinating. Delving into her darkest thoughts, Rose wanted to know how he would feel inside her. Her legs needled, falling asleep, but that was all they did. They didn't run like she told them to, just as her gaze didn't waver.

"Shane, what's that?" the woman asked.

It was Rose's phone ringing again.

Ignoring the sharp pulse at her core, she brought her gaze back to the man's face. *Shane.* Even his name was hot. She shook her head, trying to pass a silent memo.

Don't say anything. One person seeing her face was bad enough.

His masculine voice sent chills down Rose's back. "It's my phone," he answered.

Without wasting another minute, Rose snatched her cell phone and rushed out of the room.

"Hey, Devon!" she shouted when she got back to the bar.

Devon faced her just in time to catch Rose's mouth.

Circling her arms around his, she angled her head to better pace the kiss. His lips tasted of alcohol and salt and, when he opened his mouth, she found that his tongue tasted similar. It was her first kiss since Simon. Nice. Sweet. Risqué, even. It wasn't what she wanted. In her mind was a mysterious, tattooed stranger. Pulling away from him, she smiled at his surprise. Rose was surprised herself. *Where did that come from?*

Your vagina. It came from your vagina.

"We should do that again." Eyes lighting, Devon slipped

29

his hand to her waist.

"*That* was a goodbye kiss. I have to go. There's an emergency I need deal with."

Rose couldn't stay in the club another second. She wanted to have sex with a stranger, but not this one. If Rose went home with him, she'd be screwing Devon with the image of the mystery man in her head. She was horny, but she wasn't an ass. She took a pen from her clutch, then jotted her number on his arm, kissing beside the digits, her red lipstick a signature.

"Call me."

As she vanished from sight, Rose gave herself a mental pat on the back for making the first move. Dialing Olive, she made her way to the front of the club. "Where are you, woman?"

"Where are *you*? I went to the bathroom and to the VIP and you weren't there. Where did you go? Narnia?"

Rose snorted. "I was in the private lounge. I'm coming down now."

"Text me next time. I thought you'd been abducted. I was about to go all Liam Neeson in *Taken*." Olive's voice infused with sweetness like it did every time she wanted something. "I have some news."

"Good news, I hope." News that would make her news sound better.

Olive's mission for her had failed. She was going home bananaless, and she blamed it on Mystery Man. Who got blow jobs in a nightclub? Rose's pearled nipples tightened even more as the after-image of the pornographic film played behind her eyes. Fuel to her already scorching body, the memory erupted her desire, warping it into something vehement and robust. Like a living thing, *need* moved and breathed inside her, demanding Rose to soothe the ache pulsating at her core.

"Firefighter Dan texted me. He wants me to come over."

Rose drew her phone away from her ear to check the time. "It's twelve."

There was a short silence before Olive asked, "So?"

"Doesn't it sound like a booty call to you?" Rose didn't want her best friend to get hurt. "I thought you guys stopped that."

"Ya, duh. We don't like each other. We just fit our bits together whenever he isn't being a first-class douche. We argue. So, what? I don't want him as my boyfriend. I just want him to park his car in my garage, to spill his sprinkles on my cupcake, to—"

"Stop!" Rose jerked the phone away from her ear, only placing it back when Olive's voice died down. Her friend had always had little shame, but it had definitely gotten worse with age. "You're so disgusting."

"Yet, you love me."

"That's debatable." She grinned over the lie. Yeah, she loved Olive, pervert and all.

"No, it's not. I'm the one true love of your life. You okay with taking the car back alone? I hate to ditch you on your first night. I can come home with you, if ya want."

She heard the hesitance in Olive's voice and tried to shoo it away with some enthusiasm of her own. "Trust me. If I'd have found man who was nine-inches, I would never see your face. Go have fun. Try to come home before eight, though. I don't want Holton"—*poor guy*—"seeing your walk of shame. By the way, mission Get Me Laid has failed. The only thing I'm screwing tonight"—ending the call, Rose tapped on her friend's shoulder, and Olive twirled with a smile that slipped into a frown as Rose continued—"is the cap to a bottle of Mountain Dew while I cry about my life and watch reruns of *The Big Bang Theory*."

"That's pathetic."

"It's *so* pathetic." *But it's less pathetic than having sex with a stranger while fantasizing about another stranger who I creepily watched getting his dick sucked.* "You want me to walk you?"

Before their club visit, Olive had told her Firefighter Dan only lived a couple of blocks away. Rose was suspicious. Had this all been a set-up? The timing and the club's location in comparison to Firefighter Dan's condo were oddly convenient.

Either way, she didn't care. She was happy if Olive was happy though she had a nagging suspicion Olive's love life wasn't as great as she led on. Olive had always wanted someone special, but he had never come along and her best friend refused to settle.

Anyway, Rose was glad she would be home alone tonight. The last thing she needed was Olive knocking on her door while she and Enrique, her personal vibrator, were pulling an all-nighter.

"Sure." Olive took Rose's hand in hers. "You'll be my knight in shining stilettos."

Leaning her head against Olive's shoulder, she smiled. "Always have been."

"Always will be," Olive responded, a skip in her step.

Twenty minutes later, Rose stood back in front of the club, trying to remember where Olive had parked. All those times she had gone to Charlotte on the weekends to shop with her bestie during high school were long forgotten. She didn't know her way around Charlotte for the life of her. She called Olive again, but there was no answer.

Knowing her, she was probably getting it on in the most inconvenient location or position possible and didn't have access to her phone.

"Hey, sugar."

Great. Now she had to deal with a cat-calling weirdo *and* being lost in a city she hated. Throw in the fact that Rose's panties were soaked with her earlier arousal, her sexual frustration was at an all-time high and Simon had left her three drunk voicemails in the past hour, it was safe to say that the first day of her new, improved life hadn't turned out as new and improved as she wished it would have. She was starting to look forward to work Monday.

Lifting her head, the air left her lungs — something that'd been happening a lot on this day — when she saw who the voice had come from.

It was him. Mystery Man. "You're the guy…" But it was difficult for her to talk when he was staring at her body in a way that reminded her of Olive's earlier comment about middle schoolers, pimples and sticking. The bright, incandescent light shone above them, so she saw him better than she had earlier. She wished she didn't. How was it possible for him to get better looking? His shirt, now buttoned, was half tucked. The sleeves were folded up, exposing strong, veiny arms. His hair was sloppy in the hottest way possible. A wicked smile lingered on his face. She dropped her gaze to his crotch, quickly glancing away, but not before he lifted a solo eyebrow of acknowledgment. Warmth banged again to the surface of her skin.

He's a stranger. There is no need for me to feel humiliated. It was an accident.

Finding her voice, she apologized. "I'm sorry about earlier. I didn't mean to…watch. I was trying to get away from the noise. I didn't know…"

"Don't worry, sugar. I won't tell if you don't."

Her pulse and clit beat at the sound of his smooth-as-butter voice.

"Don't call me that." She liked it way too much.

He swiped a hand down his gorgeous laugh lines, his smile turning more seductive.

"Tell me your name, then," he insisted. "I think I have the right to know the name of any woman who's seen my dick."

"I didn't see that much." She'd seen every glorious inch.

"Tell me your name, sugar."

Rose wanted to strangle the tiny spark of hope blossoming inside her.

How could she be turned on by a guy she'd caught getting a blow job thirty minutes before? *What is wrong with me?*
"I'm…"

Why was she nervous? She'd peeped on him, okay, but he didn't seem angry. The only one here who was flustered was her. Remembering she was a professional woman, a sensible adult who could tell the difference between a hot guy and bad news, she answered with resolve, "You don't need to know my name." His was attention she didn't want.

His smile reached all the way down to her toes.

"Well, Peeping Tom, my name is Shane, Shane Williams. I'm about to head to a bar a couple blocks down to get some drinks. Want to join me?"

"Peeping Tom?"

"Since you won't tell me your name, I had to improvise. What do you say, PT?"

"Why should I go?" Why was she even considering the idea?

Maybe because Shane had the neighborhood bad-boy appearance that had always been unattainable in her pristine existence. She had been the good, studious girl. She had never partied or done drugs. She'd worked her butt off, neglecting friendships and relationships, until she'd gotten accepted to university. She'd fallen for her closest friend with the intention of settling down indefinitely.

Until recently, Rose had followed all the rules.

She didn't want to follow the rules anymore. She wanted to break them.

Would going out with a complete stranger—who could have been a lunatic or murderer, for all she knew—be considered doing so?

"I figured you could buy me a drink since I covered for you earlier, PT. You know, no one has ever walked in and seen me having sex, oral or not." He smiled his wicked smile. "I think that constitutes friendship. What do you say?"

"I'm not a Peeping Tom. I told you it was an accident. If I'd known you were getting your freak on, I wouldn't have opened the door. Why didn't you lock it, anyway?"

"You look lost, too. You from around here?"

"I'm from North Carolina." Rose crossed her arms over her chest. "Just not Charlotte."

The corner of his lips raised. "I'm gonna be heading to the

bar now."

Shane walked past her without looking her way, and she caught a whiff of his cologne. Goodness, he smelled amazing. She could bury her head in that smell.

"Follow me or not. It's your choice."

Observing the foreign buildings, towering like giants on either side of her, she gnawed on her lower lip. She rubbed her palms together before bringing them to her face, blowing out hot air until her fingers were toasty. Wind breathed in her direction, tugging with it faceless sounds of faraway cars revving their engines and drunken laughter in the distance.

Would it be so bad to buy him one drink? She *had* watched him during a very private act. She'd never want to be spied on the way she'd spied on Shane. Also, the prospect of being on the streets this late at night, alone in her search for Olive's car, was making her uncomfortable. Charlotte wasn't a dangerous city, per se, but she figured it better not to take any chances.

"I'm not sleeping with you."

"Had my fun tonight already, sugar." Throwing his head back, he lent her a smile and a wink that had her midsection salivating. "Think we both did."

Was he implying she'd had fun watching him?

"Has anyone ever told you you're conceited?"

He pronounced "I might have heard that a time or two" like "I might-ah heard that a timer two." His accent didn't have the same nasally pitch of a North Carolina native.

It was a low, honey-sweet accent that Rose knew could only be found in a place like Georgia or Louisiana. Her favorite type. She could almost hear him cooing sinful encouragements into her ear while he embedded his cock in her body, as deep and rough as his tongue had rolled over each syllable.

"I'm serious. Drinks don't mean you're sleeping with me. You're not." Rose wanted to sleep with him. She wanted to run over to him right now and ask his cock if it wanted to go on a date with her vagina, but she couldn't sleep with a guy who'd already stuck himself in one person tonight. It even sounded sleazy.

Stopping before he could cross over to the next block, he shifted to face her. "Sugar, you tryin' to convince me or yourself?"

Rose had no clue why she was so attracted to him. He *was* attractive, but he was also the opposite of her type, which was good, church-going guys who loved country music and rode horses in their spare time. Not ones who looked like they enjoyed bending rules and having sex in nightclubs. Running his fingers through his tasseled hair, he showed her another smaller tattoo on the back of his hand in the flat area between his thumb and index finger.

"Both of us," she said, wanting to feel as naughty as he looked.

With confidence, he let his bold gaze wander over her body as if he were challenging her statement.

She shivered.

He smiled. He'd won. "I see."

If he was going to stare at Rose like that the whole night, she was in trouble.

Chapter Two

"Jack and Coke."

Shane glimpsed sideways to the blonde he'd met outside the club, giving her a huge smile. Jack? Damn, did he like a girl who could drink right. Under his gaze, her cheeks went pink, and she brushed her hair behind her ear, turning her gaze from his to review her hands. Whatever the hell that had been, Shane liked it too. Wetting his mouth, he leaned over the counter.

"I'll take the same thing, Bub."

Bub Fowler, Shane's cousin, gave the woman—he'd decided to call her Blondie—a questioning glance before returning to Shane, who shrugged in reply. He didn't normally introduce girls to his family, but he had some questions for Blondie, so he didn't want to see her off just yet, and after dealing with Amy's bullshit, he'd needed some hard liquor. He'd decided to kill two birds with one stone, and it just so happened that the only bar on this side of town open late was his kin's shop.

Was it Shane's fault that when he exited the nightclub he'd run into the wide-eyed stranger who seemed as helpless and frustrated as she had when he'd caught her watching his and Amy's earlier performance? Was it his fault he had a weakness for innocent-looking beauties?

He brought his gaze over her full frame.

Her sweet face with its bow lips and its button nose looked innocent as hell. Had him thinking she was about to pull out a Bible or start singing hymns. Everything else, however...

All he could think was that she was like iced water after a

long day sweating.

Her barely there dress did little to conceal her tight nipples. He passed his tongue over his lips again, seeking the texture of her perky breasts. She wasn't a skinny stick-model, either. Rail-thin girls were not Shane's type. No, Blondie was the perfect balance of thin and thick. She had wide hips he imagined would settle well on his lap and long legs he'd give anything to have wrapped around his waist. And, hot damn, those heels. Shane was curious what she'd look like with those heels on and nothing more.

Who the hell was this woman?

From the second his eyes had opened to discover Blondie, he'd known he had to have her, which was a shit feeling when another girl had her mouth around his dick.

Sure, the room had been barely lit, but Shane had seen her lovely face, her trembling legs and her vision that had fallen to the girl at his thighs and come back up to meet his with…

Well, Shane had seen lust before.

To think that Blondie had been turned on watching him get off caused Shane to want to pin her against the countertop, push that cute number up she called a dress and—

His train of thought abruptly halted as Bub set two glasses on the bar top.

"Here you are, cuz."

Shane tossed the drink down, keeping his eyes on the liquid ring the cup left against the chestnut-shaded wood. *Where is my mind right now?*

He didn't know this girl from Eve.

"In a rush or something?" Those big green eyes with their yellow starbursts captured his, making his stomach knot a thousand different ways.

"No rush, sugar," Shane assured her with a wink.

A catch of breath, a roseate flush and the averting of her gaze to her manicured nails made Shane feel like the Big Bad Wolf and her the girl in red—or, in this case, black—who'd stumbled into his forest with a basket of sweets. Shane drank in her figure, curiosity and hunger mixing in his belly like Jack and Coke. He paused on her copious breasts, which fought for containment against her tautly drawn top. They *did* look sweet.

"What's your name?" Shane tried to distract her with conversation so he could adjust his hard-on with a little shift in step. It didn't work. She didn't give him her name, and his cock was still stiff as a plank of wood on his leg.

'I'm not sleeping with you.'

Shane suppressed a groan.

He blamed his current single-track mind on him donning the worst set of blue balls in history. One minute Amy had been getting him off and, the next minute, she was screaming at him for getting a text message from his *sister*. He knew he shouldn't have taken her blindfold off. Okay, fine, the *I miss you!* text could have been interpreted the wrong way, but he would have happily explained himself if Amy hadn't been trying to damage her vocal cords with the force of her damn screaming.

Shane didn't yell over angry women. He valued his life, which was why he wasn't able to get a single word out before Amy had zipped off somewhere or other, leaving him in his current, painful state that Blondie and her fuck-me heels sure weren't helping.

Shit. Amy was nothing but drama. Everyone who knew her had told him that. But when a hot girl wanted his attention, it was hard not to oblige. He liked fucking, and as long as the girls he was taking to bed remembered it was *just* fucking, he was fine answering their every sexual want and need. Amy had said she was okay with their non-exclusive relationship. Apparently, she'd been lying. Why couldn't women be honest about what they wanted? Blondie had.

'Both of us.'

She'd failed in convincing Shane of anything but her attraction to him.

'Drinks don't mean you're sleeping with me. You're not.'

If there was one thing he hated more than anything, it was

to be given rules. That's why he'd run away from home. It was why he'd become his own boss. The only good thing about rules was figuring out how to break them.

"Wanna play a game of Eight Ball?"

She flung her gaze toward the pool tables. "I don't know how to. Never played."

He was hoping she'd say that. "Follow me. I'll teach you."

Picking up two cue sticks, Shane handed her the one with the least worn-down tip. After chalking the stick and racking up, he roamed around the table, making sure everything was set correctly. Eight Ball was a serious game for Shane. It was all about calculation and challenge. Intellect. If he was going to teach someone the basics, he was going to do it right.

That meant he needed another Jack. He always played better tipsy.

"Bub, bring me another," he hollered across the room.

"Sure thing."

Blondie frowned. Reaching into her purse, she pulled out two crisp twenties. "This is all I brought with me. I had more but I spent it at the club. Don't drink too much." *She really thinks I'm going to make her pay?*

"Sugar, I'd never make a pretty lady pay the tab. Now, get your ass over here. This is the only time a man is going to teach you how to shoot some balls, so you gotta give me your undivided attention, ya hear?" *Damn, her smile was gorgeous.*

"Don't appreciate the demand, but I'll bite."

Oh, I bet you do. Shane shook the thought from his head. "Want me to break?"

Twisting her hair around her finger, she lifted her shoulders. "I don't know what that means, but sure. Show me how it's done."

Shane broke. He loved the sound of the cue ball thrashing its way across the green landscape, the blurry colors zooming in different directions. It was meditation. Some days he'd spend hours huddled at Bub's playing Eight

Ball. When he needed to clear his head, this was how he did it. "I'm stripes, okay? Your objective is to shoot in all the solids except the black, using the white cue ball. Only pocket black after all the solids are cleared. Got it?" Picking up the beverage Bub had set on the edge of the table, Shane brought it to his lips.

"It sounds simple enough." She leaned down to the table, giving him the best view he'd seen all night. He bet her ass looked fantastic naked. His dick got thicker the lower she bowed.

"The first and most important lesson is"—he smiled inwardly when she tensed as his hand went to her lower back—"aim while you're standing. Don't bend. Find the stroking line with your eyes before you get down in your stance."

He didn't take his hand off her back when she straightened her spine. He let it linger, liking the way she shivered too much to move. Leaning in close so that his hip just slightly touched her ass, he lowered his face. He kissed his cheek to hers, and his whole body moved with feeling, sparking like a flame breathing into existence. Flashes of her watching him at the club filled his mind, meshing with the warm buzz of liquor.

"Now, sugar, I want you to pick a solid number."

He raised an inch and saw her throat move as she swallowed hard. "The five."

"Good choice. Five, then."

The shot was long but clean. A beginner could make it. "Create the line with your eyes from the cue to the five. Let me know when you got it."

"I have it."

Shane didn't know how she could create a line with her eyes closed. "You sure about that?"

Moving her attention to the table, she concentrated on her task. Shane could almost see through her eyes, see her connecting the dots.

More excitedly, she told him, "I'm sure."

"Spread your legs." The challenge and appeal was all too clear.

"What?"

"To get into stance, spread your legs," Shane said innocently. "Then you're going to bend and face your target at slight angle. Lower your head to the cue stick. Keep your holding arm pointed ninety degrees and keep that wrist loose." He backed away to give her room to move.

Her legs went wide as she assumed the proper position. "What else?"

Not wanting to be the creepy guy who rubbed his dick into an unaware girl's body, he kept his erection at an appropriate distance. The rest of him, not so much.

Covering her side, his chest was a blanket against her back. *Hot.* She emitted so much heat. Her fingers left scorching imprints in his as he helped her hand over the cue stick.

"Today you're going to learn the closed bridge. Wrap your index finger around the cue stick and rest it on your thumb. Like this..." He moved her fingers so that they sat at the correct angle. "Perfect. Just like that, sugar." Would she take notice of his now-husky voice? "Does the angle feel good for you? If you don't like it, we can change positions." Softer, he said and ran a finger up the side of her thumb, "I want it to feel as good for you as possible."

She gasped, the pool stick wobbling in her hand.

With his nose beside her temple, he could smell her girly shampoo. It made Shane think about her showering—her naked. It was becoming difficult to think about anything *but* her naked. Normally, he had control over his lust. Not tonight. Tonight, his desire ran looser than, *fuck*, apparently, his morals. What was going on with his head? He was a pig hitting on a girl after she'd seen him getting off.

"Of your hand, I mean." He cleared his throat and hoped the air, too, would clear, because it was stifled with their intermingling warmth that made him feel high. "Change the position of your hand."

It was a long while before she said yes.

Moving away from her, Shane shook off his dirty thoughts. He picked up his cue stick and leaned forward to demonstrate. "I'm gonna teach you how to work this."

He held his fingers in a closed bridge, performing a basic stroke.

"We start off doing soft strokes." He cringed as he repeated the words in his head.

Had Eight Ball always been such a sexual game?

Blondie echoed his movements, the wood gliding fluidly through her fingers. "Am I doing it right?"

Shane doubted she could do it wrong. "Fantastic. You're a natural. Keep stroking it nice and smooth like that."

Her movement halted, and she brought her eyes to his.

Twin mirrors of lust poured through him something like fire as they stared at each other in open assessment. No bullshit. No ambiguous flirting. There was an almost daring interest playing in those green globes of hers, as if she wanted Shane to make a move. He wanted to. He could.

Shane would only have to lean forward to kiss her.

She'd kiss him back. He'd slide his tongue into her mouth and his hand up her outer thigh, slowly drawing closer to where her legs met. Shane pictured himself shifting his fingers under the band of her panties and between her pussy lips, which would be wet and as hot to the touch as her skin had been. He'd be close enough to feel her legs shake while he stroked her spot. Cupping the nape of her neck, he'd tug her bottom lip between both of his and glide a finger inside her inviting heat, maybe two. In and out, he'd draw them. What would her moans sound like?

Blondie opened her mouth and nothing but a breathless sigh came out, leaving his question half answered and his cock fully erect. Swallowing hard, Shane tore his gaze from her. Their connection broke, but the air was still as heavy as what he was packing downstairs.

The sexual tension, so present that it was almost tangible, weighed down on him so that moving was difficult. Before the last threads of his rationality fled and he took her against the table, he gave them distance. He wouldn't come on to Blondie. She'd already told him she didn't want sex. If she changed her mind, she could come to him.

He liked breaking the rules, but not in that sense. Shane would never initiate something with someone unless he had their verbal approval.

"Can you do me a favor?"

"What is it?"

"Close your eyes," he said.

"I may not play pool, but I know you're not supposed to close your eyes."

"Shoot with your eyes closed. Think of the line, though. See without seeing."

Shane grinned. She looked suspicious. What she didn't know was that if you had your line correct and had a clean shot, you could get the ball in its pocket without any visuals.

Hesitantly, she shut her eyes.

"Steady form. Nice and slow," he reminded.

She stalled. She shot. Shane's heart clenched. The five-ball rolled in slow motion across the table.

Blondie jumped, raising her cue stick in her hand like a trophy. "Holy shit!"

Relief flooded him. *Thank fuck*. That would have been embarrassing.

"It worked. I did it. I did it!" She gripped his shirt, hopping.

Instead of pulling away when a jolt of energy wired through his body, he rubbed his thumb across her cheek. Her gleaming expression turned into an embarrassed one as she responded to the unexpected contact. "You had chalk on your face."

"Oh." She stepped away, sweeping her gaze across the room and evading his.

She didn't have anything on her face. He'd just wanted to touch her…like some fucking weirdo. *What am I thinking? How could this stranger have me acting like a high schooler seeing his first pair of tits?* He had seen plenty of tits. Blondie laughed, still seeming embarrassed, and Shane forgot about any tits but the ones that would press against his button-down if he stepped forward a little bit. She was cute and sexy all at once, mysterious, but their conversation had been so easy and natural that it was like Shane had known her his entire life.

Combined with her genuine smile and honest eyes, her quick tongue was at variance with her sweet exterior. A contrast. She was a siren. Shane was certain of it, just as he was certain that he'd fall under her singing spell any day if it meant being able to take her home.

Chapter Three

"Was she your girlfriend?"

They had finished their game of Eight Ball with no more accidental or purposeful touches, and the night was coming to a quick end.

It took Shane all his might not to beg her to go home with him.

Usually, he stayed away from sleeping with strangers, but as the night had progressed, he cared less and less if she was one. Incapable of forgetting the way he'd caught her watching him at the club, yearning planted in those baby-doll eyes, Shane wanted to see that same expression while his cock was buried inside her. "Awfully personal question for someone who won't tell me her name."

Placing down her drink, Blondie gave him a tempting-as-hell smile. "Avoiding the question? That means she was your girlfriend."

He pursed his lips before he showed her a smile of his own. Honesty was always the best policy. "I don't really date."

After having come home from abroad to find who he had thought was the love of his life in bed with one of their 'friends', Shane had vowed off relationships. He preferred it that way, mostly. Sometimes it was lonely, but that wasn't information she needed to know.

"You don't date or you can't? Are you married?"

"Me? Hitched?" His head jerked to either side, trying to throw away the thought. "No way, sugar. Why you so curious about my relationship status?"

Choosing to avoid his question, Blondie tucked the rim

of her glass between her lips and drank. When she decided to resume her interrogation, she asked, "What does your tattoo mean?"

"Which one?" The one she'd seen when his shirt had been undone?

"The one on your hand."

Reflexively, he peered down to the tattoo.

In the slot beside his thumb on the backside of his hand, not on the web but lower, was a small but detailed portrait of a Redback.

To most people the spider looked menacing with its talon-like legs and prominent red stripe. To Shane, the tattoo was perfect. It revived memories, both bitter and heartwarming.

"I had a friend name Lennon down in Louisiana. We met overseas. He jumped in front of a bullet for me in Iraq. Saved my life. He didn't die." *Then*, he didn't add. "The bullet got him in the spine, made him a paraplegic." His breath shook as the memory unleashed a pain he'd long become acquainted with.

"He, um…" Shane shifted in his seat. "He had a fixation for spiders. I used to not like them so much myself, but while he was in therapy, I read him books about different species. That was what he was into. I learned a lot about them. Such amazing creatures. This one is my favorite. A Redback."

"It's beautiful, Shane."

He crinkled his nose. *Beautiful?*

Women didn't think his tattoo of a venomous spider was beautiful.

"My brother Holton had a tarantula growing up. She was a"—she tapped her chin—"I *think* it was a Chilean Rose. Maybe it was a Curly Hair. I don't remember. Tarantulas are really cute, right?"

Her eyes glistened playfully. For the first time since they'd met, Shane was interested in more than sex with her. She *liked* spiders?

Blondie went on, "They're not dangerous at all, either.

It's a bunch of fear mongering. You probably knew that already. When I was younger, my brother taught me not to be squeamish when it came to nature. We spent a lot of time outdoors as kids." She grinned, and he loved that talking about things like spiders excited her as much as it excited him.

"How long were you in Iraq?"

The air shifted, becoming heavy and oppressive.

Shane brought his hand to the back of his neck. The uncomfortable weight in his chest made his shoulders cave and his breathing thin. Rocks and sand crunched below his feet.

"Two tours. Three years," he confided, his voice haunted by memories of death and dust. She reached for his hand and started stroking a line against his knuckles.

"For what you did for our country, thank you. I have nothing but admiration for brave people like you who are willing to put their lives on the line to protect us at home."

Brave? Him going to Iraq hadn't been an act of bravery.

Shane had been born a no-good Williams boy who lacked a future outside of his pop's mechanic shop nestled in a small town in the bowels of Georgia. When he'd graduated high school, he had signed up for the SEALS, determined to run away from the insanity of his household. Really, he had been trading one insanity for another.

"Thank you, sugar." Shane needed to switch the subject. He wasn't okay with speaking about his tours of duty. "Enough questions about me. Where are you from?"

"I want to know more," she said with a cute pout on her lips.

"You can know more when you answer *my* questions."

"Ellenboro, born and bred. What was it like to serve?"

Shane paid no attention to her latter remark. "That's not too far. What are you doing in Charlotte? You live here now or visitin'?"

She absently stirred her finger around the edge of her drink. "Relocation for work. I live outside of downtown with my best friend, Olive."

"What's a girl like you doing alone at a nightclub, if you don't mind my asking?"

She folded her arms. "What's a guy like you doing getting sucked off at a nightclub? Probably not a rare occurrence, is it?"

Shane liked that she went right for the punch. "I like to be adventurous."

"Be adventurous with the door locked."

"And miss out on the potential of having a pretty woman getting caught admiring my cock?" He winked, his mind full of the image. "I think I'll pass, PT."

"Are you always this honest?"

"If there's one thing I can promise you, sugar, it's that I'll never lie. I hate liars." Shane nodded with resolve. He'd dealt with enough them to last one lifetime. "Now, what were we talkin' about?" Shane grinned wide. "Being adventurous, right?"

If just to avoid commenting, she began answering his initial question. "I went out tonight because I was celebrating with Olive, but she left to go to her guy friend's..."

Blondie didn't need to finish her sentence. He understood what she meant.

He tried to keep the disapproval out of his expression. Her friend had left her alone in an unfamiliar city to get some action on a night they were supposed to be celebrating?

Before he could make a smart-ass remark—he always found that his tongue ran faster than his brain—he continued to probe her for information.

"What do you do for a living?"

Panic flared across her features, and she retracted her hands from the tabletop. Behind her blonde, fanned-out lashes, her vision glazed over as she went off somewhere in her head. Her silence stretched over two minutes, knitting him with uncertainty. He should tell her to forget about it. His elbows scraped the wooden counter when he sat back against his chair, opening his mouth to tell her she didn't have to answer him if it made her uncomfortable.

However, she spoke before he could. "Sorry. I was thinking about something else." She shook her head, causing waves of hair to bounce around her face. "I oversee and implement sales and marketing strategies for digital platforms. Apps. Websites."

"No way."

"Way." She took the rest of her drink down in one relentless gulp.

"Hot damn! I think fate's playing us for chess."

Head tilting, she frowned. "What?"

"Fate is playing us like chess pieces, sugar. After the SEALS, I studied computer science. Did some full-stack development and freelancing here and there. Not in it anymore, but I'm in something similar. I work on creative with plenty of marketers."

Shane didn't mention his exact job title.

His executive position wasn't one he threw around to strangers. He'd been with plenty of gold diggers in his day, and it wasn't an experience he wanted to repeat, not that he assumed Blondie was one. It'd become a habit to keep quiet about his accomplishments. He was no millionaire — didn't want to be, either — but Shane did well for a small-town boy, making enough money that some women were willing to use him for it.

"Who would have thought we had all this in common?" Shane loved how her eyes lit up before going dark when he leaned in for a close-up. "I think it's a sign. You should tell me your name, so I can invite you on a proper night out. See how much more we have in common."

"I don't go *out* with people."

"We can stay in, if you'd like," he retorted, faster than he was proud of and lower than he'd intended.

There went her blush again. It blossomed like it sensed spring around the corner.

Damn, but wasn't she the kind of innocent that tempted big bad wolves like him? He rubbed his lips, wanting to taste hers. Devour, more like it.

Below his steady observation, her mouth parted.

As if she couldn't bear the scrutiny of his wandering eyes, she allowed her own furtive gaze to recede from his and flitter across the room like two green butterflies.

What had that been about not coming on to her? "You're awfully pretty, you know that?" *Yeah, fuck that.*

"I..." She appeared befuddled before her eyebrows crinkled. She frowned, and even that was pretty.

"You're trying to hit on me after what I saw earlier? You have *zero* shame."

Shane shrugged, a smile settling over his lips. "I'm ambitious. When I see somethin' I want, regardless of the circumstances, I go for it. What about you?"

She placed her drink down like she was trying to stain the wood. "I'm ambitious," she cocked her head, narrowing her green eyes, "but I don't see anything I want."

Not remotely defeated by her remark, Shane moved the conversation forward. "Where do you work? Maybe I know the place."

His career had made him well-connected in Charlotte, albeit in most of the creative circles.

Shane didn't like to brag, but he was damn good at his job. His many awards and acknowledgments were proof of that. After four years of freelancing for companies all over the world and what felt like a decade heading the design team for a high-profile client in Manhattan, he'd settled down in his mom's hometown, where some of his distant family still resided, to help his friend start a company.

Because his business partner handled the logistics side of the firm—screw that, Shane wouldn't be caught dead doing paperwork—his work here was stress-free and fun, strictly on the creative side. He'd founded a business, yeah, but it hadn't been a big deal. He'd provided the money only. Not even his employees knew. He kept quiet about it and did everything behind closed curtains, answering to no one but himself. He made his own rules and wouldn't have it any other way.

Blondie opened her mouth to respond, but Bub yelled over her.

"Closing time! Hop on, yonder lovebirds."

Shane scowled at him, more because he was forcing them out than because Bub had used the term 'lovebirds'.

Gathering her belongings, Blondie started off her chair. "I had fun."

"I'll walk you back." He didn't want to leave her company.

"You don't have to."

"I don't let pretty ladies pay for tabs or walk alone this late at night. Let's get going. Night, Bub. Catch ya' tomorrow noon."

"I'm still not sleeping with you." Blondie turned, raising both eyebrows, as he caught up with her. "So don't try anything funny."

"I think you have a dirty mind, sugar."

"Don't call me that." Her teeth chattered.

The January air was chilly, so he couldn't imagine how Blondie must have survived with nothing but a sheath dress to keep the cold at bay. He wished he had a jacket, but as an idea sparked in his mind, he was glad he didn't. Feeling bold, Shane draped his arm over her shoulder, bringing her against his side, where there was plenty of warmth for her to cling to.

Much to Shane's surprise, this perfect stranger did the strangest thing. She leaned into him, shivering, small and needing his protection. Although it was protection from nothing but the wind, Shane became prideful, smiling as if he'd just won a prize. Feeling uncomfortably at ease, he held her closer and with more confidence. *Just because she's cold*, he reminded himself.

"Dirty mind or not, there is no way I'm sleeping with you after what I saw."

* * * *

The front door of Shane's apartment burst open. *Finally! Fucking finally!*

He rushed inside, kicking the door closed with his foot after he entered. In his arms was a sexy blonde who'd kept promising she wasn't going to sleep with him.

He didn't know how it had happened.

They'd found her car and he'd gone to say goodbye, then that goodbye had turned into a kiss and a touch that had sunk lower. Now their bodies banged on the foyer wall like two wrecking balls, making a picture frame fall somewhere at their sides.

He didn't care. There could be an earthquake and Shane wouldn't give a damn. He could only focus on his need, growing so large that he was seconds from exploding. Shane didn't know if he was going to make it to the bedroom in time. She hugged her arms around his neck so tightly he couldn't move his head to do anything but kiss her. That was okay with him.

He smashed his mouth against her softer, plusher one. Poking his tongue along the seam, he cupped her neck as she widened her lips to allow him leeway. Shane let his hands wander over her top, shove aside her dress's intrusive fabric. Wrapping his tongue with hers, he slid his hand over her breasts, cupping her on a groan. The nipples he'd been able to see through her fabric turned to stones in his palm.

Letting go of the kiss, he whispered, out of breath, along her cheek, "Jesus, sugar. You have perfect tits." *Perfect.*

Kneading her breast, he slanted his mouth on hers—its suppleness, its weight added pressure between his thighs. He pinched her nipple with two fingers, chuckling as her moans picked up. She pushed her chest out, her whimpers launching pleasure up his cock.

"Oh, that feels amazing. Keep touching me like that," Blondie groaned.

"I'll touch you any way you want me to, sugar." Shane lifted her away from the wall, only to stumble back like a drunken fool and slam into his front door.

Cradling her ass, he hauled her up his body. She climbed him like a tree, curling her legs around his back and pushing her dress higher by his torso.

"That's right." He tugged her closer. "Get your ass up here so you can feel how hard my dick has been for you all night."

She squealed, giggling as he squeezed her ass cheeks, her smile lighting up the darkness.

Lust rang through Shane's ears, loud and demanding, when he swirled his hips, pushing them up to grind his erection against her panties.

"Oh…" she gasped, tilting her head back.

Shane leaned forward. He opened his mouth on her neck.

"You like that?" He lifted his hips with more purpose.

Blondie trailed her fingers up his shoulders and through his hair. "Yes."

Taking a trip down her throat, Shane was thankful he made it to her breasts without jizzing his pants. Her nipples had turned so hard they were like rock candy in his mouth. He kissed one, slowly and methodically, then moved over to the other, pulling her whole areola between his lips where he massaged it with his tongue. Grinding. Moaning. Back banging into the door, Shane breathlessly searched to feel and taste everything he could. When he made his way back to her mouth, their tongues clashed in a heated duel, the excited roll of her hips becoming harder and wilder and carrying him one step closer. Damn, she was hot.

Shane was afraid his clothes would burn off because the two of them were making so much fire. He was also afraid the buttons of his pants would pop loose any second, because his erection was pushing angrily against the fabric, as if pleading for freedom from its oppressor.

Somehow, they made it to the couch. Not the bedroom, but good enough.

Shane lowered her on the cushions. He sat on his knees at her front. "Take it off."

Without question, she pulled her dress over her head. He yanked her panties to the floor.

"Damn," he murmured, his hands seeming to move on their own to outline her curves. "Every woman should look like you." She had a wonderful body.

Truer words had never been spoken.

She may have been sitting on it, but Shane could tell her ass was large and thick. Not that he was just seeing it now. He had gotten plenty of glimpses of its heart-shaped form earlier. Her breasts were succulent fruit, plump and mature. Her stomach wasn't hard or toned but was soft and womanly. He loved that she had hips he could grab hold of and thighs the right size to squeeze his waist hard while he plowed his cock deeper. "Absolutely beautiful."

Shane took a moment to admire her gorgeous figure, her clean pussy, soaked and shaved, and the raw need in her eyes before placing his hands below her legs and hauling her to his mouth. Running his tongue through her gentle folds, Shane spread her aromatic juices from the top all the way down to her entrance that he dipped slowly into.

Moans hurled like slingshots from her throat the faster he devoured her.

Shane sucked and kissed every inch of her pussy so that her creamy liquids smeared all over his lips, coating the inside of his mouth. Her clit was his toy, and by reading her responses, he found out the best way to play with it. She bucked her hips, gifting the air with a delightful sigh the second Shane locked his lips around the sensitive nerves.

Heat and goosebumps spread under the pads of his fingers as he moved them up her thighs, opening her wider so he could have more room to sink farther, until his tongue was sliding in and out of the area his cock would soon fit. The flesh vibrated when he groaned.

Fuck, she tasted sweet. Honeysuckle good. Shane rubbed his tongue through her moist canal and he circled his thumb across her flesh over and over. Breathing in her pleasant fragrance, he continued upward. Shane replaced his tongue with his finger and his lips found home at her clit, kissing and massaging. Before long, Blondie arched her back against his couch, shouting her climax, and goddamn, it was like she'd won the lotto.

He wished every woman's response to an orgasm was as ardent as hers.

Unlocking from her, he smiled and stood. Shane removed his clothing, proud of her open appraisal of his body. She licked her lips like she'd done at the club, and he couldn't take it anymore. He handed her the condom he'd taken out of the pocket of his slacks.

"Put it on me."

By her stunned look, he didn't think she'd ever been told to put a condom on a man before. He tossed the idea aside. No way was he thinking about what she had or hadn't done. Right now, she was his, and he was crazy for more of her.

Shane groaned as Blondie's hands moved down his erection, covering it with the protection that he was already filling with his pre-cum.

With the condom rolled to his base, he scooped her up and sat himself on the couch so that she was on top of him. His erection grew harder, his breath catching when he caught sight of her slick pussy, pink and pretty and waiting for him. "Come on. I want you to ride me."

Chewing her lip, she grabbed his shoulders. "Just... Just let me know if I'm doing it right. I don't have a lot of experience." Her voice rang with doubt.

He stilled. "You're not a virgin, are you?" *No.* He couldn't *deflower* her.

"No" — the corner of her lips descended — "I'm not."

His entire body went liquid smooth.

"Sugar, nothin' you could do will be wrong. Just lookin' at you is enough to make me come. Now get your sexy ass up here." He dropped his hands so he could fit her in his palms. "I need to be in you *now*. You taste so damn good. I can only imagine how good you're going to feel."

Holding onto his cock with one hand, she stroked herself with his erection before holding him at the appropriate position. Her eyes snapped to his. Was that hesitance he saw?

"You want this, right, sugar?" *Please... Please say yes.* His body was alert and high strung. "Sugar?" It came out in a wheeze. He would stop if she asked, but fuck, he didn't want to. "Talk to me. If you don't want this, I won't continue. It's okay—"

"Yes. Yes." She nodded. "I need this. I need *you*. Please, yes."

He needed no further motivation. Taking control of her movements, he made sure their bodies were aligned. He teased her opening, and the second he pushed inside her, he knew this was going to be one of the best sexual experiences of his life. Her pussy *strangled* him.

Shane had never been in someone who'd felt this good.

She lowered herself with half-closed eyes, crying out and jumping up, clearly fearful of taking on his entire length before trying to push down again. He was fearful, too. He wanted to ask her again if she was a virgin, but there was no way he could talk.

His ability to do anything but feel his body slowly stretching hers had long departed. After a few harrowing seconds of jerking and whimpering and Shane gripping her tight, Blondie managed to root Shane deep inside her pussy, the best pussy he'd ever been rooted in.

He was already sweating and groaning. She probably thought he was insane, but it took *effort* not to free himself inside her after the first couple of pumps. He didn't know how he managed. Taking her hips, he aided her strokes, not bothering to go slow or soft. He fucked her hard.

As her blazing-hot pussy raced over his girth, she used her long nails to scratch his skin sore. Her breast was smashed into his mouth, nipple bouncing on his tongue.

He thrust harder, her wetness sleeking his entrance, and she yelled his name repeatedly.

Shane had never liked his name so much. He wanted her to say it louder, as loud as she could, but she quickly shushed herself, as if ashamed of getting carried away.

No, to hell if Blondie would hold back from him now. He gave her ass an encouraging slap.

"Louder!" he groaned.

She liked it, too. He did it again, smiling as her voice rose.

Sinking his fingers into each cheek, Shane crushed her ass in his hands, bringing her up and down on his lap until he was entering her faster than his heart hammered against his chest.

The tight spasm of her orgasm gripped his cock, and her body quivered in his arms, just seconds before his own orgasm hit him — a baseball bat knocking the wind out of him. Shane came hard, intense relief flushing through his body. A groan ripped from his throat. She contracted around his cock, wringing him dry, sucking him for every ounce he was worth. He laughed. She felt so good that he couldn't help but laugh. Their breath came out heavy but short, their bodies still moving in unison as they trickled down from their high. But Shane wasn't finished, not even close. When they'd successfully caught their breath, he gathered her in his arms and paced to his bedroom.

They entered the room. He rested her on his mattress. The sterling spray of moonlight cast over her features.

"Spread your legs." Shane slapped the inside of her thigh.

She opened wide.

"That's right. You're spoiling me. If you keep listening to me so well, I'm going make you do more — "

"Shut up and kiss me again." The grin in her eyes found her lips — so did he.

Delving her tongue into his mouth, she gave his neck a hug, pulling him down. He tumbled toward her, laughing again. Man, this was fun. Fun sex. All sex should be fun sex. Shane liked it. He liked her. He didn't even know her name, but he liked her.

"Getting demanding already?"

She giggled and it was cute. It made him laugh more.

"Demand all you want, sugar. As long as it ends with my cock inside you, I'm A-okay."

She wasn't giggling any more. She was sucking in air like his words had somehow collided with her lungs and pushed out all their oxygen.

"I'm lovin' that pussy. Want more of it. Tasting it and fucking it."

The sound of her gasping made him wild.

He pressed his lips down on hers, soaking up her cries of enjoyment as he shifted his hand against her mound and over her clit. The little crowd of nerves swelled under his pliable fingers, then again, below his restless tongue.

This time Shane put on his own condom. He crawled above her body, licking along the soft angle of her breasts and neck. He gripped the back of her hair.

She brought her legs around his waist, holding him tightly like they were a bow and he a present to be wrapped. Shane grunted when he slid his cock amid her inner warmth.

With her snug channel contracting tighter around each movement, she brought him higher and higher still, every time his hips tapped her inner thighs. He took her slowly, not wanting to rush.

Whereas, the first time, he could only think of the end result—an explosive climax—this time, Shane needed to explore. He wanted to feel the push, the pull. He wanted to hear, in detail, the sweet sounds coming from her mouth as he burrowed deeper and slipped out slower. The build was long, the reward consuming. His skin glided on top of hers so close that her strong heartbeat moved on his chest. A furnace of heat surrounded them until they were melding together. They melted into the sheets.

Winding his fingers in the back of her hair, he brought her face toward his, her lips closer. All night, they kissed and fucked as if they were anything but strangers.

* * * *

Ring. Ring. Ring. Ring.

Groaning, Shane slapped his alarm. It wasn't his alarm, though. It was his cell phone. Someone was calling. Deciding to ignore it, he flipped over in his bed.

His body was as tired as if he'd carried a bag of bricks across town. He could sleep for an entire year after last night. He smiled. He wanted more. His cock was in love.

Reaching over, ready to hide his fingers inside Blondie's little pussy, he froze when he realized there was no one there. Shane sat up, stretching his eyes wide to greet orange tentacles lashing across his bedroom. Squinting against the sun, he tugged the covers off his naked body and walked around his apartment.

Where had Blondie run off to?

After finding his place empty—as he usually preferred it—he journeyed back to his room. That was when he saw it. A piece of paper lay on his nightstand.

I had a good time – PT

Anger, hot and fierce, rushed through him. *'I had a good time?'* That's all he got?

He'd given her four orgasms that had had her shouting at the top of her lungs, and she'd had a *good* time? She had snuck out while he'd been sleeping? His clock read ten a.m.

Shit. How could he have slept through his alarm? Did his seven a.m. wake her up? Was that when she'd left? Who left without saying anything?

You do.

Sure, he'd left girls right after sex, but it wasn't a secret as to what they should and shouldn't expect from Shane. He had never been the breakfast-in-bed type.

At least he had extended the courtesy of exchanging names. Shane didn't know anything about the wide-eyed stranger who'd given him the best night of fucking in his life. She'd just up and left?

Was Blondie like him, only sex and no relationships?

Thinking so upset Shane. It made him feel dirty and... used. He laughed. Someone had made him feel *used*? It was something he'd never experienced before, and it was as shitty a feeling as it sounded. Was this how the women he slept with had felt? A weight, like the bricks he'd carried across town, sunk into the pits of his stomach as he repeated the question.

Settling back on his bed, Shane stared at his ceiling fan rotating so fast it made him a little dizzy. Why was he acting like a pussy-whipped teenager? So what that she had left?

She should have gone. She had walked in on him getting sucked off in a nightclub. That didn't exactly scream 'good idea'. Just like her, he should leave it alone.

This was probably what he deserved.

A no-name girl to show up one night, beautiful from her pink-painted toes to her dark-blonde ringlets, and fuck him with her perfect pussy like he'd never been fucked before, only to disappear without so much as the scent of her girly shampoo to keep him company. Taking his phone off his nightstand, he saw a missed call from Jenny, one of his late-night women—no strings, just friends.

Shooting her a text, he canceled the plans they'd made to see each other tonight.

A one-night stand is making you go soft? Who the hell are you? the rational part of his brain asked. The irrational answered, *No. It isn't a one-night stand.*

There was something between Blondie and him. She had to have felt it, too.

He didn't want a relationship, not a romantic one, at least, and neither did she, but Shane had another proposition for her, a less passive—less clothing—one.

After he retracted the bedroom shades with the remote on his nightstand, he gazed over downtown Charlotte. The sun, bouncing off the surrounding buildings, was warm syrup pouring across his skin. Below him, people scurried along the sidewalks, too far to be anything but small, abstract shapes. She might have been one of them.

He plucked his phone from his nightstand then proceeded to scroll through his contacts, pausing when he found the number he was looking for. A plan formulated in his mind. Did he really want to do this? Shane pressed 'dial'. If it meant getting Blondie back in his bed, the answer was yes, and Blondie *would* be back in his bed. Shane was certain of it.

Chapter Four

"Look what the cat dragged in." Lifting her nose from her cereal bowl, Olive snickered and gave Rose an expression comparable to the one Rose made every time she watched *The Real Housewives of Atlanta* and Porsha and Cynthia decided to go at it.

"Don't you dare get started." She arrowed her glare at Olive, who closed her mouth, pursing her lips.

Creeping her gaze over Rose's bed hair and unaligned dress, Olive smiled, and her smile, like an advertisement for teeth whitening, was bright and shining with awareness.

"Good night?"

Heat rising in her cheeks, Rose released a hefty groan. Her best friend would want all the details, and all Rose wanted was to have a hot shower and get some much-needed sleep because she sure as heck hadn't gotten any the previous night. Olive smirked at her as if she could tell.

Picking up her steps, Rose scurried through the hallway.

"This discussion is *not* over!"

Rose rolled her eyes at her friend's words.

After closing her bedroom door, she began trading her clothing for a comfy robe. She tiptoed through the hall and into their shared bathroom, where she barricaded herself.

Rose had a headache and what, during her ten-minute ride of shame back to Olive's townhouse, she had begun to call a *vagina* ache. Having a night of unadulterated sex was supposed to have cured her cobwebs and fueled her like gas did an automobile. She should be able to run on that single sexual experience alone until she found something more permanent.

She had gone over a year without sex, so it wouldn't be difficult, right? Wrong!

So wrong, in fact, that if wrong was the bullseye, Rose had shot through the center, past the target and into the woods beyond. Now that Rose had had sex — passionate, sweaty, erotic sex — she wanted it more than ever. Shedding her robe, she dropped it to the floor then stepped into the shower.

Her sleepy body revived with thoughts of her steamy night with Shane and his monster erection, which she now thought deserved a medal.

World's Best Performance, the medal would say in bold lettering.

Rose reached down, her body reacting to her touch. Breasts sore. Nipples saluting. Veins humming with activity. She wished it was *him* touching her.

'I'm lovin' that pussy. Want more of it. Tasting it and fucking it.'

Did that man know how to dirty talk or what? Second medal. *World's Best Dirty Talker.* He was deserving of that medal, too. Finding a good dirty talker was like finding a four-leaf clover, or that's what Olive had always told her. In a sea of many, few would unearth the lucky charm.

Rose was proud to be one of the gals who'd gotten lucky in more than one way.

'Every woman should look like you.'

She took a good, long peek at her body. At a size fourteen, she'd never had the best confidence. Heck, she'd been called chubby growing up. Her weight was one of her biggest insecurities but, with Shane, it was like she was the sexiest woman he'd ever seen. She lifted her lips, smiling, but dropped them immediately. She disliked that she'd never been able to conjure the feeling of being sexy on her own or with Simon. Simon had never called her sexy or told her he thought her body was nice — not that she should have been seeking anyone's approval but her own. Even knowing that, she couldn't help but be happy. The way Shane had responded to her was like magic. Like, with a wiggle of her finger, he would evaporate into a puddle at her feet, but in the same instance it could happen vice-versa. Shane touched her, and she was pudding.

Had he been truthful about everything he'd said?

Or had it all been an 'in the moment' thing?

She decided it didn't matter. Who cared if she'd ever see Shane again? Parting her wet and tender folds, Rose started twirling her finger over her sweet spot, trying to mimic how he had expertly played there. *Strum, strum. Stroke, stroke.*

Her legs became heavy. Blocks of pleasure stacked at her center, soon consuming her.

"*Oh!*" Rose moaned, a sound of pure bliss as another orgasm racked her.

She arched off the slippery tile partition, her mind numb with pleasure.

Stars flared behind her eyes and between her legs that were wobbling as if she'd downed a whole bottle of Jack Daniel's. It was the second orgasm she had given herself, mind-blowing because she'd been reminiscing about her night in Heaven with a handsome stranger.

Cracking open her eyelids, she could hardly see in front of her because so much fog had crowded the shower. Rose drank in the hot steam. She was lightheaded. Her body, drained of energy, hung somewhere between consciousness and unconsciousness. Her heart beat hard but smooth, mimicking the water slamming against the floor. Shane had created this unquenchable desire in her, one that she was afraid her fingers couldn't satisfy.

"Rosemary Louise, I know you're not moanin' the holy word in there!" Olive's shout derailed her thoughts. "Is that why you've been in the shower for thirty minutes?"

Has it been thirty minutes?

"Get your butt on out here. Holton pulled up with the furniture."

Rose groaned, not wanting to come to terms with the reality of her busy day.

Olive had given her a to-do list.

After she helped Holton move in her boxes, she would have a nail and hair appointment with Olive. At noon, they were meeting friends from college for a downtown brunch. Once home, she had to unpack her things—and she had a lot of things. Then she needed to get back to work, studying Mr. Moreno. Usually she loved her schedule more packed than a Clemson vs. Gamecocks arena. Not today. If she had her way, she'd stay home and do nothing but laze around and think about her amazing night. Closing her eyes, she pictured Shane's lips on her skin and his erection, so wonderful and thick, driving her to the best orgasms of her life. Her night with Shane had been everything she had needed. He had been flawless, a conductor working her body. They had created beautiful music—his grunts, her moans, the slapping of skin and the quick sip of air, not to mention *his* body. Shane was the definition of masculine and *hot*.

One look at his tight skin, the dangerous tattoos outlining his cuts and curves, his broad shoulders and lean waist had Rose dripping like a popsicle under a fervid sunshine. Just as she determined to do something about the lust bowling up her skin, the bathroom door jiggled.

"All right! I'm coming, already." *And not in a fun way.* Rose sulked, twisting off the shower head. The abrupt halt of water brought her back to reality.

Her nighttime fling with Shane had been just that—a fling. No matter how much Rose wished she could bottle his intensity and have it whenever she pleased, guys like Shane—bad-boy players with bodies that killed and smiles that resurrected—were a one-time deal. They conquered and moved on. It was best that way. Shane was a drug Rose could get addicted to, and for that reason alone she needed to stay far away. The icy air seeping into her skin as she made her way out of the shower was another thing that placed her back in the *now*. Simon hated turning the air-conditioning on. It wasted electricity, he'd always complained. *Simon.*

Until Shane had brought up her job yesterday, she hadn't thought of Simon once, and when she had, the thought of her ex had been a short one.

Uncomfortable with the fact that Shane could accomplish something that her partner of five years had never been able to, Rose was cut by a sharp sense of betrayal.

Was it okay for her to have enjoyed herself so much with a complete stranger when her relationship had ended only two months before? She considered calling Simon. Never being one to do well with hangovers, he probably felt horrid right about now, but she had to remember he wasn't her responsibility any longer. Shoving back all thoughts of her past was something Rose would have to get used to doing—and soon. She got dressed then joined the others.

They began unloading.

"Here ya go, Cookie Monster."

Rose coiled her fingers around the borders of the cardboard box her brother handed her, but she didn't move to take it inside.

She was stunned and had been stunned since she'd found Holton sitting on the couch at her grandmother's, looking nothing like the young boy he had been when she'd left home eight years before.

Holton gave Rose a quick show of his pearly whites, crinkling the corners of his eyes as he grinned—a mirror of how her own features moved.

"First time you've seen me all dressed up, ain't it? If you'd come home every once in a while instead of holing yourself up in Houston, you would have seen it sooner."

She knew her brother well enough to realize he meant no harm by his comment. It still struck a chord, though—lots of chords if she were being honest, if only because it was the most accurate response he could have given. She and Holton had seen each other plenty while she'd lived in Houston, but it had always been him coming to her. He'd had no reason to wear his uniform to Texas, and she had missed his inauguration into the police force three years back because of work.

Work. Rose sighed, thinking of all the Moreno & Blu research she'd yet to do.

Simon had told her she was in love with her job, not him. Did Holton feel neglected by her, also? While Rose was strengthening her career, Holton was beginning his. If he were as busy as she had been at her start, he didn't need any distractions. That was how she had justified it.

In truth, she had been too scared of North Carolina to come back.

Holding the box closer to her chest, Rose used it for support as she watched her brother walking in and out of Olive's townhouse, furniture in hand.

His uniform, fitting tightly around his biceps in a crisp midnight blue, made him look grown up, like a man. Rose was immobilized with grief. Tears gathered in the corner of her eyes, their fall impending. She'd missed so much. She'd missed *him* so much.

Looking back on what her life had become, she couldn't help thinking that she'd traded in her family for her version of perfection. The accusation was tart and ugly. She loved Holton more than anything. She never wanted to abandon him. In her quest for perfection, had she?

"We don't got time for you to stand there admiring my good looks. I got work soon. We gotta get a move on." Holton nudged his head toward the house.

Eyes going soft, he offered Rose a sympathetic smile. "It's okay, Rosey. You're here now."

"God, you're good."

He had to be clairvoyant.

Rose went back to work. She needed to remember that her new life was more than a new job opportunity and a changed relationship status, but a chance to spend time with her family. As Rose worked, she made a promise to herself—a promise she would keep—that she wouldn't leave this place until her family knew, beyond any and all doubt, how much she loved them, even if staying here and knowing what it would do to her tore Rose apart.

It had all begun—her nightmares and her anger—the summer before her freshman year of high school. Her life had changed forever. An innocent trip to camp—the same trip she'd been making every year since she'd been twelve—had turned into a horror story she'd dream about for the rest of her life.

Pain ripped through her heart so acute that Rose became short of breath. Her vision dimmed, obscuring everything but the memory of the assault. As nature's sounds had amplified in the nighttime, her pleas for help hadn't been enough to disrupt the North Carolina air. The soil she had played in as a kid and the rocks she'd skipped across the water had flattened against her shoulders, smashing into her back.

Catching herself on the metal rail, she would have fallen down the stairs if she hadn't dropped a box of clothing. Laundry colored the grass—some shirts green—Simon's favorite color—and some blue like the one she'd worn *that* night.

"You okay?" Olive ran up to her.

"I'm fine." She hid her shaking hands, interlocking her fingers. "I wasn't paying attention."

Olive exchanged a look with Holton before facing Rose. "Why don't you sit down? We're almost done."

"I'm fine." But she wasn't fine. She would never be fine while she was in North Carolina. *He* was why she hated this state, why every second she was here, she felt nasty—impure. Knowing *he* was here, even if he was locked away for life, was enough to make her want to leave and never return.

Holton hooked his elbow around her neck and leaned her into the pit between his chest and arm. "Can you do me a favor, Cookie Monster?"

Rose nodded.

"Make me some iced tea, will ya? Like you used to make

it. Dang, I missed your sweet tea. Olive and I will finish up here, and when we do, I want a whole pitcher to take back home with me. Got it?" He was trying to distract her, and it was working.

"Got it."

Feeling reinvigorated, Rose did as instructed, making her way inside and taking out the biggest pot she could find in order to boil water.

Olive and Holton had finished unpacking and were talking in private by the time she was done making two pitchers of her sweet tea. "Remember to refrigerate it before you gulp it all down." She handed a warm pitcher to her brother. "No putting ice in it to cool it off."

"I can't make any promises." Holton eyed her mischievously. "If y'all need anything, just holler at me." He climbed in his truck, his gaze lingering on Olive before turning to Rose. "Good luck Monday, Rosey—not that you need it. You're gonna kick ass."

Emotions climbed up her chest, making it hard to breathe. She placed her hand over her heart, rubbing there like the motion would make it hurt a little less. She needed to tell her brother the truth about her move. She didn't want to keep hiding it from him. Really, she needed to tell everyone.

"Love you!" Rose yelled, but he was already backing out of his parking space.

Beside her, Olive rested Rose's head on her shoulder. The wordless exchange brought Rose to tears. Her brother had grown up so fast, and she'd missed it all. How could she have allowed this to happen?

"It's okay. Just let it out, Rosey. It's gonna be okay."

Together they watched Holton drive off, and when his truck disappeared, Olive grabbed Rose's shoulders with gentle affection, holding her at arm's length. "Brunch? Alcohol? Boys?"

Heck, yes. Rose needed a distraction, and all three sounded wonderful. Releasing her, Olive brought her fingers to Rose's cheek where she cleared her tears.

"Brunch, alcohol and boys it is. Now, let's get you into something sexy. Girl rule number one is confidence on the outside boosts the confidence on the inside."

That was how Rose found herself in a scanty outfit again—a short skirt and button blouse, an opera-styled necklace and kitten heels. Drowning in mimosas and the latest gossip, she and her girlfriends sat at an outside table for four in the middle of downtown.

Rose forked up some of her French toast and strawberries and shoved them in her mouth, making *yum* noises as she chewed. Brunch was, in her opinion, the best meal of any day. Allowing the sweet cocktail to wash away the strawberry syrup on her tongue and the negative episode she had had earlier, she gave a contented sigh.

"Tell me everything." Olive wiggled her eyebrows.

Beth and Mandy glanced up from their plates of Belgian waffles and sunny-side-up eggs as if they were about to exchange scary tales over flickering candlelight.

Rose wasn't the kiss-and-tell type. Sex was private and not to be shared.

Those were her normal beliefs and her brown-nosed friends were all too aware of them. She scanned each of their faces, their curiosity as apparent as ever. She saw it clawing at them like they were desperate to be vicariously whisked away by the details of Rose's trip to Heaven.

With three pairs of eyes staring at her, there was a huge amount of pressure on Rose, but the bottomless mimosas had put her high on the tipsy-Richter scale, so she couldn't help thinking what did it matter if the girls knew about Shane? It was a one-night deal, and Rose wanted to relive it as much as she could. This was a way to do so. She wiped the sides of her lips with a napkin then placed it neatly over her crossed legs, patting it down before returning her attention to the group. She gave the ladies a charming smile that told them to perk their ears because this was going to be good.

"Firstly," Rose said, giving a pause for dramatic effect,

though she didn't need to embellish the story to make it amazing, "that man is an animal" — she bit down on her lip as she recalled Shane's panty-dropping aggression—"in the *best* way possible."

Their responses were all immediate and hilarious.

Olive elevated her arms, thanking the heavens that her best friend had finally gotten a good lay. With a light brush, Beth swooped her hair over her shoulder and leaned forward on her elbows, eager for more. Mandy fanned her hand beside her face, preaching something about those being the best kind. The tell-me-more in their gazes gave Rose the boost she needed to continue.

"We went to a bar where he introduced me to his cousin."

"Cousin?" Mandy's eyebrows raised. "Was he good-looking?"

"Introducing you to family on the first date?" Beth brought her drink up.

"It was his cousin's bar," Rose continued. "His cousin was good-looking, yes." Truthfully, Rose hadn't paid much attention to Shane's kin. She'd been too focused on the heaping pile of sex beside her who had been beaming out his alpha male pheromones at a rate that had made Rose want to strip off her clothes like they were burning her alive.

"What happened next?" Olive eyes were animated, mouth open in amazement.

What happened next? Shane had dazzled her, that's what.

With his attentiveness fixed on nothing but her, she had been prone to falling for the illusion that she was the only girl in the world, and it had gotten worse as the night had gone on.

Every time Shane had spoken, he'd thrown flirt-bombs Rose's way, wearing her down until she had been nothing but prickling anticipation in five-inch heels.

There had been times when Rose had wanted to hit his innuendo-filled head with the pool stick for being such a pervert or for not shutting the hell up and taking her against the pool table.

She was still debating which.

Either way, Rose concluded that the man was an expert at wearing ladies down.

She'd expect no less from a player. He'd spun his lines all night with conviction and confidence, like someone used to having things done his way. He could've been deceiving Rose, but he'd a way of talking that had made him sounded genuine and genuinely interested in her life.

She had more than fallen for it.

Her sexual deprivation, which she was sure had spawned its own ego at this point, had been helpless to his charm. By the time they'd found her car and he'd hugged her goodbye — Rose's nose pressed to his chest, inhaling his masculine scent — her impulses had taken over.

Whisking her fingers through his hair, she'd brought her lips to his, allowing her mouth and her hands to tell him exactly what she'd wanted. He hadn't hesitated to respond in kind.

"Anyway" — she came back to herself — "we ended up drinking and talking for a while. It got to be around three in the morning. Like a gentleman, he escorted me back to my car." Where she had charged him, full-blown horny. *Leaving that out.* "After that, everything happened so fast. We were at my car saying our farewells, then I was pinned against his wall."

"*Pinned*?" Holding her hand to her lips, Olive sealed her eyes, shaking her head like she was so proud of her girl. She *would* be proud of Rose's conquest.

"How big?" Mandy jumped with excitement.

Rose tried to conjure up an image of Shane's penis. "I don't know." A gusty exhale shot past her lips. "Big enough, that was certain." She couldn't remember what his penis looked like in graphic detail. It had been dark, but she only remembered that she had been in awe of its size. Rose fastened her thighs together as the ache between them pronounced itself. She may not remember what it looked like, but her vagina sure as hell had no issues recalling the half-pain, half-pleasure his award-winning member had left behind. "I wasn't focused on Shane's size then." She hadn't been focused on much else but the sexing part. "He was much bigger than Simon, though. Simon said he was six inches."

Olive threw her hair over her shoulder. "That asshole wishes he was six inches."

"You didn't measure it?" Beth stared at Rose like she was insane.

"Is that something people normally do during a one-night stand?" Rose's nose scrunched as she thought. "How would you even go about measuring it?"

Mandy crossed her arms and leaned back in her chair. In the most nonchalant voice, she replied, "Just put his dick on your face. That'll tell you."

Christ! Rose stole a look across the patio, hoping no one would overhear the inappropriate conversation they were having.

"No, use your arm." Beth gripped her lower arm. "Go down there and put your arm or hand beside it. Kind of awkward if he's small, but it's easy."

Olive held her hands out, as if to say 'let the expert speak.' "Rosey, this is serious." Her friend was such a drama queen. "You need to know what you're working with, even if it's information you only keep to yourself." She snickered at the girls. "If you want to measure a guy's penis, here is what you have to do... Wait, are you pro blow jobs or against them?"

"Who the hell is against giving a blow job?" one girl said and they scowled in unison.

"Trust me, it happens. Personally, I haven't blown every guy I've slept with. My mouth is for special use only. I'm not going to lend it to just anyone. That's where I pray." Olive beat her eyelashes in a girly display of innocence.

She was so full of crap.

"And your vagina isn't for special use?" Rose cocked

an eyebrow.

Olive threw her head back, laughing. "That's different! My vagina has penis needs. My mouth only has food and liquid needs."

"Oh no, my mouth has penis needs." Mandy took the mic. "I love giving my husband blow jobs. He turns to putty the second my lips touch his cock. I can ask him for anything, and he'll say yes. 'Baby?' — she put on a playful voice — 'Can I get those new Jimmy Choos?'" Snapping her fingers, she had the grin of a satisfied woman. "Works every time, ladies."

The group shared laughs before silencing themselves to enjoy the rest of their meals.

After the waitress appeared to fill their drinks with more orange goodness, Olive progressed, "Enough nonsense. Let's get back to the dick sucking. Pro or con?"

Nervously, Rose chuckled. "Pro?"

"Yes! That's my girl." Olive clapped, clearly feeling the alcohol. "Okay, next time you sleep with him —"

"There won't be a next time." Rose's voice was firm. She didn't want Olive to mistake her night of passion for anything but.

"But? But?" Olive's happy expression faltered.

"Why are you looking at me like I took your candy away? It was a one-night stand. I'm not going to see him again. I didn't even give him my name."

"You didn't give him your name?" Olive's disbelief was momentous.

"Pause." Rose lifted from her chair and dug in her purse, searching for the source of the sudden ringing. "I've got a phone call. Might be important." She stepped away from the girls with a sigh of relief. The number on her display screen was unfamiliar, but she recognized the Charlotte area code. "Hello?"

"Rose?"

It was a male.

"This is she. May I ask who's speaking?"

"It's Devon from last night. We met at the club. You gave me your number and kissed me, not necessarily in that order."

The cowboy?

"Oh!" Rose had forgotten about Devon. "Hey, Devon, how are you?" If she spoke slow and easy, maybe he wouldn't hear the guilt in her voice.

"Fine, thanks. I wanted to know if you'd like to grab dinner with me tonight."

"Is that Big Dick?" Olive howled from the table.

The patio guests turned their eyes toward her best friend then to her, almost like they were waiting for a response.

Rose covered her receiver. "No, ladies and gentlemen, it's *not*." Those watching her turned their heads away, hopefully in shame. "Now, shut up, Olive."

She was going to strangle her best friend. Walking out of the courtyard and to the sidewalk, her view of her friends and their table was blocked by a wall of greenery.

"You there, Rose?" Devon asked.

She placed the phone back to her ear. "Yeah, um, dinner is nice. I have plans later on." If you could consider unpacking her belongings 'plans'. "What time were you thinking?"

"How about six? Are you free then?"

She didn't want to have dinner with Devon. It didn't settle well with her, going out with someone when she'd spent the entire night sexing it up with another person, not that she owed Shane a thing. They weren't together, and she'd never see him—

"PT?"

She jolted. "Shane?" Rose's mouth dropped open, and the mimosas she'd downed were doing a little dance in her stomach. She couldn't believe it.

Shane was staring right at her, surprise and dark excitement on his face.

"Why are you here?" It was all Rose could think to say.

"Big Dick!"

She about screamed when Olive's voice came over her

shoulder.

Glancing around, she gave her best friend a *shut the hell up!* glare, but Olive wasn't having it. She wasn't focused on anything but the six-footer in front of Rose. Before her best friend could reach them, Rose jogged over to her. Grabbing Olive by the shoulders, she redirected her toward the restaurant, determined to save herself the humiliation of Shane finding out how much she'd been bragging about his—

Intersecting her thoughts, Olive not so quietly released a delightful giggle punctuated with slurs. "That's him?" She formed an okay sign with her fingers. "A-plus."

Rose quietly cursed her friend for being so obnoxious when she drank. "No, Olive—" she began to say but the other line chirped.

"Rose?"

Crap! She'd forgotten about Devon. Twice. Holding the phone against her ear, she discharged an impatient breath. "Yes, I'm here." She needed to end this phone call before her tipsy friend did irreversible damage. "Sorry. It's kind of a bad time. I'm at brunch with my friends. You know how girls are when they have a few." Nervousness laced with her weary laugh.

"Yeah, I have a younger sister myself."

"So, six, yes?" What was she doing? Devon seemed like a nice person—the type of man she *should* have slept with—and she'd only be jerking his emotions around by going to dinner with him, knowing nothing would come of it. Rose didn't have time for a relationship and, considering last night, she was uncomfortable sleeping with another random person. One-night stands were not her norm. Other people could do it all they wanted, but it'd remain a novelty for Rose.

"Great!" Devon answered. "Can you text me your address? I'll pick you up."

His excitement made her feel worse. "Devon…"

"Devon?" Olive asked, the influence of alcohol making

her voice shrill.

"I'm on the phone, Olive."

"You're with your friends, so I'll let you go. See you tonight."

Before she could reply, the line went quiet. "Shit!" She stared at the screen.

As she went in search of Olive, Rose was startled to find Shane standing in front of her. Had she been that distracted by her best friend and Devon that she'd not seen him walk closer?

"Big Dick, huh?" Playful and accusatory, the words sunk right to her core.

Rose inhaled a sharp breath, in the process, sniffing his rich-smelling cologne.

Shane smelled strong.

Not strong as in pungent, but strong as in manly, earthy and *delicious*. Would rubbing her face in his shirt be weird? Speaking of shirts, those muscles, toying with the clean, black fabric of his top, made her body tingle in inappropriate places. On some sort of twisted instinct, she almost reached out and grabbed his bicep. It was so large and coursing with powerful muscles she'd have to hold onto it with both hands. Dropping her gaze to the center of his jeans, she pictured what rested beneath. Her vagina ache came back full force, its effects crawling up the areas his mouth and tongue had so thoroughly traveled the night before. She would have to hold that with two hands as well. Her legs shook as she stared up his trim waist. An arrogant smile waited on his face.

"Done checking me out?"

In need of water, Rose swallowed. Why was she seeing him? Had she somehow summoned him with her excessive thoughts? "What are you doing here?"

Instead of answering her, he lifted his lips like he could tell how much his presence was affecting her, like he sensed how wet her panties had become just by *thinking* about what they'd done and in how many positions they'd done it.

"I wasn't expectin' to find you so easily." His grin nearly knocked her off her feet. "I had an elaborate search plan and everything. Good thing I did find you, though." His gaze trekked over her body. "You look better each time I see you. If we weren't in public, I'd have you all over again."

"Being in public has never seemed to stop you," Rose dared to tease. *Am I crazy?* Two seconds ago she'd made plans with another guy and—

"I guess you're right, sugar."

His eyes detonated feelings inside her that she'd boxed in for so long, lustful feelings that made her want to enact her wildest fantasies with him—for him.

He might be a stranger—maybe it was *because* he was a stranger—but Rose wanted him to take her in his arms and kiss her like he'd done the night before.

"I *am* feeling adventurous," he noted.

"I'm totally watching a scene out of a movie right now." Olive sighed, reminding Rose that she was still there.

With Shane in her vicinity, it was rocket science to think of anything but—

'Demand all you want, sugar. As long as it ends with my cock inside you, I'm A-okay.'

"Is this the friend from last night that you were talkin' about?" Shane tossed his gaze over her head, returning to her within seconds. "Olive?"

Pride shaped her friend's grandiose smile. "Talking 'bout me to your one-night stand?"

Shane obscured his hands in his pockets, giving Rose a look of pure lust, then passing his bad-boy grin to Olive. "Not a one-night stand if I have anything to do with it."

Rose waved her hand in front of her face. Someone upstairs had to have turned up the temperature because it was hot out here. She checked Shane out again. *So hot.*

"I heard you're an animal," Olive said pointedly.

Embarrassment charged up Rose's face when Shane raised his eyebrows. "Olive!"

"That's all well and good," Olive went on, "but if you

don't treat my girl right, I'm going to have to kick your ass because I'll let you know something. I'm an animal, too. A momma bear that'll eat your head off!"

Rose grabbed her friend by the arm. "I'm so sorry. She's drunk." Rose was starting to feel the excess mimosas herself, or maybe it was Shane's presence intoxicating her. "Wait here. Hold on. You didn't answer me. Why are you here?"

"I was actually—"

"Hold that thought," Rose said, ignoring the drop of Shane's lips. "I have to sit this one down. I'll be back." Ugh, that sounded way too excited.

Taking Olive by the arm, Rose jogged down the sidewalk. Making a sharp turn into the restaurant's courtyard, she found their table. She pointed to Olive's seat. "You sit your happy butt right here, Olive. You got it? You so much as stand up to tinkle and you'll regret it."

"Yes, ma'am."

It was hard not to laugh at Olive's toothy grin. She might be a jerk for yelling out inappropriate things that Rose didn't want Shane to hear, but she couldn't be upset at her friend.

The situation *had* happened before, in reverse.

"Tell him I said it is nice to meet the person who popped your Simon cherry."

Goodness. "There is no way I'm telling him that."

When Rose made it back to Shane, what breath she'd been able to catch was stolen from her. Shane was one mouth-watering specimen. If she'd ever seen him again, without the cover of darkness, she figured she'd fly in the opposite direction like a bat out of hell. She'd been lust-struck last night. This morning, she'd clearly remembered that she didn't like tattoos, blazers or aviator glasses, like the ones that settled on the top of his bed-tossed hair.

Rose was all about simple—blue jeans and cowboy hats—or, at least, that's what she used to think. It was brighter than her foreseeable future outside and Shane, tattooed and wardrobe on point, was sexier than ever. Rose blinked, clearing her throat. "Why are you here?"

"Those your friends?"

Following the direction he indicated, Rose found Beth and Mandy sneaking peeks at them from behind the wall of vegetation.

"I don't know them at all," she seethed, giving the girls a grimace.

They rushed back to the courtyard, their laugher combining with the sound of morning traffic, birds chirping and Rose's heart beating like tribal drums.

Thump. Thump.

"You sure, sugar?"

"Pssst!" Whispers came from her behind her back. *Seriously?* "Psst. R—"

"What?" Rose yelled, twisting around before Beth could give away her name. Maybe not giving Shane her name was ridiculous, but to her, doing so would make last night too personal. It would make Shane more than a stranger. With her life more complicated than a Pinterest DIY project, she didn't have time for any new friends, and apparently, she didn't have the patience for old ones.

"Beth"—she clenched her teeth—"I'm trying to speak with someone."

She chuckled, and Mandy popped her head into Rose's view. "Is that the one?"

Shane pointed toward a charcoal Mercedes, not a pickup truck like the Southern boys she loved, parked behind him. "Come on. My car is right there. We can speak alone."

"I'm not supposed to follow strangers," Rose said, trying to remind herself that was what they were to each other, regardless of whether they'd spent last night pretending they weren't.

"Who says?" He cocked an eyebrow.

"Everyone knows that rule."

His eyes flashed, a burning desire swarming their depths.

"Do you always live by the rules, sugar?"

She did, but something about him kept making her want to change that.

"Come with me and I'll show you how much fun you can have breaking them."

Her heart clenched.

"Is it?" the girls continued.

Crap. They were still there? What were they? Kindergarteners? Rose followed Shane to his car, turning back to give them a fast nod —*yes, it is!*

"Hop in." Shane opened his passenger door for her.

Quickly righting herself, she made her face ultra-serious and smoothed down her skirt before slipping into the car. "Thank you."

The car door closed, locking the two inside.

Shane was all business. "How much did you tell your friends about me?"

She peered out the windows. The temperature was just as hot in here as it was outside. Maybe it wasn't a good idea, getting in a car alone with him.

Readjusting herself in her seat, she turned halfway to face the man she had been positive she would never see again. "I don't know what you're talking about." Her cheeks fired up.

"Ah, you're embarrassed? How cute."

She scowled at him, the warmth in her bones putting her on edge.

"I'm glad you were talkin' about me, because that means you had a *good* time." He grabbed his phone off his dashboard. "What's your number?"

"Why do you need my number?"

"We're going out," he said, like it was the most obvious thing in the world. "Tonight."

Thump. Thump.

"What?" He wanted to go out with her? *Tonight?* "Don't assume I'll go out with you because we had sex. I'm not going out with you. I don't even *know* you."

"Getting to know each other is the point in going out,

sugar. I want to know you."

Arching over to Rose's side of the car, he rubbed his lips over her cheek.

Thump. Thump. She pinched her eyes closed at the abrupt contact, grasping the buttery leather cushions of her seat.

"We don't have to go out if you don't want to." His whisper burned through her. "We can skip that part and get to know each other in my bedroom."

"You arrogant—"

His hearty laugh unsettled the air. "It can be in your bedroom if it makes you feel better." She sighed as he placed his hand on the inside of her knee. A car door slammed somewhere in the distance.

Thump. Thump.

Shut up, heart!

Lips so close she could sense their heat, he whispered, "I only figured that with your roommate there, you'd want to be somewhere more private. I plan on making you scream again, sugar. I want you screaming my name each time I bury my *big dick"* – he emphasized the nickname—"inside you. You sure you want to subject your friend to all that noise, sugar?"

"Why" —she set her jaw, trying hard to focus on anything but his hand smoothing circles over her leg but, holy hell, it felt good—"do you insist on calling me that? I don't like it."

"I wouldn't have to call you that if you'd tell me your name."

Warmth bristled over her skin as he placed his lips to her earlobe. Instead of yanking away from him, she lowered her eyelids until blackness surrounded her—and pleasure. Bending her head to the side, she gave his mouth more room to roam.

"Names aren't important," she said, but it was a mumble, hardly audible. "Shane, I don't think this is..."

He squeezed her thigh, sucking her earlobe between his lips before dropping a hot kiss behind her ear. Prickles assaulted her breasts and neck, her nipples rising to attention.

"Why is that, sugar?" Shane's voice was deep and husky, fire against her skin, as his kisses grew bolder, turning into little bites that made her legs shiver and her clit tighten with awareness. Her breasts heaved beneath her top when he lifted his hand a few centimeters up her skirt.

"Because I'm a one-night stand?" he asked.

He pulled back. A hedonistic gaze greeted her own, and the way he was looking at her, like he was trying to scour her of all doubts that he was anything but uninterested in extending their night in paradise, made her stomach simmer with wanton sensations.

Yes, Shane was a one-night deal.

Call her anal, but she had a five-year plan that had gotten off track when she'd lost her job and her fiancé. She had to get her life together again. Boys like Shane Williams weren't a part of that five-year plan, not with those eyes and that smile. He was trouble through and through, and she didn't have time for anyone's trouble but her own. "Why are you even here?" How did he come to be in the exact same place as her at the exact same time? Rose didn't believe in coincidences.

"You don't remember where you are?" Eyebrows stretching up his forehead, he shook his head. "Bub's is down at the corner, less than a block away. You don't recognize the area?"

Oh. Rose evaluated the unfamiliar streets. She'd been out of it last night when they'd walked to and from the bar. How could she have been expected to memorize her surroundings when there had been a stunning male hanging over her shoulder? "You mean you're not stalking me?"

His whole face changed when he laughed, becoming brighter. The hard angles softened with warmth and Rose lost her breath.

"Charlotte is a small city, and I frequent this part of town often, sugar." Lingering on his face, his smile turned wicked.

Rose's chest grew heavy when he came closer then pressed long fingers against her inner thigh again, harder, making her squirm. She stared outside the car. Could people walking by see? But the windows were tinted. The huge Jeep parked in front of them concealed the street view.

"I saw you when I pulled out of the sports bar. After last night, I'd recognize that ass anywhere," he teased. "If anyone is stalking here, it's you, PT. Not that I'm complaining. Running into you saves me a lot of time."

Shane had seen her and pulled over?

"Saves you a lot of time for what?"

"You know, sugar. I heard that if you keep meeting the same person coincidentally, it's fate."

Fate? How about crappy luck?

"Shane, we are nothing more than strangers. We can't be anything more than—" She gasped as her lips flattened under his, unable to quiet the moan that ruptured from between them.

He was scrumptious. The taste of beer and chocolate followed his tongue. Heat plunged into her mouth and down her body. All she wanted was to taste more.

Just one kiss wouldn't hurt her, would it?

Grabbing his hair, Rose accepted the kiss. She slid her tongue against his in a sensual stroke. She brought her hands to the side of his face and loved how his jaw moved with the kiss and how his breath picked up speed when she dropped her fingers to his chest. Trailing her fingers against his smooth shirt, she let them explore the chiseled muscles below and she kissed him harder, excitement mixing with a growing sense that what they were doing was wrong. Voices came from outside. She dug her nails inward, surprised by him stealing and sucking on her bottom lip. Letting her fingers fall to his, she gripped the hand on her thigh. He groaned, and a moan vibrated up Rose's throat. He was every rule she'd never broken and all she wanted to do was take a walk on the wild side. And she was. Rose was walking on the edge of a cliff. If she allowed him to keep kissing her this way, the consequences would be unforgiving.

Deviations in her five-year plan were unacceptable. Last night had been a one-time deal. Tomorrow—hell, maybe an hour from now—she'd regret letting him get under her skin, even for a second. One-night stands didn't spill over into afternoon make-out sessions. But as his skillful mouth descended, she forgot all arguments as to why he was wrong, because how could something wrong feel so good?

"Open your legs." He brought his hand up her skirt, his growl tickling her collarbone.

Rose shivered, hating that she wanted a guy she'd met just yesterday to do naughty things to her in the front seat of his car on a semi-busy afternoon, but she pushed away that feeling. She wanted to break every rule in the book, to live. And, for some reason, she trusted Shane. She needed the passion and recklessness he offered like nothing else.

She spread her legs for him, and her knee hit the passenger door.

The warm glow of sunlight cutting through the front windshield was nothing compared to the heat of his body. Shane moved at the invitation, and she held her breath while he inched closer toward the delicate flesh hidden by her panties. When his fingers drew over the soaked-through fabric, he curled his lips to a smile against her neck.

"Look how wet you already are for me." He hooked his fingers around the lace.

His knuckles making contact was like lightning jarring up her spine. Sensations drowned every neglected part of her, and she sighed. He rotated his fist above her clit. The friction was marvelous, and if she'd been able to say a single coherent word, she would've told him so.

"Lift, sugar."

Ignoring the honk of a car horn somewhere close by, she pushed against the back of her seat and raised her hips.

He dragged her panties down her legs and past her knees.

The soft fabric fell to her ankles, and she lifted her feet so he could slip them off. He reached to the floor to take her underwear then bound them around the knuckles that had rubbed over her middle. He skimmed that same hand back up her leg, traveling under her skirt. The contrast, the smoothness from his skin and the rough material on her thigh, was one of the most arousing things she'd ever experienced.

Panties gone... Morals gone... Rose was officially off her five-year track. The deviation came with a rush of adrenaline.

"You'll get these back when you come over tonight."

"But..."

Her protest got stuck in her throat when he carried his fingertips through her watering center. Circling. Stroking. Her arousal dripped against his knuckles and his hastening breaths moved along her skin. He gave her careful caresses, slow and teasing.

Gyrating her hips, she shuddered as his ring and index finger spread her labia wide. Between the stiff pliers, his middle digit skated through her soaked divides, up and down.

"Does that feel good, sugar?"

The words burst through her haze of desire. *What am I doing? Oh, Christ.* She had to stop.

With the intention of pulling him away, she laced her fingers around the wrist working below her clothing. She didn't shove him off but kept him in place with her disobedient hand, squeezing him tightly. He toyed faster with her body.

"Jesus, I want you right now. I'm so fucking hard watchin' you like this. Feel me. Feel how hard you make me." He reached across the armrest and brought her hand to his lap.

A groan slipped past his lips when she ran her fingers over the visible strain in his pants. The jeans were rough, and he was thick below her fingers. Rose's insides clenched. The guarded flesh, hot and iron-hard, branded her with a vicious need.

"Want it inside you?" he asked.

Focusing all his attention on one spot, Shane massaged the bundled tissues at her junction. Her head fell back on her headrest, her whole body stiff as he built her up. Another sigh emptied into the car. The air became heavy, bearing down on her, and tension spread through her limbs. Moisture bathed her skin, the leather seats burning below her thighs. Her stress built, a stress that could only be revealed with lips and fingers.

Yes.

An orgasm brewed low in her belly. Her vocal cords tensed, stealing her answer.

"I can't hear you," he gritted out. "I said, do you want me inside you like this?" He thrust a finger all the way into her body, pressing his hand into her labia.

Rose whimpered, whiplashed by pleasure. Her whole body pulsed with it and that pulse grew larger and brighter as he began a slow and steady rhythm. Pulling back, he inserted a second finger, and her whole body trembled. He moved them through her interior in tandem.

He wet his lips and his eyes closed for a millisecond before they opened with flames. "Play with yourself."

Surprise made her gasp, but Shane didn't miss a beat. Right beside her ear, he growled, "Put your hand on your pussy and rub yourself while I fuck you with my fingers. Do it now."

She wanted to say she was hesitant. She'd never touched herself in front of someone before, but she wasn't scared or nervous at all. Trapped in his car in the center of downtown, Rose was unbelievably turned on. Loosening her grip on his wrist, she dove her hand under her skirt, finding her spot. She'd spent years holed up in her bathroom touching herself when Simon had been too busy or too tired. At one point, Rose had begun to hate masturbation for what it symbolized, the lack of desire in her failing relationship.

Back then, she'd fought for the simple pleasure, not

wanting to allow an unhealthy love life to strip her of her sexuality. As Rose began creating shapes right above his deep plunges, she stared into Shane's smoky eyes, unfocused like she assumed hers were, and she was thankful she had fought back then, because if she hadn't, she wouldn't have been able to share this moment with a man like him. She didn't know a lot about Shane, but she had concluded— even if she couldn't explain why—that when he loved, he loved hard, and he would never leave the woman he was with to feel unsatisfied or inadequate.

"Do you like that?" he asked in a low rasp. "You want me harder?"

Because she refused to speak lest he hear the emotion in her voice—the emotion that told her he was someone she wanted to know also—Rose nodded.

Shane buried his fingers deeper. Air rushed up her lungs.

Sneaking a peek at her mouth, a warning he'd soon kiss her, Shane muttered something under his breath then he moved like lightning. Rose groaned as their lips met, the satin slopes of his mouth nestling where hers seamed.

"All day," he uttered across her parted mouth, "I haven't been able to stop thinkin' about you, how good you fit around me. I thought I was crazy, that I'd dreamed you."

Beats of heat pushed through her legs, making them quiver. On a groan, he fit his tongue into her mouth. The kisses there, the slamming inside her and her own fingers working at her tenderized flesh, was too much for her to bear.

Overwhelming. The bite of pleasure was unparalleled, rending through her and smudging her surroundings. The winter sun behind his back became fuzzy.

"I saw you today, and it was like seeing a mirage. I had to touch you—to know you were real, that last night was real." Shane's movements gained momentum, turning into angry injections, merciless dives into her body, until all that existed was *him*.

God, it's too much.

Rose fought to be released from the unrelenting sensation. She tightened everywhere, the purge of vibrations barreling their way up her skin in sharp and euphoric wakes.

"Let me see you come, beautiful." His voice was a turbid cloud of lust, deep and demanding, spurring her toward the precipice. "Come all over my fingers and your panties, so I can have something to keep me sated until I take you tonight," he growled and, like her body mysteriously seemed to do for him, she obeyed.

The rope of pleasure snapped and splintered. Heat flushed from inside her, and vibrant waves made her shake with their power. Her legs clasped, and she moaned his name.

"That's right. Fuck, that's right, beautiful."

More. The word was on the tip of her tongue, but she stayed silent, scared that if she spoke, she'd go down a path she'd never find her way back from.

* * * *

After she had gotten a hold of herself and Shane had wiped his fingers with her panties before tucking them inside his pocket with a wink, he grabbed his phone again. Rose recited her number in a daze, her heart still going at full speed. She didn't know what frustrated her more — that she could get used to this feeling or that she *wanted* to get used it.

Shane placed his cell on the dashboard and adjusted himself in his pants. Then he stepped out of the car, filled with the musky aroma of their intense session, and he went around the back.

Dewy air blew across her as he opened her door. Rose took a refreshing breath and stepped out. Her legs, wobbling as she shifted out of the passenger side, could give out at any moment.

How long have we been in there?

Shane held her hand in his, twining their fingers as he walked her to the restaurant's entrance and carried on conversation like they hadn't performed illicit acts in his car. Rose gazed up at him, nerves shot, then back down to their locked hands. Sharing intimacy was supposed to make people comfortable with each other. She gnawed on her bottom lip, her telltale sign of discomfort.

It wasn't that she *disliked* him touching her. It was that she liked it too much.

She kept forgetting Shane was a stranger.

She didn't know him outside of a couple of encounters.

He was the ultimate oxymoron, familiar but foreign. He made her feel safe, but at the same time, he put her constantly on edge. When her heart beat around him, it beat in his direction.

In only a day, his lips had become a signal for her attention.

Rose had never been in lust with someone, and as far as it went, she hated it.

The out-of-control feeling. Her endorphins overworking. The incapacity to settle. She always wanted more. If this was what passion was like, she took it all back. She didn't want it.

Why would anyone *want* to feel this way?

Rendered helpless with the touch or the aimed smile of another person? She didn't like being defenseless. Troubled by the effect he had on her, Rose tried to pulled away from him.

Shane wasn't having it. "Not so fast."

Releasing her hand, he let his fingers fall down her hips, trailing chills. Trailing need.

In an impressive display of his strength, he grabbed hold of her waist, lifting her to his brick-wall chest. He kissed her, but not the way a stranger kissed someone. Shane kissed her like they were two lovers reuniting. It was a full body kiss, contouring his muscles over her breasts and stomach as if her body were made to fit with his. His mouth was hotter than the sun on her neck. Ringing her arms around his shoulders, she wove her fingers through his hair. She kissed him with fervor. She moaned, and the sound circled around her cheeks and vibrated their tongues. Why couldn't she get enough of him?

Like he remembered they were in public, Shane broke apart their kiss, keeping his nose beside hers and his panting breaths inches above her lips until the dizziness passed. He lowered Rose and her heels made a pointed *click* as they hit the pavement.

"You think you came hard a few minutes ago?" He plucked a strand of hair from her forehead and tucked it behind her ear, reminding Rose what it was like to be wanted, desired. It was terrifying.

"That's nothing compared to what I've got planned for you tonight." Dark eyes letting her feel the truth of his words, Shane stared down at her as if she already belonged to him. "I'll text you the details."

Gulping, she swayed a little on her feet and nodded.

He seemed to like her response, his haughty smile showing approval. With one last peck on her lips, Shane freed her. He got into his car and drove away. Rose stared at the area his Mercedes had occupied for an unwavering moment. Pulling out her phone, she found numerous unread texts from a number she assumed was Devon's. She'd made plans with two people tonight, and she had no clue what to do about it, but there was one thing she knew for certain. Under no circumstances would she ever allow herself to see Shane Williams again.

Chapter Five

"Stop looking at it like it's about to grow fangs and bite you in the ass!" Olive whined from her spot on the bed. "You look great. You're wearing it. You *have* to wear it."

Silky black threads of lace played against Rose's fingertips, rough but somehow smooth. A nervous layer added texture to her voice, making it higher-pitched than usual. "If it's not underwear, then what is it?" Her vision rose from the sheer lingerie, hugging her body as if the fabric were lonely, to stare at the reflection over her right shoulder.

"Seriously, Rose, you need to get out more. It's called a garter belt, and when Shane sees it, that boner of his is going to launch faster than a firecracker on Fourth of July weekend. *Bam!*"

There was a thud as Olive threw herself on the bed, giggling.

Squaring her shoulders, Rose frowned as her friend sank into the foam mattress and all but disappeared in a mess of cinnamon sheets and plush pillows.

"Olive?" Using her elbows, she sat up. An impish smile emerged on her face.

Olive's eyes gleamed a radiant amber, almost golden. She blinked, failing to appear virtuous. "Yes, best friend?"

Rose bit her tongue to hold back the string of blasphemies rolling around her mouth like sour candy. Olive was doing it on purpose, wasn't she?

"Devon." For the fifth time, Rose corrected her. "It's *Devon.*"

As expected, when Rose had told Olive she wasn't going out with Shane tonight, or ever again, but instead was having dinner with another person she'd met at the nightclub the previous evening – she thought it best to break the news to Devon in person that she wasn't looking for anything serious – her friend had been nothing short of blown away. Since they'd come back from brunch, Olive had been bombarding her with questions that, not wanting to explain herself, Rose had countered with evasive answers. Minutes had ticked to hours, and Olive still hadn't given up.

In fact, she'd become more relentless in her attempts at deciphering the truth, in time, resorting to guerrilla war tactics that Rose had no chance in negating.

Exploiting the benefits of her Ph.D. in psychology, Olive had asked what seemed like innocent questions but were really miniature pieces of a jigsaw puzzle, which had obviously come together in her mind to form a whole myriad of nonsensical conclusions.

Her overactive imagination had narrowed it down to two choices – either Rose was feeling Shane Williams already and was frightened of being serious with a guy that wasn't her 'Mr. Perfect on paper' or Devon was better looking and better equipped.

More tenacious than the provocative garter belt adhering to Rose's waist and hips, Olive went on to weigh the possibilities of either alternative while Rose had come up with her own set of conclusions. Either Olive had been binging way too hard on *Law & Order* recently or, in her past life, she had been a sergeant. Her interrogation skills – eerily accurate – were out of this world, making Rose feel sorry for anyone who'd been at the receiving end of her best friend's drilling gaze. Terrified that she might get a hemorrhage from Olive's persistent scrutiny, Rose gave in, confessing a partial truth and praying that Olive wouldn't press her for more.

Why hadn't she known better?

As soon as her friend had found out that Rose wasn't interested in Shane because he wasn't her type, Olive had kept accidentally forgetting Devon's name. Though coincidentally, Rose noted with a hint of irritation, she seemed to remember Shane's name fine.

Rose didn't care if her friend agreed or not. Even if this wasn't a date, she would always choose cowboy boots over dress shoes...and thick arms that made her want to melt into a pool of hormones, seductive tattoos that swirled over a set of abdominal muscles sexy enough to turn her brain to mashed potatoes and a smile she could stare at—

"I don't get it!" Her friend's voice was a jagged current, cutting through her thoughts, and Rose blinked, refocusing her eyes to find Olive pinning her with a frown. "I just don't, Rosey."

Her best friend would never understand.

Olive was the live-every-day-like-it's-your-last woman. There was nothing wrong with that mentality, but not everyone had the luxury of being able to take risks.

Or being hurt and coming out unharmed.

"What don't you get?" Rose decided to indulge her friend a while longer. It shouldn't be long before Devon arrived.

"Why go out with some country bumpkin who wears *cowboy* boots to a club instead of the guy who rocked your world *numerous* times?" Olive stared at her with eyes that dared a challenge. "Including once this afternoon in the middle of our brunch session. Rosey, you don't just let your French toast go soggy for anyone."

"How am I supposed to respond to that? I already told you how I feel. Besides, it's not a date."

"I think you're lying."

Of course, Olive thought she was lying.

"Based off what I saw earlier, you do have *some* sort of romantic interest in Shane."

A finger lifted, silencing Rose before she could wedge in a retort.

"There is no denying body language, Rosey. Not only that, but the sexual energy around you two was sweltering. I could practically see it. Actually, I *could* see it, in his pants!"

Rose faced the mirror again, realizing too late that

her move back home had come with a side of immodest wardrobe and free, but unwanted, counseling from a licensed sex therapist.

The consequences of having a friend who gave sex advice for a living was that the advice didn't stop when she left her job. Rose didn't need counseling. What she needed was to get her life back on track. She needed someone who could offer her more than sex. Someone comfortable and compatible. Safe.

"It's clear the guy has a hard-on for you the size of Texas, and given that you let him get you off in his car in *broad daylight*, I would say the feeling is mutual. I get that you want order in your life, but denying yourself because of a repressed—"

"I'm not denying anything," she cut in.

"Rose, I didn't…" Olive opened her mouth then closed it.

Memories of her past horror swamped her.

The rancid taste of nausea filled Rose's throat and slid over her tongue like grease. The familiar surge of pain gushed through her bloodstream, drenching her with poison.

His snaggle-toothed grin and his eyes, blacker than tar, stared into her soul. The tearing sound of her shirt ripping open… His voice was like gravel. The man's touch had left a permanent stain on Rose's skin. No one saw it but her.

Olive was wrong. She'd never been so lucky as to repress the memories of her assault. They came back—night or day, rain or shine. They always came back.

"I'm sorry. I didn't mean it like that."

That had been a fight Rose had lost in the past, one that had contaminated her to this day. It may have made no sense to other people, but she needed her five-year plan. Good country husband, Fortune 500 job, a house on a ranch, two children, the all-American family, normalcy, success.

"I know. It's okay."

She'd failed back then—failed to protect herself and failed to tell anyone the truth until he had struck once more. Failure wasn't an option for Rose—never again.

"My night with Shane was fun, but that's all it was, a fun night that I don't plan on repeating. Don't read too much into what you saw earlier. There has to be some repercussions to being the first man I was with besides Simon" — *and him* — "but that's it."

"I want you to be happy." A weak smile accompanied Olive's defeated tone.

"I know you do, but really, I don't see anything happening with Shane."

She took her outfit off its hanger then slipped on the fine material.

Rose had told her friend this dinner was strictly PG, but Olive had still insisted on her wearing her cranberry cocktail dress, chic and elegant, with thin spaghetti straps. Her hair was designed in a classic updo, curled tendrils hanging around her neck.

As she smiled at her reflection. Her lips, highlighted in dark burgundy, looked swollen from Shane's prior kisses, or she could be imagining it.

The promise he had made Rose before he'd left her with a kiss replayed in her head, bringing chills down her shoulders and breasts.

She blew out a breath and grabbed her evening bag, starting down the hall toward the sound of knocking at her front door.

* * * *

Gripping his cell phone, it took all of Shane's strength not to hurl it against the restaurant's wall. The muscles in his jaw ticked as he curled his hands to fists.

What the fuck am I doing?

He stared at the bottle of champagne, the empty flutes, the uneaten bread, the bouquet of roses that reminded him of her red-blotted cheeks and all the other cliché shit — the dessert menus and movie tickets — that went along with going on a date. Had he really gone through all this trouble for some girl who wouldn't even give him her name?

I'm pathetic.

"Would you like more water?" The waiter presented Shane with a silver pitcher.

The poor guy couldn't hide his frown. He might as well have spoken it out loud. "She stood you up, bro. Go home."

Hear that? Even the waiter thinks I'm an idiot.

"No," he announced, his voice curt and his pride eroded by the sharp tap of his watch.

Displaying his wrist, he checked the time again. Every muscle in his body went rigid, filling him with outrage. Burning. Ferocious. Temples pulsing, he placed his fingers on the drumming veins in his forehead and began a light massage.

Why did he keep doing that? Looking at the time and simultaneously reminding himself that he'd waited for over an hour would only serve to intensify his anger.

Twice in one week he'd been used by a woman, the same woman. *Twice.*

Instead of going out and finding someone to screw his ego back in place, Shane was sitting at a table with his eyes glued to the vacant chair in front of him as he tried to determine where he'd gone wrong. Maybe she *was* a dream, a recurring nightmare—his personal nightmare. Shane couldn't count the number of times he'd been told by lust-scorned women that karma would catch up to him. If only he'd known back then that when karma came, she'd be wearing a little black dress and the sweetest smelling perfume, Shane would have reformed his ways faster than a sinner on his deathbed. Fine. He could admit that sometimes he did things that wouldn't exactly win him a Boy Scout badge—this afternoon being a shining example of one—but he never committed to something then bailed, and he definitely had never stood a woman up.

'Cause you never took one on a date.

That wasn't the point. He might be a player to some and an asshole to others, but he respected people's time. Had he been too intense when he'd seen her earlier?

Shane had planned on getting in touch with the club owner, Rob Anderson, an acquaintance of his. If Blondie had had VIP access at Base, which she did or she would've never caught him in the private lounge with Amy, then she or her best friend Olive had to be on the list.

He could have found her that way.

The afternoon had come around and Shane had been due to see Rob later that night.

Sometime before noon, Malcolm—his friend and work partner—had met him at Bub's. Every Sunday, before his cousin opened shop, the three of them sat around the bar drinking and shooting the shit. They would talk about the past week and their upcoming one.

Always, Shane had to remind Malcolm that there was to be no business talk at the table. Malcolm was in a long-term relationship with paperwork, and getting him excited about any other subject beside his work or his woman was a feat akin to finishing a marathon.

Today, by some miracle, Shane hadn't needed to ward off topics about finances, marketing strategies or monthly projections. He had bet his ass it had something to do with Bub spewing gossip quicker than he filled his cup with a new draft. His cousin's interest in the cute, blonde friend from the previous night had been a colossal annoyance, but Shane had kept silent with his beer and double chocolate pancakes. Weird combo, sure, but hella good.

"Our boy's a little quiet over there, don't ya' think?" Bub had asked Malcolm, his shaggy hair waving as he'd nodded, answering his own question.

"She must be somethin' special." Malcolm had taken a bottle of Samuel Adams from Bub, "Did you sleep with her?" The question had reached his eyes before it'd bowled off his tongue.

The memories had reverberated through him, tingling over his chest and drawing his muscles tight.

"Probably did." Bub had inserted his two cents, rubbing

down the inside of an empty beer glass before he'd tossed the rag over his shoulder. "You should've seen him, Malc, like a puppy dog. He was all big-eyed and drooling. Looks like our buddy finally got struck by the bow."

Shane had grimaced when Bub's mouth had shifted into a grin.

"It was bound to happen sooner or later, man."

Struck by Cupid's bow? Me?

The only bow that had touched Shane was the one between Blondie's legs. Shane had forked some pancakes and slammed them into his mouth, letting the rich chocolate and sweet batter knock away any chance of him responding.

Struck by Cupid's bow, my ass.

"Y'all boys are awfully curious about my sex life," he'd said. "Not getting any from your wives?"

The two had broken out in laughter. They loved the married life. Freaks.

"Hey, hey, everything with the Mrs. is good over here," Malcolm had assured, a smirk turning his lips. "Maybe it's because she's pregnant, but Nina has been horn—"

"Shut it!" The shout, loud and alarmed, had bounced around the desolate bar. "Serious, man?" Shane had complained. "No one wants to hear that."

"I second that," Bub had said, but his wife was pregnant, too, so Shane didn't know which comment he was seconding. He sure as hell hadn't asked.

Pregnant. Shane cringed.

He preferred not to have kids *or* a wife. Why would he?

Single life suited him well. Shane didn't want or need another person cramping his style. So what if sometimes he wondered about what it'd been like coming home to one woman, one woman that was all his. Why complain when everything had worked out so far? Anyway, his heart wouldn't be broken if no one got close—his last relationship ending as it had, Shane had never since been interested in another woman outside of his bedroom, and the open-minded ladies who came into their sexlationship, knowing what to expect, had become good friends to him. There was a pestering voice in the back of his head, some crazy bastard yapping, telling him Blondie had been interesting *before* the sex. He was resolved to ignore it.

After he'd finished at the bar with his friends, Shane had pulled out of Bub's, only to find Blondie pacing the sidewalk less than two blocks away—skirt loose, skin looking impossibly supple in the sunlight. He thought he'd fallen asleep at the wheel, dreaming.

She'd been a vision, long hair whipping in the breeze, framing her baby face, green eyes wide and so bright he could see them clearly from his car. Cutting across the intersection, the steering wheel swerving in his palm, he'd made his way to her. Never in Shane's life had he parallel parked so fast. It'd been hard for him to contain the excitement of seeing her again as he'd stepped out of his car, approaching her with caution. She hadn't noticed him walk up.

The thing was, in spite of being thrilled that he'd run into her again, he'd still been angry about that morning. It had infuriated him that she had disappeared without a word—turned out she had a forte for pissing Shane off—and he'd carried that anger into his conversation with her. With his cock twitching, gaining girth as he'd listened to her best friend reveal how much Blondie had enjoyed herself with him, Shane had wanted to let her know what she had missed by leaving so early. Thankfully, using the help of her friends, he had been able to lure her, like the greedy wolf he was, unsuspectingly, to his car. In the heat of the moment, Shane had gotten carried away.

Touching her, hearing her moan and feeling her response to him were all too addicting.

Shit. She had responded so well.

Liquefying under his hands and lips, she'd said his name with breathless urgency. Shane had lost it. Words had started to leak from his mouth like he had no filter. He'd told her how much he wanted her. There was something about Blondie, something he couldn't quite shake.

The need to get to know her was as pertinent as the need to quench the burgeoning thirst of his desire. He had to find out why, since he'd woken up that morning, she hadn't escaped his mind. The sex? The laughs they'd had? She was hidden behind a veil of mystery. If exposed, would he still feel this incredible draw? His new and bizarre infatuation scared him.

Had it scared her also? Had Shane pushed her away?

Taking out a wad of bills from his jacket pocket, he clenched his jaw. The money felt dirty in his hand. Shane had never liked money. It only caused problems. His parents used to fight about their finances all the time.

Shane was from a family of car dealers.

Trevor, his older brother, had dropped out of college to help with his old man's business, which was salvaging old vehicles, fixing them up and selling them for profit. If he hadn't run away from home when he'd been eighteen, Shane would be sitting on his ass in Georgia right then, fixing up some rusty piece of metal he'd pawned from the junkyard. Instead, he'd chosen a life free of restrictions and his old man's rules – and his old man's fist when he broke those rules.

Once Shane had made a name for himself, he had offered to help pay off his family's debt. His old man had refused, not one for pity. When his father had passed a year ago, he had left the shop in Trevor's name. Trevor would take care of it best, and when Shane had insisted his older brother let him help the dealership out, his brother had conceded.

Shane sorted through the stack, exhaling out a sigh. He tossed a hundred on the table.

Screw it. He would've spent more had she decided to show up.

Blondie was right. He was nothing but her one-night stand. Why was he trying to force more? It wasn't like he wanted anything from her but sex, right?

Maybe it was best she hadn't shown up, because

eventually she'd be just another woman he slept with and left. Though the pang in his chest said otherwise, Shane stood, and as he walked through the restaurant, he deleted her number from his phone. The hostess extended her hand to grab the entrance door for him.

"I've got it." His face never left his phone as he strode past her. What was up with these places forcing their employees to act like servants? Shane could open his own damn door.

"I get off in ten."

He stopped.

Tossing his gaze over his shoulder, he skimmed the woman who'd spoken to him, a slender blonde staring back, her azure eyes potent with interest.

He tilted his head and slanted his gaze to pause on her work shirt, tight enough that he could appreciate her busty outline. He was fully aware that if he fucked her in the back seat of his car with the scent of another woman still staining the leather interior, he'd be a bad guy, the worst type. Karma would destroy him, shred his heart till it was next to nothing like he'd been accused of doing to numerous late-night girls.

Winded with thoughts of his wide-eyed stranger, he tightened his hand over the door handle. Kissed by the winter, it was cold to the touch. "Do you now?"

Untucking her bottom lip from between her teeth, she looked up from his crotch. "I do." Her eyes glistened as he handed her a smile.

Let karma reign. Let her come and try to destroy him.

Chapter Six

Biting her nails, Rose listened as the elevator passed each floor, ascending higher.

Her nerves were frayed beyond recognition. She was jittery, frantically tapping her fingers away at her ebony pencil skirt. Below her sweater, her heart was on overdrive. The *swish, swish* in her stomach that threatened to expose the shiny floor to last night's supper and the drip of sweat between her breasts were prelude to her first day as marketing director at Lambda Digital. She couldn't remember the last time she had been this anxious.

There was a *ding!* and she jerked her head up in time to watch the reflective doors yawn open, revealing her to the ninth floor.

Whoa.

Exiting the elevators, she took in her surroundings, stunned to silence. The crisp smack of her stiletto heels against marble announced her arrival, and a woman, brunette with light-brown eyes, lifted her head from her iMac. A broad smile lightened her concentrated expression.

"You must be the new manager, Rosemary Berkowitz."

Stomach churning—she didn't expect them to know her already—Rose forced a smile, kindly correcting the receptionist, "Rose is fine."

Behind her, on an otherwise gray-painted wall, the word 'Lambda' was drawn in bold graffiti and underneath a clean-cut font read, 'Build Your Digital Community'.

Rose had never liked graffiti. It reminded her of rebellion, something criminal.

As she shortened the distance between herself and the

receptionist desk, her eyes were hooked on every vibrant, twining curve. *Awesome.* There was elegance in the wild text, elegance she'd never imagined associating with street art. Obviously designed by a talented professional, the loud sketching, that matched the red, orange and dark blue colors of Lambda's brand, managed to look professional but concurrently gritty and daring. Rose had never seen anything like it.

It was an art piece representative of the company itself, no doubt.

The unsettling mix of nerves and anticipation that had been knotting in her stomach ever since she'd woken up this morning intensified. Start-ups were cool and hip. Rose was corporate.

She already felt out of place.

Standing from behind the counter, the receptionist grinned, seeing the direction of Rose's eyes. She circled the desk, coming to stand beside Rose.

"It's gorgeous, right?"

"It's something," was what she managed to reply.

"Wait until you see the common area."

Maybe reading the panic of Rose's face, the brunette made quick work of assuring her. "It's not bad, I promise. If you like this, you'll love it. By the way, my name is Tiffany."

Rose accepted Tiffany's hand, smiling, this time genuinely, when her firm shake was reciprocated. *A woman with a solid handshake?* Rose liked her already.

"At times, you will see me man the front desk, but I do it by choice. I'm in content marketing by trade." She beamed, her pride shining through. "I'm so glad you're here."

"I'm glad to be here." Rose followed Tiffany as she led her down the hall.

"You'll have to excuse my excitement." Dropping her voice, she confided, "There aren't a lot of women here, so when I got word you were coming, I was ecstatic. Seriously" — she sighed — "jumping out of my seat excited. Being in an all-boys club gets old after a while."

Rose frowned, but it wasn't directed at Tiffany. She understood her completely.

In all the time she'd spent as a digital marketer for a handful of top-tier tech firms in Houston and Austin, she had come to the same conclusion. Women were scarce in her field. It was an unfortunate reality she'd dealt with for years. "I think we'll get along great."

Tiffany tossed a hearty smile over her shoulder. "Me, too."

"What's it like working here?"

Tiffany paused, pursing her lips in thought. "I may sound full of it, but I'm telling the truth when I say it's by far the best place I've worked. Thanks to management, it's a laid-back but productive environment. We mostly use the scrum framework, so everyone works independently, but we're also a collaborative effort. There's never a dull moment. Be forewarned. Everyone who has worked here falls in love with this place." As if Tiffany had reached into her head and pulled out her innermost thoughts, she added, "Whether they want to or not."

Rose picked up her pace as Tiffany resumed her strut and said, "I'll take you on a tour of the facility now. You'll be able to meet the team, and I'll introduce you to the office manager, Jim Salah. I think he told me earlier that Mr. Fletcher was expecting you at ten."

"That all sounds good."

Down the hall, she heard gusty laughter and people talking.

Here it was. The moment of truth.

The communal area was much larger than the common space at her firm in Texas had been, and there was so much going on that Rose couldn't decide what to take in first.

When she finally settled on something, it was the high-backed chairs that circled floor-to-ceiling columns. Resting on every sofa was an assortment of Lambda-brand colored cushions. Solo desks and group tables spread strategically throughout the open floor plan. The space was vast enough for running laps. Beside her, a wall-sized window offered a breathtaking view of downtown.

Fun. If Rose had to characterize it, fun would be the best word to use.

Directly in front of her was a game room decked out with a popcorn machine, rows of classics like Pac-Man and Dragon's Lair and a pool table, which—she blushed—reminded her of Shane. More graffiti lined the wall. This time it was large enough to cover every square inch. The text was audacious and alluring, like the piece in the lobby.

There was plenty going on, but nothing seemed forced or cluttered. As a matter of fact, it was like everything had been expertly placed for optimal employee comfort.

One by one, she was introduced to everyone.

Each person identified themselves as either creative, sales, search or software development, and they all sounded eager to have someone new on their staff. Before Rose realized it, her nervousness had vanished into giddiness, and her hesitance at not fitting in had disintegrated to excitement.

The start-up was nothing like she had expected. Maybe working here wouldn't be so bad. It would certainly, if anything, be an unforgettable experience.

After Tiffany made her acquainted with the staff, she was shown to the front again to meet the office manager.

"Rosemary, I presume." Jim was young, no older than mid-twenties. He wore casual clothing, slacks and a knit sweater, sleeves rolled up. Tattoos inked his pale arms dark.

"Rose," Tiffany said, before she could.

Showing his teeth, he smiled and corrected himself, "Rose, my apologies."

"I'll catch you later. It was awesome meeting you, Rose. We should catch up for lunch sometime."

Rose agreed. She'd love that.

Tiffany went to join the others, shouting when someone called her name.

Laughing, Jim picked up a clipboard from the receptionist's desk. "It's kind of crazy around here sometimes, but it's home. I think you'll like it."

"I think I will, too." For the first time since she'd left Texas, she was hopeful.

"You'll be meeting the executive members at ten." Jim glimpsed his watch. "There's still time. While you're waiting, you can sneak a look at your office. I know Fletcher wanted to show it to you personally"—he gave Rose a sly half-grin—"but we can keep it our secret." For the second time, Rose was led through the common area, which was, for all intents and purposes, the entire office, but this time they walked farther down and past the game room. Jim guided her through a funkily painted walkway she hadn't noticed before, probably because she had been too preoccupied ogling the main space.

"This is the conference room." Opening a door to their left, Jim held it wide so that Rose could see inside.

She was given another fantastic view of Charlotte.

In the middle of the room was a large table and, on the wall, a projector screen and a white board. Equipped with everything one might need for a meeting, it seemed simple enough. Shutting the room off, the two continued down the short path to the executive offices.

"Here we are."

Walking into an octagon-shaped lounge, they came to a dead end.

"Your office is there." He pointed to the closed door on the right. "When you get done taking a look at it, you can wait in the conference room and fill out your employee paperwork. Mr. Fletcher should be there shortly. I've got to run, but if you need anything, don't hesitate to ask."

Then he was off.

She buckled her fingers over the door handle. Twisting it, she pushed in.

The office was phenomenal. The downtown display was superb, making her envious she couldn't wake up to the view. Stepping inside, she laughed. Huge desk. Personal computer. Wooden floors. Decked-out sofa. *Mini-fridge?*

She could get used to this.

Some minutes later, Rose sat behind her desk, filling out her W-2 information, glad that everything was starting to look up.

Her not-date with Devon on Saturday had been a total disaster. After he'd hit on the waitress and tried to feel Rose up under the dinner table, she'd easily decided not to pursue anything with him. She was also missing Shane's company, but it didn't matter because she was through with men, through with anything that could distract her from her goals. She was only semi-sad that her sex life had been put on the back burner when it had been starting to boil, but it was for the best. Focusing on fixing her career after being dubbed a leopard in her field was where she needed her attention to be. After all, how else would she get a position at a Fortune 500? Later she'd worry about marriage and kids...*and the man with heavenly biceps who I can't stop thinking about.* Bringing her pen to her mouth, she began to chew on the end.

As of late, Enrique had not been cutting it. Her vibrator couldn't hit that spot Shane—

Her pen clanked on the desk when it fell. Voices moved down the hallway, coming closer to her. *Crap.* She wasn't supposed to be in her office.

The last thing she needed was to make a bad impression on her first day. Her door was ajar, but not enough to be noticed...*unless someone is paying attention.* She only had to stay quiet long enough for them to go to their offices, then she could sneak into the conference room.

"What did you end up doing Saturday?"

Rose tensed as someone asked.

"Her name was Monique," someone else answered, his laugh throaty and warm.

"You're a pig." That person sounded familiar, but Rose couldn't place his voice.

"So," the second said, his tone resonant, "who is this chick we're supposed to be meeting today?" *This chick?*

Was he talking about *her*? "I've got a twelve o'clock I need to prepare for. Gonna talk web dev with Tim. Ocean View Realtors is looking to rebrand."

Why do they both sound so familiar?

Rose debated standing up and trying to sneak a glance through the crack of her door.

Um, heck no. What if they catch me?

"Marketing director," one of the men said.

She recognized him now. The CEO, Mr. Fletcher. She'd spoken to him on the phone during her interview.

He continued, "Your new boss."

"My *what?*" the second man said.

She was taken aback by the other man's surprise.

It was like he didn't know Rose would be heading the marketing and creative department. Would Mr. Fletcher hold off on telling a staff member such vital information?

"She is your new boss," Mr. Fletcher said firmly.

There was a moment of pause, then, like a switch of a blade, his sharp voice sliced through the silence, "You are fucking kidding me."

Rose flinched.

"Nope." There wasn't an ounce of sympathy in the CEO's voice.

"I'm not going to work under some crazy chick who punches her employees when she has bad cramps."

Bad cramps? What? She sucked in air and dug her nails into the sides of her chair. Who the hell did this guy think he was? She was a second away from pushing out of her chair and introducing herself as the '*crazy chick who punches her employees when she has bad cramps*', but she forced herself to stay still.

I need this job. I need this job. It became her mantra.

"That isn't what happened, and you are *not* to bring it up to her."

With a locked jaw, she sat back in her chair. It looked like her new job wouldn't be as easy going as she'd thought. Rose had screwed up—big time, she got that—but her screw-up didn't give him, Mr. Asshole, the right to speak about her that way. No matter. Rose had worked with jerks before. She'd let this guy know who was boss.

Tears touched her cheek, and she wiped them away with an inner curse of disgust. Who cared if he had a point? Who cared that, if she was in Mr. Asshole's position, she too wouldn't want to be underneath someone who'd gotten fired for assaulting their employee?

"You saw her résumé." Mr. Fletcher had a soothing voice, and it calmed her.

"I didn't need to see her qualifications to know that she is a huge risk to a company that can't afford taking risks right now." His words, regardless of how true they were, stung Rose.

"You didn't look at her résumé, did you?" the CEO scoffed. "Did you do a search on her, at least?"

"I might have..."

"Which means you didn't. Jesus, why do I even bother? Regardless of her past, she *is* an asset to Lambda. If we want to grow, we need her. We need another person working on implementing strategies besides me, and since you are useless when it comes to anything but creative, I found her. Luckily, I might add."

"Then why is she not *your* boss?"

This guy is such a brat. He's complaining to his boss about having a boss?

"*This* is the price of expansion. *This* is what we need for Lambda's future."

"We can find another way."

Find another way to what?

"I make the business decisions here," Mr. Fletcher said.

"Remind me why, again?"

The balls on this guy!

"You *are* going to behave yourself." The warning was clear, but why would Mr. Asshole need a warning like *behave* to begin with?

She hated when people lacked respect for the chain of

command. *Why hasn't he been fired already?* If it had been her that he was speaking to so disrespectfully, he would be cut quicker than a dead end.

"I don't like this."

"You don't have to like it. The decision wasn't yours to make. That's why you're there, and I'm here."

Rose heard keys clinking together.

"Don't look at me like that. Just because we're friends…"

They were *friends*. No wonder he hadn't been fired.

"It doesn't mean I'm going to take it easy on you. My job is to do what's best for Lambda, and quite frankly, someone looking after you might be a good thing."

She thinned her eyes. Rose wasn't aware she'd signed up for a babysitting position.

"Now, stop being a child. She is overseeing all of creative and sales, not just you."

"For your sake and because I am willing to do what it takes for our future, I will play by the book. But know that she is only my boss in title. I don't work for —"

"You're being ridiculous."

Rose couldn't agree more with Mr. Fletcher.

"I've spoken to her plenty of times. She's a good kid, and I guarantee you'll like her. Actually, I know you will. It was one of the reasons I hired her."

Rose didn't know what insulted her more, that one of the reasons she had gotten hired was because Mr. Asshole would approve of her or that the CEO was under the impression that she would actually get along with this prick in the first place.

"I hope you're right."

He's not.

"Next time you hire someone, I'm gonna be there," the voice stated.

Mr. Fletcher laughed. "You say that now, but we both know it's not true. Also, since we're on the subject, she's pretty. Don't try to sleep with her."

Rose stiffened.

"Damn, I'm not a raging horn-dog."

Was Mr. Fletcher seriously warning this guy as if he didn't have faith he could control himself? Rose might have a dubious moral code when it came to her relationship with employees, but she didn't sleep with them. And, not to sound like a prude, but she wouldn't sleep with Mr. Asshole even if he wasn't her employee.

"All I'm saying is, we need her and I'd hate to see her go." His warning was as clear as day.

The conversation ended when two doors closed.

She used the time to sneak out of her office and into the conference room. When the conference room door was shut, she leaned against it. Heart slamming inside her like it was in a one-on-one cage fight, she had been under the naïve notion that no one at Lambda, except Mr. Fletcher—and maybe the office manager, Jim—had known about what had happened in Texas. How stupid. Her incident was a Google search away. Did they all know? Did they share his opinion?

The wall clock ticked in a mock countdown. Soon she would have to face the guy whose cruel words she could still feel splicing through her. How could Rose work with him, knowing he didn't respect her? That he was her employee but, at the same time, he wasn't. He was friends with the CEO, which meant if the CEO had to choose sides, it was obvious whose side he would be on.

Striding to the window, she stared at the city below. She could do this. She *had* to do this. The door knob wiggled. Even though she wanted to puke, she stood strong and kept reciting it.

You can do this. You can —

"PT?"

Every hair on her arm lifted. *Impossible*. Confusion swept over her in a furious wind. She was hallucinating. The universe was playing a trick on her.

Distinct footsteps closed in on Rose, yanking at her heart. A hand touched her shoulder and she jolted.

"PT."

The confirmation in his voice made shivers run down her spine. *Oh, God.*

How could she not have recognized that voice? How could she not remember her body reacting to its depth, its heavy baritone? His harsh exhales on her neck, like the biting lash of his palm on their first night alone, caused her pleasure and pain.

As if he sensed she was too scared to move, he turned her himself. The shock on his face didn't take away from the fact that he was the most handsome man she'd ever seen. Mr. Asshole. Shane.

'I did some full-stack development and freelancing here and there in college. Not in it anymore but I'm in something similar. I work with plenty of marketers.' Their conversation at the bar came back to her.

Dumbfounded, Rose stepped backward. It was an out-of-body experience, seeing him in front of her. What had he said in the car? A mirage. A dream. Dress shoes. Navy slacks. The button-down he wore was folded up to his elbows. All Shane. No dream at all. He was here. Real.

A wisp of the hypnotic tattoo that covered his waist and drew up his back peeked out from beneath his shirt as it stretched up the side of his throat. The Redback came into view when he raised his hand as if to touch her, as if to see if she were real, too. Behind them, a dark-skinned man entered the room and shut the door. "You two know each other?" Mr. Fletcher took a seat.

Managing to close her mouth, she answered him with a shake of her head. She avoided the flare of anger in Shane's brown eyes. "I've never met him in my life."

We're playing that game? his expression asked.

"Sorry." Shane moved away from her, his smile seeming to come with some difficulty. "You look like a friend of mine. What did you say your name was again?"

This wasn't happening. She couldn't stay at Lambda. Rose couldn't *work* with him, the asshole who had no respect for her, who she'd *slept* with. "I didn't."

Mr. Fletcher passed his worried frown between the two. "Rosemary, this is Shane Williams, our head of creative. Shane, this is Rosemary Berkowitz, our new marketing director."

"Rosemary." He said it slowly, as if savoring.

"Just Rose."

"Rose."

The word carried heat like a pair of lips at her ear, lips he'd brought down her throat, around the high camber of her breasts and swooped over her stomach before coming to rest at the throbbing peak of her anatomy. Reaching out, Shane offered her his hand. With Malcolm watching them, Rose had no choice but accept it and no choice but to overlook the spark that shadowed his fingertips, trailing down her arm.

Smiles like Shane Williams' smile were dangerous. They should be categorized under weapons of mass destruction, causing the widespread incineration of women's panties, especially the grin he wore now. Promising misconduct, it focused on her. It was like she'd entered an arena — like some sort of game had been initiated the second he'd grasped her hand, and, by the way his perceptive eyes toured over her physique, Shane had to know exactly what she did. He had the home-field advantage.

"It is nice to finally meet you, *Rose*."

Chapter Seven

Shane wasn't paying attention to a word Benji was saying as he sat in the common room with the rest of the creative team, recapping their meeting with CTO Tim Macmillan of Ocean View Realtors. How could he when Blondie, *his* Blondie, was feet away, engaging in what appeared like a wordless argument with the printer and fax machine.

Feet might as well have been miles as Shane cut glimpses at her while still trying to appear immersed in the conversation at hand, something about super-targeted ads and user-generated content. He should have been paying attention, but as he minded the way Blondie's—no, Rose's—ass was flattered by a snug knee-length skirt, he couldn't count his cares on a single hand. There had to be some screwed-up sort of fate at play here. Their meeting not once or twice but *four* times by accident? Her waltzing into his company and introducing herself as his boss, of all things, and having the gall to look him in the eyes like she had forgotten about the night they'd spent doing their own type of engaging—Shane's favorite type, clothing optional.

Her stray sighs drifted to his ears. Had this woman never worked a printer before?

But, call him a cocky bastard, Shane doubted it was the printer giving her hell, but him. Did she feel the same way he did right now? Astonished? Curious? Confused?

Pissed beyond belief?

Maybe it was only him who was seeing flames, but after she'd stood him up Saturday night, he never thought he would see her again, let alone work—

"Shane?"

"Huh?" He turned back, finding Tiffany leaned toward him, hands interlocked and sitting on her crossed legs with her head slanted to one side, as if she were awaiting an answer.

"We should focus on driving social ads, right?"

"Yeah." He cleared his throat, putting together bits and pieces of the conversation he'd missed. He was drawing a blank. "How about we reroute all their social traffic to a landing page? Create a full screen design, high impact, and with a call-to-action that directs to their products."

"That's what I just…"

But the conversation dropped to background noise as he glanced over to Blondie again. Bending down to insert more paper in the machine, Blondie gave Shane the most tempting view, breasts spilling forward. Turning sideways into a fresh stack of white printer paper. Her shirt gaped wider and her bra—

His chair jolted violently, waking him up from his daydreaming of everything his mouth could do—had done—to those breasts. Reaching out, Shane gripped the side of the table and pulled, slamming the front legs of his chair firmly on the ground. He hadn't realized he'd been tipping back in his seat to begin with. His team member's eyes were bulging out of their sockets, probably because they weren't used to their boss off his game, but Blondie did that to him.

"You okay there?" Benji asked as Shane stood.

"I'm fine." He caught Blondie leaving the printer room, heading toward her office. "Send me an email summarizing everything. I've got something to do…"

Heading in the direction Blondie had gone, Shane trailed down the art-littered hallway, colored with graffiti he'd drawn when Malcolm and he had first opened Lambda. He hadn't expected to dress up the whole place, but when Shane had started the blockbuster out front, he'd had a hard time stopping at the reception area, the addicting fumes influencing him farther down the halls until he had been high on them and the walls were bright with wild style. He had just passed his office door when his phone rang from inside. He looked between his closed door and Rose's.

Stopping in his office, he picked up the phone. "Shane Williams."

"Why don't you answer my phone calls?" His sister's voice, pitched higher than a foul ball, exploded from the other line.

Imagining her face, scrunched up by frustration like it always was when her tone raised decibels, Shane smiled, settling himself on the edge of his desk.

"I'm at work, that's why." His own voice carried all the fondness of missing his younger sibling, who lived hours away. He and his sister were close, and they spoke a lot, but he wanted to see her like crazy. Speaking to her always brightened his day. With the bombshells that'd been dropped on him today, he could use some brightening and maybe some beer, too.

"You're always at work." Her irritation was thicker than her Georgia accent. "Guess what? Heath booked our plane tickets. Eric can't wait to see you."

Samantha and Heath, her husband, were parents to his sparkly eyed nephew Eric, six years ago. His favorite member of the family, Eric was the only kid Shane had ever liked.

He'd been trying to convince Sam and Heath to move up to Charlotte. Shane would give anything to see the little man growing up, but Sam loved her job as an elementary school art teacher in Atlanta too much to move. Sam was relentless, but Shane wouldn't give up just yet.

"You're supposed to give me time to guess, Sam."

"Whatever. You're excited?"

Gone from his hometown since he'd been eighteen, he had more than gotten used to being away from his siblings for long periods of time, but they were due for a visit. Usually Shane made the drive to Georgia to see Trevor and Sam every four or so months, but with the recent growth of

Lambda, he hadn't been able to commit to the long drive. "Of course I am."

"So, how've you been? Anything new in your life? New friends, perhaps?"

Shane scoffed. If there was one thing his sister wasn't, it was subtle. Vocal on her opinion of Shane's single lifestyle choice, his sister tried to change it at every chance she got.

"Everything's the same up here." He rubbed his knuckles into the back of his neck. "Listen, Sam. I gotta go. I've got work to get to." He couldn't handle a speech from her on manhood and family right now, and she would give him one. She always did.

"Yeah, I hear ya. I'll speak to you later, okay? Tell Bub I say 'hey'."

"Will do. Love ya." After they'd hung up, Shane remained still, contemplating his next move. Blondie had walked into his life again and, coincidence or not, Shane saw it as opportunity. Standing from his desk, Shane heard Malcolm's warning. Don't try to sleep with her, huh? Well, everyone who knew Shane knew he had this thing with rules.

* * * *

"He called me a crazy chick."

On the other line, wind cooed in the background. Olive must be on her break. Five hours had passed since she'd found out her one-night stand was now her permanent co-worker.

Everything was a shitstorm.

Rolling her pen beneath her finger, she made sure it wouldn't touch the white sheets in front of her, hesitant to finish her employee paperwork.

"Um, hellooo." Olive laugh was pure amusement. "You *are* crazy. That's why I love you."

She lifted her head from the desk. "Yeah, but he isn't supposed to know that."

"Anyway, why quit when you're already doing your job so well?" Olive teased. "You're the best boss he's ever had, and it's only the first day."

Rose groaned and a giggle from her friend sequenced.

"Seriously?" She almost ripped out her Bluetooth. "I asked for advice because I'm having a literal life crisis, and you're no help at all. Aren't you supposed to be a doctor?"

"I teach couples how to improve their sex lives." Rose swore Olive was grinning. "Are you sure you want my advice on this one? Because, sweetie, I can hear you at night, and I'd say your sex life needs some improving. Word of advice… Give Enrique a break."

Rose didn't have the energy to be upset with her friend's sassy comment.

"You're right," she said, defeated, demoralized. *Dick-whipped.* "About the advice, not Enrique." Rose tossed the pen aside, frustrated. "Leave him out of this."

"Rose, you need this job. I know you do. You're not leaving."

"Really? Because I am seriously considering it."

No matter how Rose looked at it, there wasn't a solution besides giving up.

Normally, she wasn't a quitter. No, never. And she didn't want to become one because of some guy. Issue being, Shane wasn't *some* guy. He was *the* guy she'd slept with numerous times, the guy whose phone calls she'd ignored Saturday night. The guy who had occupied her shower-thoughts this morning and yesterday morning and—

She peeked up as her office door opened. Speak of the devil and the devil will come. "Olive, I have to go." Her eyes narrowed when he entered the room.

"What are you doing here, Shane?" Her breath was shaky from where her thoughts had been heading, and the way he caressed her with his eyes ensured that her voice would continue its rebellion.

He closed the door behind him and leaned against the entrance. The room became smaller with him inside, hotter.

Rose shifted. She tried not to think about how good he looked, but God, he was gorgeous—a glass of whiskey Rose wanted to drink down in slow pulls. The five o'clock shadow suited him well. His hair was short and styled in a way that made him seem like he'd been running his hands through it, and maybe he had. Maybe Rose had frustrated him so much that he'd been pulling at it all day. The thought made her want to smile but his molten expression, searing her skin and unfurling desires she'd rather keep hidden, made her lips stay sealed. He looked upset. His narrowed eyes kept her from moving, speaking.

"You stood me up." The accusation was sharp.

Her throat constricted.

Without replying or meeting his eyes, she stood with the purpose of walking him out, but he came forward as she stepped around her desk, blocking her with his large frame.

His anger was a furnace inside her office. She licked her lips and brought her shaking hands together. Okay, she didn't think she'd see him again, so she'd blown him off, but...he was one to talk. Now that she was aware that Mr. Asshole was Shane, his conversation with Mr. Fletcher filled out. Rose may have been a jerk for standing him up but he sure rebounded fast. "I'm surprised you weren't too busy with Monique to notice."

"Where were you?"

"I was on a date." No reluctance followed the statement. Screw it if he was mad at her.

His face darkened. "Say that again, sugar. I don't think I heard you."

"Don't start with the 'sugar' stuff, Shane."

She had a moment of uncertainty, fearing what he might do as his jaw hardened and his eyes, churning hotter than lava, thinned so that they were almost closed. He looked like he wanted to either tear through her office or rip off her clothes. Which frightened her the most?

"Do you know how long I waited for you?"

"I hope you waited all evening." Rose instantly regretted

saying it, but she kept her face calm. She breezed past him, about to show Shane out but he grabbed her forearm.

"What are you—?" Panic seized Rose the second she turned.

Shane forced her to the front of her desk, the hard edge of wood sharp on her backside. She slapped his hand. Tried prying his fingers away from her arm. They were meta, digging in, immoveable. She ground her teeth. His eyes boiled. "Let me go."

Her heart drummed faster.

Holding onto her eyes, he grabbed her waist.

Pencils and pens shook in their silver jar as he yanked her up so she was sitting on her desk. Eyes widening and stomach fluttering, she spread her hands out at her sides. Rose glanced between him and the door. Malcolm's warning to Shane flashed through her mind.

'I'd hate to see her go.'

"S-Shane."

He stepped between her legs, forcing them wider. Her skirt raised past her knees. His top was opened a button to expose lightly tanned skin. She focused on that, his chest rising and falling and the sound of his angry exhales, instead his face, fearful of seeing what expression he was making, fearful of losing herself to the look. Before she could protest, Shane came closer. He pressed his erection onto leg. A jolt of excitement shot through her.

Her eyes closed for a moment. Enough time for him to lift her hair off her collarbone. Shane pushed it behind her shoulder. He brought his ragged breath beside her ear, down her throat, then he captured the base of her neck in a kiss and a bite that ended on a growl. *Oh, I am so screwed.* A slow and magnetic burn began in the places they molded together.

"Shane."

"No." Frustration marred the word. He combed his fingers up the back of her hair and gripped her scalp with the obvious intention of making her listen and it worked.

She snapped her mouth shut, only opening it again to moan as he rubbed himself against her. Every inch of Rose's body tightened. Inner strings pulled tight.

"No speaking to do anything but answer me, *Rose*."

Her nipples had gone pert. Her lower body throbbed with activity. She reached backwards and her employee paperwork slid below her hand. What was she doing? Why couldn't she stop? Shane sighed her name, his lips skimming over her jaw, and her barriers — her plans — dropped like a cloak and puddled at her feet. Selfishness took over.

"What I want to do to right now…" He sounded as if he were lost in a fantasy, envisioning it all.

"Glad you know my name now, Shane? Took you long enough." Rose laughed when he raised his eyes to hers, a drunken sound she didn't recognize.

He toughened his hold on her hair, making the pain more acute. "Do you know how pissed off you make me?" His voice, raw and violent, spoke to something primal inside her.

She bit her lip, but her moan snuck through, loud enough for Shane to know she liked what he was doing. Echoing the roughness used to crush her to her desk, he slammed his mouth to hers, throat rumbling as he wasted no time curving his hands over her waist. Rose's breath quickened. His lips claiming hers, her body squeezing and rippling with delight.

Desperation and fury made them move faster. Shane deepened the kiss. He squeezed the back of her thighs, grinding hard. Her head fell backwards. Her shoulders hit the desk. She fingered his belt. The sound of his zipper descending. He ripped her shirt out from her skirt. His lips were everywhere, quick and hot. The room spun. He yanked her against his open slacks. She barely noticed Shane raise her skirt until his fingers were below her soaked panties.

There was a light tap behind him.

"Rose?" Mr. Fletcher's voice was muffled by the door.

Shane stumbled as she shoved him away. Faster than

she had ever stood in her life, Rose straightened herself, slightly dizzy, and smoothed her skirt, reality sinking in as she patted down her hair. "Give me one moment, Mr. Fletcher." Her voice was as unsteady as she.

What. The. Hell. Is. Wrong. With. Me.

"It's fine. Meet me in the conference room in ten. We've got..."

She didn't hear the rest of his response.

The shame roping in her stomach tuned out everything else. How could she let this happen? Vibrations came from Shane's pocket, making her freeze, and he tugged out his cell phone.

Putting his fingers against his closed eyes, Shane answered the call. "Malc."

Rose didn't know what Mr. Fletcher was saying, but she imagined it was something along the lines of, "Screwing the newcomer on her first day?"

"Yeah." His gaze was relaxed as it drifted to Rose.

How could he sound be so calm after what had just happened? Maybe he had that much experience.

"I'm at lunch. I'll be up now." Shane ended his call.

Trembling, but now for a much different reason, Rose clenched her eyes shut and took an enormous breath. Following a couple of minutes of freaking out, she was able to come to her wits. Opening her eyes again, Shane was in front of her, his face inscrutable.

Her first reaction to his nearness was to lean in, which was why she needed to quit. She would find another way to fix her reputation.

What if this is the only way? It couldn't be.

"Rose."

"I'm sorry, Shane, but this was a huge mistake. This can't happen—"

"You're wrong." The intensity in his eyes made her turn away. How could she ever face him? How could she be so stupid? "It wasn't. There's something here, between us."

"There's not," she said, even if it wasn't true. "If you're

looking for a friend with benefits, look somewhere else, because this will never happen again." With that, she left.

For the second time that day, Rose snuck out of her office and to the conference room.

The whole way there she was coming up with ways to tell Mr. Fletcher she couldn't work at Lambda. In the reflective glass of a wall-length portrait, she checked herself out to make sure her hair was fixed and her skirt was in place before joining the CEO.

She took a deep breath.

Mr. Fletcher's face lit when she entered. "How are you liking it here, Rose?"

Rose marched across the office then pulled out a chair. She managed a professional voice. "I like it. Everyone is nice, umm, and helpful…" *But I need to quit because I don't think, after punching my employee in the face, my track record could take me sleeping with another.*

A breeze drifted through the room as the door was opened. "Shane."

She stiffened as Mr. Fletcher greeted Shane.

"Now that you two are together, let's get busy."

Was it just her or did *you two* and *get busy* just sound wrong in the same sentence?

"We need to talk Moreno & Blu."

"Rose, were you able to come up with any presentation ideas? It's your first day, but the deadline is only five months away. At one month behind schedule, we're already competing with firms who have gotten their entire content down. With our recent growth, it's been hard to take on multiple projects, but now you're here" — he smiled, making Rose feel worse that she couldn't stay — "and the staff will be working with our other clients while you spearhead the Moreno & Blu project."

"Yes, I've been profiling Matthew Moreno for some time now."

"What do you have?" Shane crossed the room and grabbed a seat in front of her, beside Mr. Fletcher. The switch from personal to professional was instant and…

Not hot at all.

Jesus, could she just stay focused for a minute?

"Rose? If you don't have anything, that's fine. We'll start from the beginning. Taking our time to be as thorough as possible is essential in order see this through to its completion."

Completion.

"No. It's not that."

Opposite her, Shane smiled like he'd a private tune into her dirty thoughts. He winked. Her lady parts responded. She pushed their enthusiasm away.

"I've a PowerPoint—" she explained.

"PowerPoint?" Shane kicked his feet onto the table, looking like the arrogant man he was. "If you think you'll get his attention with that, you've got another think coming, sugar."

"I don't think calling me that is appropriate."

"Rose is right." Mr. Fletcher gave Rose an apologetic nod. "Shane, please keep in mind that we are in a professional setting. Nicknames are not work-appropriate."

"*Rose.*" There was an edge to his voice that crawled under her skin. "No PowerPoints."

How could he discredit what she was bringing to the table without so much as hearing her out?

"*Mr.* Williams, both Matthew Moreno and Brendon Blu"—Matthew's husband, who wouldn't be participating in the judging, something Rose didn't understand at all but also didn't question—"have been known to value the simplistic over the grandiose. I've profiled them—"

"Neither of them is going to be impressed by some prep-school presentation, sugar. Sorry… *Rose,* I mean." Shane scoffed. "I'll have to get used to calling you by—"

"That's enough, Mr. Williams."

"Oh, she's feisty," he said to the CEO then turned back to her. "Feisty Rose, you'll have to get used to how things are done around here. I say no PowerPoints and that means no PowerPoints. Creative" — he pointed at his face — "remember?"

She sucked in her cheeks to keep herself from telling him where to shove that finger. Now she was glad she'd stood him up.

"I'm sorry. Who is whose boss here?" First day or not, *one-night stand or not*, she'd not allow someone to disrespect her.

Shane's eyes constricted. "Excuse me?"

Before World War Three could break out, Malcolm spoke, a trace of a smile on his lips like was enjoying their banter — or maybe he just enjoyed someone standing up to this ass. "Though yes, please, Shane, keep in mind that Rose will be making the final decision on future projects, Rose, it is important that we use Shane's expertise here."

Expertise in what, being a pompous jerk? She refrained from asking that. Barely. "I'm sorry, Mr. Fletcher, but what knowledge does that person have that I can't acquire?"

"*That* person?"

"Shane, please." Mr. Fletcher held up his hand. Closing his mouth, Shane rolled his stupid eyes.

"Prior to his position at Lambda as head of creative, Shane led the design team at Moreno & Blu Associates in New York."

Because he must have read the look of pure amazement on Rose's face, Shane gave her a smug grin. "I assure you that Matthew wants more than a PowerPoint."

First-name basis?

"Needless to say, you and Shane will be working on this project together. When you go to New York, you'll be presenting as a team, representing all of Lambda."

Mr. Fletcher was going on, but everything else filtered out into the background. *Shane worked with Matthew Moreno?*

"Yes, I worked with him for six years," Shane answered the disbelief on her face. "You can close your mouth now."

She narrowed her eyes. This man worked with one of the most powerful event planning CEOs in the world? What were the odds? Her working with a man directly connected to the person who could change her life…

Wait. This was it.

Her silver lining.

How could she turn this opportunity away?

Shane and Matthew had worked together for six whole years, which meant her chances of success doubled—no, quadrupled. Hope surfaced.

She could fix everything.

When she hadn't respond, Shane took over the conversation. "You and I will start from scratch. Get ready, Rose. With only five months left, we've a lot of catching up to do—a lot of late nights ahead of us." The innuendo glazed in his eyes.

All she needed was five months.

If she could resist him in that time and get Moreno & Blu as Lambda's client, she'd have enough to fuel her in her search for another job. The only question was, how the heck was she going to resist Shane for five months when she couldn't even resist him for five hours?

Chapter Eight

"Rosemary fucking Berkowitz."

The dart left his fingers, whizzing through the air before embedding itself, with a sharp splat, deep within the bullseye. A perfect simulation of what, over the past four weeks, Rosemary Berkowitz had done to his manhood.

"Hot damn! That's the game," Bub shouted behind him. "Shit. Looks like the next round is on me. Remind me never to bet you on darts when you're pissed."

Dipping his lips into the sudsy bubbles of his drink, Shane gulped down the amber ale. He rested the empty glass on the bar top, darting his tongue over his lips to remove the excess. It wasn't the first time Rosemary Berkowitz had driven him to drink midday. It probably wouldn't be the last.

"This woman must have gotten under your skin good." Bub set a fresh draft on the table beside Shane's fisted hand. "I ain't seen you throw a dart that hard in your life. It's kind of funny, though, you gotta admit — your one-night stand ending up being your boss."

His cousin's smile wavered as Shane flashed him a look of warning. "My boss?" Rose was as much his boss as he was *just* head of creative at Lambda Digital.

Bub lifted his hands in acknowledgment.

"Hey, cuz, don't get mad at me."

Shane could tell he was trying to make his voice sound apologetic, but he couldn't displace the grin warping his expression. "You know what I mean."

There was a rumble in Shane's throat that he drowned with a second swig of beer.

Keeping his fingers rounded over the dewy glass mug, he grumbled, "Why are you even bringing her up?" Couldn't he escape her for a goddamn minute?

For weeks, there hadn't been a moment of his life that his iron-willed 'boss' and her voluptuous ass, sculptured to perfection, didn't occupy. In the daytime, she was walking around the office spouting orders in the form of passive-aggressive suggestions and, at night, she was in his bed, in his fantasies, shouting out his name.

"Me? You're aware that you've been here for the past two hours whispering *'Rosemary fucking Berkowitz'* under your breath like you're tryin' to put a hex on her?"

"Shit." *Has it been two hours?*

Checking his watch, Shane confirmed the time. He rolled his shoulders, trying to work out the kinks in his back. Within a month, tense muscles had become his reality — tense muscles and a stiff cock that no woman could move, save her. Normal sexual activity had come to a whopping dead end once Shane had realized that sex with his normal chicks didn't excite him as much as the idea of pushing that pretty blonde 'boss' of his against her desk and having his way with her. Tension trickled down his body, concentrating at his middle. Pent-up frustration. Screaming muscle. Sore cock. Headache like he'd been slammed in the temples with a Louisville Slugger.

Four weeks summed up in four statements.

"I've got to get back to work before..." He trailed off. Never in the past would Shane have formulated that sentence. He had to get back to work before *what*? Before his boss blew up his phone? Chastised him for taking a two-hour break?

He could already see himself falling down the rabbit hole. Years of working his ass off to be his own manager had come to this? He didn't know how much more he could take. Following her orders? Having to answer to someone *other* than himself? No, this shit wasn't for him.

The frosty air hit him square in the face as he migrated

outside.

He breathed in, awakened by its sharpness. Puffs of steam flowed past his lips and ice cracked under his boots as he began his walk back. Shane loved the wintertime. It was one of his favorite seasons, but he couldn't wait until spring bloomed. When the wind was warm and filled with the scent of nature, Shane was the happiest. In less than a month he could shed his jacket and undock his mountain bike from his bedroom wall. The second the snow cleared, he'd take a trip to Dupont State Forest. He'd take Rose with him. They'd hit the trails together.

On those rare moments when she wasn't busy reminding him that he was her underling, she'd shown interest in things like nature and mountain biking. The woman was from North Carolina, home to the most serene landscape in the country, and she had never taken the time to marvel at it? Smiling, he pictured her face gleaming with joy and her hair pushed back by the wind as she peddled down the woody forest's slopes. She'd said she wanted to try it, so Shane would show her how it was done. There was a discrepancy between their mentalities, he'd noticed.

He liked to live. She liked to work.

Not realizing that you could do both at once, Rose kept busy, as if without her late nights and her calendar books she was nothing but a jade-eyed girl from a small Southern town that no one had ever heard of. That wasn't true. She was so much more. Did she realize her eyes twinkled with curiosity and a need for adventure every time he brought up the trails or rope courses or kayaking? Did she realize he could tell, when they were alone, that she let her eyes wander freely over his body? He flashed a look toward his ringing phone. Her name took up the display.

His chest tightened.

Her name. *Rose.* What a fitting name. Red, like the color he always saw when she neared, red from her cheeks or red from his anger, but beautiful. Always beautiful. "Hello?"

"Where are you, Shane?"

131

He used to like that Rose cut to the chase. Now he put his fingers on his temple and tried to keep his voice as calm as possible. "I'm on break."

"Your break has gone on for two hours. I think it's officially over. Can you please come back to the office? We have work to do, and for once, I'd like to leave early."

"Yes, *boss*." The words brimmed with sarcasm. Sooner or later he would have to sit down with Malcolm and sort something out. He didn't want Rose fired. Hell no.

What Malcolm had said was right.

She was an asset to Lambda, adaptive and innovative. She'd help dig them out of the hole the expansion had created. But the chain-of-command thing Rose was milking more than her tight pussy had milked his cock during their first, and only, night indoors had to stop. She could nail her 'big boss' hammer on some other poor man because he was going to go crazy if this kept up.

Having a father who'd punish him if he came home a minute late, Shane never wanted to live by someone else's rules again. That included the rules his *boss* gave him.

Week one of her employment had been miraculous.

When Shane had seen her in the conference room, he'd almost fallen to his knees. He had thought he'd been slipped a drug and entered an alternate reality. He couldn't believe she was really there. Week two had been a challenge. Flirting with the idea of working beside her, Shane had been on his best behavior. A furtive glance here and a meaningful smile there seemed to work in his favor until she started ignoring him. The third week had been a pulse behind his eyebrows. Dealing with his new work regime in which he came to her for approval and final decisions was something he needed but didn't want to get used to. Now, the fourth week of him being under her authority, Shane cringed. The mere thought was nothing but a pain in his ass and an ache in his dick. Fuck, he had to see a doctor or something.

In a perpetual state of arousal, his cock stalled at half-mast. Not every order Rose barked was a turn off. When they weren't directed at him, Shane was kind of turned on by her relentless will. The no-bullshit attitude looked good with dirty-blonde hair and bright eyes, which only served to frustrate him more.

Pushing past the revolving doors, he noticed the difference in temperature immediately. The building's warmth submerged him. And more frustration. More arousal. The corporate offices, shit, *everything* that used to remind him of his accomplishments now reminded him of one thing—one person. Rosemary fucking Berkowitz.

Shane crossed the lobby.

"Hey." Shane trudged off the elevator and to the receptionist desk.

"What's up, man? I thought you'd headed out for the day," Jim said.

"No, I was on break." Shane slouched against the tall desk's wall. "Boss is going to have me by the balls." Everyone loved his nickname for Rose, just like they loved seeing her fulfill the nickname. Well aware of his opinion on rules, they liked watching Shane suffer a little too much.

"I took two hours at Bub's. Completely lost track of time."

"Nah." Jim grinned. "Rose wasn't mad when she came looking for you earlier. Anyway, you already missed her. I don't think you have anything to worry about."

Shane cocked his head. "Missed her?"

"Yeah, she went down about ten minutes ago. Said she was going to pick up food."

Went to pick up food? Had she not gotten off the phone with Shane less than five minutes ago, telling him to get back to the office? This woman… *Is she trying to piss me off?*

"Oh." He made sure to sound casual. "I'll catch her later."

As he walked to his office, his thoughts abound with irritation, Shane reached into the front compartment of his pants, fondling the lace hiding there.

Rose's panties, the ones he'd taken the second time he'd seen her, had been in his pants like this on the same evening she'd stood him up to go on a date with another man.

That Saturday, after he'd gotten home late, he'd thrown them into his laundry basket, and the next morning his wide-eyed stranger had become his co-worker, and her panties had turned into the last thing on his mind. A couple of days back, he'd found them. The lady Shane paid to clean his apartment had washed, folded then tucked them neatly into his dresser. Unearthed, they enticed memories that ran like magma below his skin. Rose brought out his anger and fervor, and they intermixed so often sometimes that Shane had difficulties distinguishing between the two — like now.

The little thong slipped from his pocket as he pulled it out then hung the lingerie so it dangled on her office doorknob. A smirk on his face and only a small care that anyone other than her would find the panties — unless someone had a meeting with an executive, no one came down to these offices, and Malcolm was out for the day on back-to-back meetings — Shane went through the door beside hers. With a sigh of contentedness, he set his feet on the top of his desk.

He waited.

Shane heard her shout before a gust of air shifted his hair. She blew through his office door, her panties almost vanishing in her fist.

"Shane!" There was hell-fire in her eyes and it was fixed right at him.

"Coming in without knocking? That's not very professional of you, sugar."

Resting back in his chair, he smiled. She closed her eyes momentarily, as if to get a grip on the situation.

"Listen, asshole. If you do something like this again, I'm going to —"

Lowering his feet off the desk, he lifted to his full height that was much taller than her and she seemed to notice. Rose froze as he stalked around his desk. Leaning onto its edge, he crossed his arms.

"*What* exactly are you going to do?"

They studied each other, unspeaking and unmoving, sparks flying like electric bullets between the two. Stressed by the reminiscent scent of her shampoo and the sound of her quick breaths, Shane toyed with the idea of striding across the room and possessing the very lips that scowled at him with rage, tempted to see her dangerous expression shatter to something sweeter.

One of the most admirable traits about Rose's work was that when running into an obstacle, she never backed down, so he wasn't surprised that she stepped toward him with her chest heaving and her fists strong at her sides. "You think I'm scared of you, Shane?"

"Yes." His answer was immediate, and because Shane wasn't one to lie, it was his honest opinion. Denial was the game she'd been playing ever since she'd stomped those stiletto-clad feet through *his* office. "You're scared of your feelings for me."

She narrowed her eyes to resemble fine cuts of emerald. "What the *hell* are you talking about?"

"You know exactly what I'm talking about." He stepped closer.

Her hair waved around her shoulders as she laughed. "He's delusional," she said to the room then turned back to him with a straight face. "You're delusional. I'm your *boss*."

His patience threatened to crack as his annoyance built brick by brick. "You're my boss, are you?" It was on the tip of his tongue to tell her how wrong she was.

Before he could speak, she countered, "Yeah, I am." Raising her chin, she was the most tempting woman Shane had ever met. "And you'll do well to remember who is in charge here."

Shane laughed and it was as harsh as hers had sounded.

That was it. He *was* going crazy. Hell, maybe he was already locked up in a loony bin somewhere having hallucinations of Miss Karma coming off her high throne and down to Earth to make his life a living nightmare. "God" — his voice was sharper than a knife — "is your sole purpose of working here to drive me insane? Because, if so, I'd say you've earned employee of the month."

"You can go to hell, Shane."

"I'm already there, sugar."

She held her head in a condescending fashion. "You're intimidated because your boss is a woman. It wouldn't be the first time I've dealt with—"

"I'm not intimidated by you, Rose." It came from between his teeth. "I'm..." *attracted to you and your feisty fucking mouth that'd look so much better opening around my cock than opening to yell at me.*

It was probably best to keep that part to himself. "You just piss me off."

"As long as I'm doing my job and you're doing yours"— she hit Shane with her pointer finger, digging it right into his chest bone—"I don't give a crap how much I piss you off."

He lowered his eyes to her hand, noticing how close they'd gotten. When had that happened? Wetting his lips, Shane glanced down at hers. Her mouth was calling to him, those thick pink lips begging to be sucked. Lowering his gaze even farther, Shane was burdened with the image of him on his knees, his mouth working between another step of lips.

She cleared her throat, making him transition his eyes back to her face. "We've things we need to do. I've got to get in touch with a couple of New York organizers to see if Moreno—"

"Sugar." How could she not feel this?

"We have to come up with a dialogue—"

He placed one of his hands on her torso, the other he raised, allowing the side of his index finger to catch her right under the chin, so he could bring her face to his. *What am I thinking?* Well, he wasn't. That was the point. He wanted to stop thinking. He wanted her to stop thinking.

"I need to set up a meeting for us with—" Shivering, her voice copied her body.

Working with Rose was burdensome for him and not because of the way she worked—the woman was a champion in the office—but because he didn't want to be under her, he wanted *her* under *him*—a flower spread above his sheets. She was the sexiest woman, made more alluring by watching her work. He loved the way she got that concentrated look on her face and how she'd chew on the end of her pen, all cute, when she was thinking about a challenging task. When she found the solution, her eyes lit brighter than the North Star. Shane laid his parted lips on the edge of her jaw, hearing Rose suck in air like it was water she'd wither without.

How was he expected to behave when she responded to him like that?

With her breasts pressed into his chest and her fingers digging into his sides, he ran the dull point of his tongue over the defined angle of her jaw, his desire blazing and snapping—a lick of fire in dry air. Was it because she had thus far been unattainable that Shane wanted her greedily, to the point of voraciousness? That Shane could take her in his arms when his office door was wide was risky, even for him. Maybe it was because she'd rejected him that the moan emanating from her as he slid his hand low to fashion a firm grip on her ass cheek, felt like the greatest triumph. Or had it simply boiled down to lust—to the animal feeling inside him that was dying to see pleasure consume those stubborn eyes?

Guiding her closer, he kissed her chin.

He lifted his head so that his mouth was close enough to hers that he tasted her minty breath, but he paused, dedicating a moment to memorizing her face, her glistening lips, flushed cheeks complemented by noble cheekbones and, above them, eyes that brimmed with fear, but lower, something like the affection she'd attempted to hide. *Gorgeous.* "So gorgeous."

Unable to wait a second longer, he leaned forward. But because everyone always told him an instance would come when he was least expecting it that he'd get the karma that'd been coming his way, Rose's cell phone went off, the chipper ring surprising her so that she jumped away seconds before their connection. His breathing staggered as she backed up.

"Don't." His pulse raced up his throat. "Don't leave."

"I can't do this, Shane." She shook her pale face. "I'm sorry. I *can't* do this."

"R—"

She turned around and ran out of the door, leaving Shane with a thundering heart, the empty heat on his chest where her body had been and her name a wish on the edge of his lips.

Chapter Nine

The car's consistent hum died as she slid her keys out of the ignition. Rose's hands were shaking. They hadn't stopped shaking since her kiss with Shane.

Almost kiss, she corrected. Silent regret came along with the statement.

Why had she stopped him?

Worse, what would have happened had she not done so?

The entire drive home, she'd tried to make sense of how they had gone from arguing to being in each other's arms. Leaning back on the headrest, she lowered her eyes and was introduced to the after scene of Shane, bowing his mouth to her cheek, his eyes overflowing with a craving that reciprocated in her loins. She sighed, the impression of his lips afire on her chin.

Shane had called her gorgeous. She didn't *feel* that way.

Rose was using him and everyone at Lambda to further her career because of a screwed-up situation she'd gotten herself into. She planned to land Moreno & Blu and get the heck out North Carolina. Once she'd done that, everything would go back to normal, and she'd be on her way toward the perfect, nightmare-free life. Success. Quiet. Lately, her nightmares were getting louder. Waking up before dusk with cold sweats, Rose assumed the terrors had something to do with her being back in the state where it had happened. Now, she realized it was guilt.

Manipulating people for her benefit? That wasn't beauty. It was hideous, and she was more disgusted with herself each day. She realized more and more that Shane Williams was everything she wanted and nothing she needed. Five-year plan?

Shane fit into her plan as much as a triangle fit into a circle.

Hefting her work bag over her shoulder, she used her free hand to open the car door. She'd rather not think about all of that now. There was a time and place to sit down and contemplate life, and it was called Happy Hour at Chinco's Burgers and Beer two miles away.

Maybe tonight she and Olive could—

Peering up, she paused. Olive was pacing on front steps of their apartment. "Olive? What are you doing out here?"

Her nervous gaze greeted Rose. "You didn't answer you phone." The worry in her voice made Rose anxious.

"It's in my bag. Sorry. I'm kind of out of it right now." Grabbing the leather strap on her work bag, Rose pulled it higher up her shoulder. "Why? What's going on?"

"I got off the phone with Holton about fifteen minutes ago. He says Simon called him."

"My ex-fiancé Simon?" Fear undulated through her, paramount and staggering. "Why would Simon do that?" she asked Olive, trying to combat the nausea building inside her.

"Rose." Olive's face was swelled with distress. What wasn't her friend telling her?

"Olive, what else?"

"Simon is here. He is in Ellenboro."

Rose's vision went dark. *Simon is here?*

Her family…

Telling everyone that her engagement with Simon had ended was high on the list of things Rose planned to do. She wanted to let them know on her terms, when she was ready. It wasn't easy admitting that she lied out of cowardice, but now she feared not having the opportunity to tell them the truth. "Do they know?"

Olive didn't respond to her question. She didn't have to.

"Let's go." Olive ran down the stairs. "We can take my car."

Following her friend, Rose clenched her fists in fear.

She swung the car door open and rushed inside. Olive in the driver's seat and Rose beside her, they started toward Ellenboro.

Between swipes at the tears on her cheeks with the back of her hand, Rose lifted the flap on her leather bag and dug inside, searching for her cell phone.

When she found it, she pressed it awake, only to find missed calls from several people—Holton, Mom, Olive, Simon and Shane. She spurted a curse. How could she have been so zoned out that she didn't realize people were bombarding her with phone calls?

She dialed Simon. Why would he come here? What incentive would her ex have to see her? The phone was a brick in her hand when she lifted it to her cheek and listened as it rang, but the one time she wanted to speak to him, *needed to*, since moving back home, he didn't answer.

* * * *

An hour went by before they pulled into her family's cottage, which sat, aged white and cozy, on the edge of a great field and behind it, mountains so large that, at the right time of day, they blocked out the sun. Her stomach dropped. Simon sat on the front porch.

Even in the distance she could tell he was drinking her grandma's sweet tea. He'd always loved her grandma's sweet tea even more than he'd loved hers. Relaxed in a rocking chair, he was exchanging words with her brother.

Both men turned their heads when the car pulled up the gravel.

Olive shut off the ignition.

It felt like ages, not months, since she'd last laid eyes on Simon. Blond hair, the same color as hers, swooped at his forehead. He widened his lips in a grin when he caught sight of her. Those charming smiles used to be one of the things Rose adored. Once upon a time, they'd made her heart flutter like it was preparing to take flight. Flash forward and now his smile made her stomach turn. Memories floated through her mind of the time she'd witnessed him smiling the same way at Jessica. Emptying from his chair, he shouted out her name.

"Rosey!" His boots and faded jeans were a reminder of a life that had long passed. He hopped off the porch.

Wondering what he would look like dressed up, she realized that she may have never found the cowboy look as attractive as what it had represented.

Normalcy.

"Hey, Rosey." She stepped away as Simon tried to pull her into a hug.

"Why are you here? Why didn't you answer my calls? I was calling you." Rose had tried calling him the entire drive to Ellenboro.

"You know I can never get a signal up here." He locked her with a gentle smile. "I was worried about you. You weren't picking up my calls."

"You decide to fly over a hundred miles because you were worried about me?" She couldn't stop her tone from rising or her anger from leaking out. "Really? Can't you come up with a better excuse? That is what a phone call is for, Simon. Actually—"

"Yes." Simon shook his head like she was nuts for asking. "Hell yes, I'd come all this way because I'm worried. Was that supposed to be a hard question? We were together for five years, Rosey. I'm allowed to worry about you. You haven't answered my calls. You haven't responded to my voicemails. Thank the damn Lord I was able to get in touch with Holt, or I'd have thought you were—"

"We were together for five years?" Long forgotten were the onlookers. "Why didn't you think about that before you screwed my co-worker, huh?" Rose and Simon had had something good. There may have not been passion, but they had been friends. Best friends. He'd ruined that. "You cheated on me!" she blurted out, like he'd forgotten. "What gives you the nerve to come to *my* home, to impose on *my* family when you broke my—"

"Cut the shit, Rosey." Simon's face turned hard and his crystal eyes—an ice blue that sliced through her—made her go silent. "I didn't break anything on you. You're unbreakable."

"What is *that* supposed to mean?"

"Rosey." Simon released an exhausted sigh.

He was tired. He had to be from his long drive. God, she was still worried about him after everything.

"Put aside our past for a moment. We break up and you leave. For a month, I try to contact you. I get nothing but static." He rubbed his hand over the top of his head, looking as drained as he sounded. "You can't tell me that if the roles were reversed, you wouldn't be worried about me." He was right. "Let's go grab a cup of coffee. We can speak privately about this."

On the porch, Holton was staring at her with an undecipherable expression. Beside him, Olive was dressed with concern.

Her brother's face might be blank, but his anger and hurt were echoed in her bones. They were twins, connected. Rose sensed his emotions like the smell of oncoming rain. She placed her hand over her banging heart, knowing Holton's beat the same.

Wiping at her runny nose, she looked back to Simon. This was his fault. He'd shown up and put Rose in this position. He'd cornered her.

"I'm sorry I hurt you, whether you believe me or not. I didn't come here to argue. I wanted to make sure you were alive."

"What?" Rose spat. "Because I'd kill myself over you?" There was no helping it. Her words were just emotional punches—no substance, but anger. Simon showing up out of the blue was the last thing she'd expected. She hadn't wanted her family to find out like this.

"That would require you to have emotions!" Outrage contorted Simon's features.

She flinched.

"You want to do this, Rosey?" A flare of anger in his face, and his tone raised. "You want to make an enemy out of me. Fine! Let's be honest with each other. I loved you for about three fucks before I realized that you'd rather suck your boss's dick than mine."

"Hey!" her brother howled.

Simon turned to acknowledge him. Holton extended his arm in a flash, the punch jerking Simon's face to the side. A groan rippled through the air.

"That's my fuckin' sister you're talkin' about!"

Doubling over, Simon cupped his nose. Blood dripped past his fingers.

"Holton!"

Her brother twisted around, the emotions on his face blaring and too much for her to stomach.

"Don't you dare, Rosey. How could you not say anything?"

"Holton, I—"

"You running off is one thing. I dealt with it."

She could take Simon yelling at her. She could take Simon talking bad about her. One thing Rose couldn't handle was Holton's anger.

"You left, and it broke my heart, but I managed to get past it, to try to see it from your perspective."

"Holt—"

"No, Rosey. You listen." His finger, pointed at her, froze her in place. "I know what that asshole at the camp did to you was bad, and if North Carolina reminded you of him, it was best you were happy. But this? Lying right to my face?"

His body trembled, green eyes darkening with anger and the contents of her stomach swished and rolled. She wanted to reach out and comfort him but he'd pull back. She knew it because she'd do the same.

"Have you been so blinded by your own pain that you don't realize you're causing other people to hurt? Or do you not care? Do any of us little people mean jack shit to you?"

"Holton!" Olive ran after him as he stalked off.

Rose couldn't move.

Everything was happening too fast. Tears blurred what she saw of her brother growing smaller the farther he walked.

"I'm leaving." Simon wiped his bloody nose, wincing. "Since I know you're fine, I won't come back again."

"I'm..." Rose watched the man she'd thought she loved and finally understood. "I'm sorry, Simon." Too busy focusing on her plan, she'd never given him all of herself. No matter what he'd done or said, this wasn't Simon's fault. It never had been. "I'm sorry."

"For what it's worth, I did care about you." His face was one of absolute conviction. "I loved you."

Taking the keys to his rental truck out of his pocket, Simon walked to his vehicle. Rose didn't watch him pull away. Her knees pushed into the gravel after she fell, pain ripping through her body. She wept.

"Come here."

"I'm sorry." Her momma nestled her arms around Rose. Forehead against her chest, Rose cried harder into her momma's sweater, cold air freezing her tears to her cheeks. Agony gripped her heart, tearing her insides to nothing. Memories of her assault came back with a vengeance – her screaming, branches scratching at her face as she ran faster. "I didn't want to fail you." Rose didn't want her momma to know she had failed again. All she wanted was to make up for her past. "I didn't want anybody to hurt again, Momma."

"Shush now, baby girl."

The hatred and sadness she'd been holding on to for this place – North Carolina – for herself, and toward *him* – the man who'd assaulted her at sixteen and had assaulted again before she'd had the courage to confess – flowed into the delicate cotton of her momma's shirt.

Melissa had been the girl's name.

She'd been sixteen, too. Months after Rose had been

assaulted by her guidance counselor, Melissa had been beaten and sexually attacked by the same man. Her injuries had been more brutal than the ones Rose had endured. She hadn't survived. Melissa had died in the same emergency room Rose had gone to, where she'd lied to the nurses and told them she didn't remember a thing, fearful he'd come after her family. Melissa had lost her life. Rose had failed. She'd failed herself, Melissa and all the women who'd come before her. All Rose wanted was to make up for that failure. That was it.

Was that too much to ask?

She was sorry, so sorry, but no matter how hard she tried, Melissa was gone, and her mother was daughterless. Her father would never be able to see his little girl's graduation walk or witness his little girl fall in love with a sweet, God-fearing man, who she'd marry and have two kids with, and they'd live on a ranch with horses and the perfect picket-fence house just like theirs.

"I'm sorry." Rose cried, pain and memories cracking her bones, until she lost track of time.

"It's okay, baby girl. I've got you." Her momma patted her hair, saying in a soothing mantra, "It's gonna be okay. Everything is gonna be okay."

And Rose wished she believed her.

Later, when her mom's shirt was washed in tears and she was exhausted, Rose showed her mom inside then set out in search for her brother. Her past had been waiting to confront her ever since she'd come back to this place. Sooner or later, Rose had to face the facts.

Melissa would be alive if Rose had had the courage to tell the truth.

Nothing could change that.

No picket-fence house or cowboy husband.

Melissa would never have the perfect life. Rose had ensured that when she'd failed to speak up all those years ago.

Coming around the barn, where she assumed Holton had

gone, Rose tried to figure out how to mend this situation. She couldn't leave Ellenboro, for work or any other reason, with Holton upset. Peeking inside, when she found the downstairs empty, she went upstairs to his room.

Though Holton owned a house in Shelby, he stayed with their momma most of the time.

At fifty-five, she was getting older, and she always needed extra hands around the place. Holton was God-sent, taking care of their momma when Rose couldn't—another guilt that wore on her.

Olive's voice drifted to her ears just as she was about to enter her brother's room. What her best friend was saying gave her pause.

"I know, Holton. I never meant to lie to you, but I can't tell Rosey's secrets. She's my best friend."

Rose stopped her hand over the golden knob.

"What about me?" Holton asked. "I thought *I* meant something to you, Olive."

"You do! I care about you so much, Holt, but Rose—"

Her voice faded into a feminine moan. *What?*

Rose vibrated, rage scaling up her back, as she heard what sounded like kissing.

"We can't. We can't do this again, Holt..." Her voice trailed off into a sigh.

Again? Pushing the door open with a bang that reverberated, Rose confirmed what she couldn't believe was happening. Olive's shout met with Holton's curse. She covered her eyes long enough to give Holton time to pull his hand out of her best friend's skirt. When she met with their image again, she tried hard not to notice her friend's puffy lips and pink cheeks.

"What the hell is going on?"

Olive sat up and came toward her. "Rose—"

"I don't want to hear a word from *you*," Rose said to Olive, turning back to Holton. "I was talking to my brother. He was about to tell me what the hell is happening."

"You will not speak to her that way," Holton ground out.

"What is going on?" Rose's head spun. "How could you do this? Me lying to *you*? How about telling me how long you've been screwing around with my best friend?"

She looked between their two guilty faces. "How long?"

They stayed silent.

"How long!"

Holton's jaw was hard, eyes tough with determination. "I love her."

Rose recoiled.

Olive's eyes widened. "Holton…"

Her brother stepped in front of Olive, and Rose shook in disbelief. What had he said? *Love?*

"You left and she was the only thing that kept me sane, and goddamn it, Rosey, I won't allow you to take that away from me because it doesn't fit into your neatly wrapped box of perfection."

"Jesus," Olive said. "Rose!"

"Don't!" Rose threw her arms up and backed away. "Don't you dare touch me. Don't follow me. Just don't."

Walking back the way she'd come, Rose took out her phone again and searched for a signal. When she found it, she stood in place, shivering, listening to it ring and hoping he would answer.

"What's up, sugar?"

The moment his voice touched her ears she could breathe again. Instead of thinking that it was impossible to care for someone after just a month she spoke, forgetting everything. "Shane—"

"Are you okay, Rose?" He turned serious. "You don't sound good. What happened?"

"Can you come and get me?"

Olive had driven her to Ellenboro, so she had no way of getting back to Charlotte. Rose refused to sit in a car with her for an hour. She'd betrayed Rose. Olive had driven a wedge between Rose and the person she'd loved most in the world. And Holton? How could he be angry about her lying? How long had both of them been lying to her?

"Tell me where you are." There was a protectiveness in his voice that, despite her feeling miserable, made Rose smile.

"I'm at home." She recited her Ellenboro address.

"I'll be there as soon as possible." A car engine cranked in the background. "Talk to me, sugar. What happened? Are you okay?"

"I'm not okay." When was the last time she'd really felt okay?

"I'm listening." His smooth voice calmed her.

The negative emotions in her head subdued, giving way to warmth.

"Tell me what happened, sugar."

"I need you." Rose admitted, knowing that in Shane's arms her problems would dissolve, because in Shane's arms everything dissolved. "I just need you right now."

Everything erased but them.

Chapter Ten

'I need you.'

Shane followed the winding road, hand curving with the wheel as they drove through the mountains in silence. In the foreground, the sky was dimming to an ashy blue that reminded him of cue-stick chalk. If he glanced down, he'd find the same bluish tint on his fingertips.

He'd come from playing a game of Eight Ball to clear his mind and ended up right at the source of his disarraying thoughts. He angled his head to the side, allowing himself to take her in, cuddling the inside of his jacket, before he turned back to the path in front of him.

When he'd picked her up earlier, he could tell she'd been crying. Shit, he'd heard her crying on the phone, but she hadn't told him what had happened. Close to twenty minutes had passed, but he could still feel his reaction, the indignation thrilling through his bloodstream and huffing out of his nostrils in fiery spouts of anger in need of an outlet — preferably on whatever piece of shit had made Rose cry. He tightened his hand, pressing his foot on the pedal. The car accelerated at a pace that matched his anger. Christ, listen to him. Shane wasn't one of those prissy men who couldn't admit when they had feelings for someone, and this wasn't high school where people just hitting puberty got all confused about their emotions. This was real life, and Shane was an adult.

He knew he was in over his head.

Rose yarned her fingers further, making them snugger between his, and a sea of heat washed over him. Shane was *definitely* in way over his head.

'I need you.'

He heard it again. He'd been hearing it ever since Rose had gotten into his car, her eyes tearing up and the sight tugged at his heart.

With good intentions, Shane had set his hand on her leg, his attempt to bring her comfort.

She'd stolen his fingers and slipped them into hers, easily, the same way she'd stolen his every waking thought from the moment she'd stumbled into his life a month ago.

"Where am I dropping you off?"

His beaming white headlights shined on a dust-caked sign that read *Charlotte 39 miles.* Shane hated the idea of leaving her like this, but he didn't know what to say to make her stay. *Let's get dinner? Coffee?* Would she even be willing to spend more time with him?

And why would he want her to?

Spending time with Rose outside of working wouldn't be putting only him and her at risk. Everything he'd built would crumble if he didn't keep their eyes on the prize— signing Moreno & Blu Associates. It was a stark reality he tended to forget in Rose's presence.

"I have a favor to ask." She removed her hand from his, and he was put off by the lack of warmth, but he didn't say so.

"Ask away, sugar."

A wordless sigh told Shane she was unsure. *Encourage her.*

"Anything you need, you've got it, Rose. Anything..." *Pipe down, man. Too desperate!* "I mean"—he shifted in his seat—"just that, if you need a friend or a..." Shane went silent, subduing a vexed groan. He was good at seducing women, not soothing them.

"You have a guest bedroom, right?"

Shane nodded.

"Can I sleep over tonight? If you have a guest room—"

"Yes." His answer, instant, needed no consideration. Besides the will to jump on any opportunity to have her at his house, it was obvious that something had shaken Rose.

If being with him made her feel better, then she could spend the night, the weekend or the whole month if need be.

"But I want you to tell me what happened."

"I missed you," she said, but she was deflecting.

He smiled. Deflecting or not, he was okay with hearing those words. What she couldn't have known was how much *he* had missed her. Not that he'd ever tell Rose, but over the weekends he found himself wishing he'd hear her preschool-teacher voice telling him to get back to work. Shane envied her organization skills and her ability to light a fire underneath everyone's asses, which made seeing her emotional all the more intimate. Whether it was purposeful or not, she was admitting a hell of a lot to Shane. She trusted him.

"I missed you too, sugar. Now, tell me who made you cry." *So I can beat their ass.*

"Pull over," she said.

"What?"

"Pull over." She unbuckled her seat belt.

"Are you okay? Do you feel sick?" He veered over to the side of the highway. Putting his car in Park then taking out his keys, Shane turned to her.

He didn't have a second to register what was happening before she pressed her soft lips and her softer moan against him. It took Shane the same amount of time to respond with mutual enthusiasm. Disregarding the consequences, he molded his mouth to the most delicious pair of lips he'd ever kissed, like he'd wanted to in his office that afternoon.

There were no slow flirtations leading up to a deeper kiss.

The insistent tug on her lips was desperate, telling Shane she was, too. He understood the feeling better than she could know. Fitting his palm over the back of her neck, he stole every breath she let out, bringing her moans into his mouth and his fingers in her hair. He kissed her like a poor man starving. He *was* starving, having wanted this for too long.

Releasing her bottom lip, he slanted his head. Shane

delved his tongue inside, and her response—balling her hands with his shirt and bringing herself closer—was his only solace after weeks of need. It made sense to go slow, savor the moment and all that shit, but even if he wasn't possessed with a savage desire that demanded he take her right there, Shane wouldn't have been able to go slow if his life depended on it, not when she felt so right.

With double the force, his mouth crushed hers. Wrapping his arm around her waist, he yanked her against his chest and she massaged her hands in his hair as he kneaded his tongue hotly against hers. He caught the golden-yellow beams of cars passing out of the corner of his eye.

What were they doing? They were on the side of the road. They shouldn't be—

Shane groaned when she crossed the space separating them. His thoughts came to an abrupt halt as she climbed onto his lap. Shane gripped her thighs and locked them beside his waist. Rose did that to him, made him forget life existed outside her fervid touch and her delicate body. She'd done it that first night and now again. Heated feelings rushed over him—lips, fingers, moans, hips—like he'd jumped into a pool of lust. His cock thickening to steel, he ground his hips into hers. Shane held her ass and helped her forward so her panties—he had to find the man who invented skirts and thank the shit out of him—slid across his shaft. Shane wasn't fond of science, but he was all for friction, and the friction they were making was so hot that the air popped, singeing. He wished he'd paid more attention in school because he thought that had to have been impossible and he wanted to know exactly how much friction created fire because, *fuck*, he was burning to a crisp.

Taking hold of her soft breasts, he dropped his face to them. He scraped his lips on the top of her curves. Shane pulled some of the flesh into his mouth, and at the same instance squeezed so that her bosom mashed into his cheeks. He groaned and the sound echoed back into his ears.

What the fuck are you doing?

153

He released his suctioning mouth with a *pop!* and dragged it across her collarbone. Shane moved his hands beneath the top of her shirt. Chills broke out under his fingers as he cupped her through the bra. He wanted it off.

Shane bared her breasts while her long hair fell into his face. Her nipples hardened in his hand. Her moans shot down his cock when he raised his hips and lowered his mouth. Beside them the windows showed evidence of their passion. Lights from emerging cars were hazy and dulled by fogged glass. His need to strip her bare and slide his cock inside her and fuck her against his steering wheel like an insatiable animal was turning his mind to mush.

No. Don't do this.

The seat was tight. The air was steaming. It lashed at his neck. She ran her hands up his arms, stroking his body with hers. He tightened his fingers around her nipples, breathing a sigh into her mouth, along her tongue. He kneaded her breast.

Stop. Shane, stop.

Like an addict being deprived of his favorite substance, it *hurt* Shane to stop kissing her. At no time in his life had he been so hard, and knowing she could make him come by her feral movements alone made it that much more difficult to think straight. Gritting his teeth with so much force he thought they'd shatter in his mouth, he released her breast from his hands.

Out of breath, he fell back to his seat cushion. "Rose…"

She leaned forward. Shane moaned at the sensation of her nibbling his neck, his dick twitching on his leg. It was everything Shane wanted. Her touching him was heaven. Stopping her? *Hell.*

With godlike effort, he took her shoulders and pulled her gently away. "Stop, Rose." He forced his tone to sound strong, even though his entire body was weak. "You don't want to do this."

No matter how much Shane wanted her, he'd never be the man who took advantage of her.

He could piss her off with a smile on his face and disobey her rules on purpose, but he wouldn't use her vulnerability against her, and right now she was vulnerable.

Frozen on his lap, Rose stared at him, silent, through rapid exhales. Clasping her hand over her mouth, she swung her head to the side. "I'm sorry. Shane, I'm sorry. I just…"

She was off him faster than she'd gotten on.

Closing his eyes, Shane tried to get a hold of himself. His cock was furious, but given they'd not had a good relationship for a while, Shane figured it could deal.

"I'm so sorry." She panicked, eyes growing wider. "I wasn't thinking."

"It's fine." A tremor in his fingers, he started the car. "I understand." *Whatever happened to her had made her emotional. She needed comforting. That was all.*

"Please, forget—"

Before he could turn back onto the highway, Shane took her cheek in his hand, brushing a stray tear away with his thumb. "It didn't happen. Okay?" He hated the words. They tasted disgusting, rioting in his mouth like he'd swallowed trash, but he said them for Rose because he cared about her, and caring about her meant he had to do what he didn't want to, if it meant making her happy. "Nothing happened, sugar. We're on our way home is all."

Bouncing her head in agreement, she managed a thin smile. "Thank you." She sat back. "Do you still want me to tell you what happened?"

"You don't have to," Shane said as they began their trip to Charlotte. "I'd like to know, but only if you're comfortable. If not, then I'm okay not knowing."

"It…" Steering her head away from him, she stared out of the window. "It all started…"

There was a delay, her quivering outtake of air, and Shane removed her hand from her lap and rested it in his. That seemed to console her.

Her shoulders relaxed. "It started when I was sixteen," she stuttered, her voice feeble. "When I was at summer camp.

Chapter Eleven

Hearing Rose talk about the time she had been sexually assaulted... There were no words.

It was a nightmare. Rage like he'd never experienced in his life coursed through him. The kind of barbaric rage that put men in one of two places—jail or Hell.

Not even when his nose had been in the dirt and his old man had been shouting at him to stop being a pussy and stand back up, had he felt so helpless. He'd thought of a thousand different scenarios where the bastard who had raped her ceased to exist by his hands—strangled to death, shot between the eyes, beaten until he was breathless. The man might be in prison for life, but that didn't mean he was untouchable.

With dim vision and chattering teeth, Shane had driven back home, and by God's mercy they'd made it to his apartment in one piece. Tossing the car keys to his valet, he'd been glad that Rose had let him escort her to his home, hand in hand. He'd needed to touch her. If Shane was touching her, he wouldn't have been able to use his hands to phone up his military contacts and see if one of his friends who worked in North Carolina law enforcement could call him in a favor.

But Rose didn't want sympathy.

She hadn't wanted a shoulder to cry on or someone to curse with—or even someone to threaten the bastard's repulsive existence. A person to speak with was all she'd cared to have, so, though he'd wanted to explode with blasphemies and maybe kill somebody, he'd bitten his tongue as she'd told her story, listening with as much calm as possible. Even after he'd showered and dressed in gym shorts and a nighttime shirt, finding Rose in his guest bedroom, her stomach flat on the bed, kicking her feet in the air as she'd spoken on the phone with her brother, he was still attempting to control the anger that coiled through his veins like poison ivy. He thought he had a fucked-up past, that he was strong for overcoming it. His old man used to beat his ass with a whipping stick, one Shane had to select off the front lawn himself, if he didn't abide by the Williams family code. Eventually, he'd put the stick down and started using his fists. The abuse had gotten so bad that Shane had run away from home, then he'd spent months training for the SEALS. Sweat. Tears. Pain beyond description.

The training had brought him to the zenith of his physical and mental abilities, then pushed him further, off an edge he had no choice but to climb back up. He thought he'd undergone perseverance. He was nothing compared to Rose.

Shane couldn't imagine what it must have been like to live with a constant gnawing at her thoughts that something so horrendous could happen to her. Scared to reveal the identity of her assaulter for fear of her family being harmed as the bastard had threatened, she'd had no one to speak to and no one to confide in. More than anything, he wanted to tell her he was here now. She would never have to feel alone again. Lips tight, he kept those words locked in his head.

Things she'd done and said in the past were starting to make sense. Her rants about the perfect life became clearer now that Shane could view them through this knowing lens.

Did she realize she was trying to live in the place of the murdered girl...Melissa? That her idea of a perfect life and Melissa's idea may have been different?

At work once, Rose had told him a secret.

It'd been one of the nights they'd stayed late and ordered

in. She'd looked at Shane from across the conference room desk with a foxy smile that had made his heart act all crazy. When she'd disclosed to him that she didn't like picket fences all that much and would have loved to live in a big condo with a view of the city like his, he didn't understand why she couldn't do that. Now he understood what she had meant. He understood her—understood he wanted to protect her.

Shane didn't know how, but he was going to make Rose forgive herself. No matter the time it took, no matter if, at moments, it seemed like an impossible feat, Shane was determined to make her see the amazing woman he saw every time he looked at her—not some failure. Never.

"How was that?" he asked as he sat on the edge of the bed.

Two hours ago, the first thing she'd done when she'd arrived at his house had been to draw a bath. The second thing had been to put a charger to her phone. With all that'd happened, she had wanted to call her brother as soon as possible, but her phone had died on the drive back.

Along with telling Shane about her assault, she'd filled him in on her old fiancé showing up at her mother's place and Holton's relationship with her best friend, Olive. After these life-changing events had occurred, she'd called Shane for support. It humbled him.

"We are going to speak tomorrow." She sat up and crossed her legs, giving him an adorable pout. "I know I shouldn't be upset with him but…" She sighed. "I don't know."

"You have every right to be upset, but don't stay upset. Be angry tonight then, when you see him tomorrow, hear his side of the story. From everything you've told me, you two are close. It's worth listening to him, at least." He smiled, even though it was the last thing he wanted to do.

"You're right."

Her grin was a punch to the chest because it didn't reach her eyes. He wanted to hold her, tell her everything would be fine. It physically hurt to stay still while she was trying to keep a cool façade.

"Who knew you'd give such good family advice?"

"Who knew?"

"You've never told me anything about your family."

"There isn't anything to tell." Shane's family drama seemed insignificant to what Rose was going through. He also didn't want to talk about himself. More than pulling her in his arms and kissing all her doubts away, he wanted to be there for her like a rock. *Her* rock.

"I've told you everything. Your turn. Spill the beans, Mr. Williams."

For pajamas, she was wearing a plain T-shirt of his and his gym shorts. No woman had ever worn his clothing before, so he didn't know if feeling prideful and simultaneously turned on was something that came with the territory or if it was because it was *this* girl in *his* bed wearing *his* clothing. Granted, as much as he would have jumped — who was he kidding? *Fucking leaped* was more like it — at the thought of finishing what they'd started in the car, Shane didn't want to focus on his selfish needs. "I want to talk about you."

"Shane…"

He rubbed his neck, frowning. "Do I have to?"

"Boss's orders."

She bit her lip but she couldn't contain her laughter, probably guessing the command would make Shane cringe. It did. The funny thing about lying was that it had no boundaries. Nothing worked quite like it. You could lie by speaking or lie by staying quiet. He wasn't one to be dishonest, but wasn't that exactly what he was being? What would Rose's response be if she found out he was the founder of Lambda?

"Okay, boss. Where do I start?"

"Do you have any siblings?"

So, Shane told her about his brother and sister who were both in Georgia. He told her that both of his parents had passed on. Letting her know *why* he'd run away was difficult.

Sympathy clouded her eyes when he spoke about the abuse. Leaving his siblings behind was his first, biggest regret, though they'd never seen it that way. Not being able to save Lennon when he'd come home and committed suicide because of severe PTSD came in second. During that part of the conversation, he'd decided to rest his back on the mattress, talking about his old man, his death the year before that had happened at the same time Lennon had died, always made his feel sick. She snuggled beside him, bringing her arm to his waist almost naturally.

Consequently, speaking became easier.

They explored his childhood and, though reluctant, Shane gave her a glimpse into his life as a soldier. He had nightmares sometimes, too, he confided. His nightmares were about his days at war. They were of blood and heat. There were moments when he'd be doing a mundane task at work or home and, all of a sudden, he'd be able to taste the yellow dust on his lips and smell copper. Then there were the guns. Most of his friends from war had come back with a new love for the automatic weapons, but he hadn't. To this day, Shane couldn't hear fireworks, balloons popping or any loud noise without being put back in that scary headspace. With delight, he'd traded in his gun for a sketching stencil.

Shane had always had a thing for drawing.

His mother had been an art teacher, and when his old man hadn't been looking, Shane had played with coloring books and drawing pads. She'd taught him how to draw well, even though his old man had never liked seeing him do it. Thought it made him too feminine.

Rose rested beside him, staring up at the ceiling, but the furrow of her eyebrows was pronounced enough that he saw it from the side of his eye.

"I'm glad you got out of that environment, even if you regret leaving people behind. I'm scared to think what would have happened if you stayed."

Luckily, Trevor and Sam were older than him by years.

Both had graduated high school. The only large adjustments they'd had to make had been moving off the farm when Shane had left. Sam had gone to college in Atlanta and become an art teacher herself and Trevor had dropped out to take over his old man's shop.

"I don't hold it against him." Not that he could if he wanted to, since his pop was dead.

Rose seemed baffled by his statement so he explained further.

"He was tryin' to teach me how to be a man. Well, what he thought a man was. It's a bad way to teach a kid, yeah, but as much as I suffered, I learned how *not* to behave. I don't hate him. I hate what he did to me." Shane raised his eyebrows. "Sure did teach me how to throw a mean right hook, though." He snickered. "You know a little 'bout having mean right hooks yourself, don't cha, sugar?"

"Oh, shut up."

She covered her head with a pillow, green eyes peeking above the white cushion, blonde eyebrows sly and raised, and his thoughts drifted to close-fitting spaces and kisses.

"Is it odd I find the thought of you deckin' a man twice your size to be a major turn-on?" Truth was everything about her turned him on. Shane liked strong-willed women who knew when and how to break the rules. "Makes me want to do bad things—"

He got a pillow to the face.

"You're a pervert."

"I'm a hot-blooded male who likes women with a little fight in them. Nothing is sexier than a woman who can punch, 'specially when she drinks Jack. Sugar, you may be the woman of my dreams. If you can take down that rough stuff, I bet you have no problem swallowing—"

Another feathery pillow swooped over his head. "Don't you dare finish that sentence."

He snatched the third weapon from her. When she went to grab another, he wrestled it away. Pouring out laughter, Shane got her in his hold but she slipped out and a pillow war ensued. Okay, jumping all over his bed like a preschooler and tossing feather bags at Rose *was* emasculating on a small scale. It *was* however made less so based on the way she'd pounce toward him, her smile playful, her breasts jiggling without a bra.

Twice he almost reached out and cupped them…for their own protection, of course.

Their pillow war was fun and not only, though mostly, because Rose had a killer rack. It was because, well, it was just fun. Hell, he'd never say those words out loud. He rationalized that his actions were the equivalent of *'real men wear pink'* except it was *'real men have pillow fights if initiated by hot woman'*. Eventually, he was able to trap her.

Resting against his headboard, he pinned her down with both arms. Her back lay against his chest, and she dropped her head between his collarbones, the top of her head brushing his chin. Both of his legs lay over the top of hers as he held her still. Their breathing was doing double time.

"You get off on throwing stuff, huh, sugar?"

"I look innocent, but that doesn't mean I'm going to take crap from anyone." She spoke softly but Shane heard the roar of aggression. "That guy at my former agency deserved that punch after spreading rumors about my relationship. It was wrong of me, but I hate drama. I… I messed up." She turned her head to him like she was seeking his opinion, but Shane was mute. "I regret it. It was immature and unprofessional."

"Don't beat yourself up." Bringing his hands up her arms and trying like hell to ignore her shiver that followed, Shane said, "I'm sorry for what you overheard your first day at Lambda. The cramps thing… You overheard that, didn't you? I was an ass." She stiffened, so he quickly changed the subject. "Tell me more about Texas. When did you leave North Carolina?"

Silence prevailed.

Then, slowly, Rose started talking. "After Duke, I applied for graduate school there. All my friends think I moved there to go the University of Texas, but the truth of it is, I moved there to get away. I would have left with or without getting accepted."

"Why don't you like it here?" Shane wanted to know all he could. "Is it because of—?" His words cut off in his throat. Shane was thankful not to be facing her, so she wouldn't see his face, the emotions gathering there.

"Bad memories."

"Have you ever thought of talkin' to someone?" He didn't want to offend her by suggesting professional help. He just wanted her to be okay. How did people cope with such horrific things?

Twisting around, she grinned, a real one this time. "I'm talkin' to you."

He laughed. She was avoiding his question. Plucking a stray lock of hair from her cheek, Shane hid it behind her ear. "Touché, pretty Rose."

He brought his finger down her neck, chest warming, and she quieted. Her irises were becoming more black than light green. Since he'd met Rose, she'd always reminded him of nature. Now was no different. Her eyes, sketched with daytime hues, stared back at him. Her scent, honeysuckles, filled his brain like a toxin, crippling his body. Her body, the one he was wrapped around, curved the way mountains do, mountains whose sole purpose was to be explored. Sunshine flowed around her shoulders. Her smile gave him the same feeling he'd gotten when he'd stood at the peak of Chimney Rock to watch the horizon wake. Resplendent. She was nature's finest creation.

"You know, Shane." She changed course, probably noticing how fascinated he'd become with her lips. "About earlier… I wasn't thinking—"

"I understand." Shane didn't know if he could take her finishing that thought. "We're co-workers, nothing else." The words stung something deep. "Want to watch a movie?"

He didn't wait for her to answer. The big-screen television

on the wall in front of them woke with multicolor as he flipped it on. He passed her the remote. "Pick whatever you want."

"Anything I want?"

She raised the corner of her lips in a mischievous way that had his balls tightening and heartbeat doing kick flips. Fucking inappropriate after their conversation.

"Yeah, whatever you want." He might regret saying that in an hour's time but he needed to get out of the room before she noticed how much she affected him, especially his cock, which was full-blown ready for shit that wouldn't be happening now or anytime soon. "I'm going to make popcorn."

Turning to her with a stiff smile, he wasn't noticing how cozy she looked curled up in his sheets. He wasn't thinking about what it would be like to see her in the same position, at home and comfy with strings of dirty-blonde hair falling against her cheeks, every single night. No. Shane Williams wasn't falling for that romance bullshit.

He stood to leave.

"Shane…"

His heart tugged. He looked around to find her lips quivering. "Yeah, sugar?"

Emotions punctured his lungs as she stared at him with a mix of nervousness and something he couldn't name. Shane didn't have a clue as to what she was thinking, but if it was anything like what was on his mind, then maybe it was best he didn't know.

"Maybe we can just talk."

Relief and warmth filled him. He nodded. "I'd like that."

She raised the covers for him and he turned the television off, returning to the bed. A soft weight on his chest, Rose closed her eyes as she lay against his heart and they talked about everything from their biggest fears to their favorite movies. Nothing was off limits.

Hour after hour passed and confessions eased off his tongue, and when Shane had spoken so much his mouth was dry and his body was weighed down from the need to recharge, he succumbed to his exhaustion and fell asleep by her side.

"Stop!"

The sound of someone shouting startled Shane awake. Years of conditioning made his body coil, ready to strike. Muscles tightening, he was alert in an instant. His vision moved around the room but was greeted by nothing but darkness.

"Stop. Don't touch—"

Beside him something was shaking. He flipped over to see Rose was swinging her head from side to side. A tortured expression was on her shimmering face. *She's asleep?*

"Rose?" Leaning toward her, he touched her cheek. His hand came back wet.

"Please."

The whimpers she was making filled him with sorrow. This was what her nightmares looked like?

"Please, don't—"

"Come here, pretty Rose." He gathered her in his arms.

With a gradual pull, her shapely figure nudged against his chest, perfect, like they were two halves that had been carved from a whole. "No more," he whispered, kissing her shoulder before resting his head beside hers and locking an arm around her waist. "No more bad dreams."

All night Shane stayed at her side, awake, ready to fight off any nightmare that dared disturb her. Only when he saw the pale sunlight sneaking through his window shades did he allow sleep to take him again.

Chapter Twelve

Shane was hot.

No, not hot as in attractive—although he was pretty freaking attractive, so much, in fact, that the word didn't do him justice—but 'hot' as in temperature. The reason Rose knew he was hot, on both accounts, was because one of his bulky arms cuddled around her waist, holding her against his chest, and one of his legs draped over both of hers.

Waking up was challenging. Having slept better than she had in ages, when orange streams of light fluttered beneath her eyelids, rousing her awake, Rose had been upset to let go of her peaceful dreams. Actually, there was a good chance she would have drifted back to sleep—she was *that* comfortable—but she noticed three odd things.

She wasn't in her bed. This bed was much larger than hers and the mattress, compared to the cheap one she had back home, was on a whole different level of cozy. She was burning. Sweat clung to her skin, and her shirt cleaved to her breasts. And there was something hard poking into her lower back and she doubted it was a flashlight. Rose shifted her hips to no avail.

It was difficult to move her thighs together to neutralize the lustful sensations that had flamed through her core ever since she'd woken up to Shane's massive morning wood.

Shocked to stillness, Rose tried not to think about how, if she were to wiggle up about three inches, her butt would be in perfect alignment with what had to have been God's gift to women. With something *that* big hanging out—pun intended—between Shane's legs, she understood why he was a lady's man, but worst of all, he was shirtless. His muscles were hard against her back, moving each time he breathed. Squirming, Rose attempted to scoot out of his grasp.

Trying to pry his arm off her waist was like trying to move a baler.

She was out of breath in seconds. *What the hell?* Was his blood infused with metal or something? Shane's limbs were solid, heavy blocks that she couldn't lift more than a couple of centimeters. When she let his arm drop, it crashed into her belly and the air whooshed out of her lungs.

She had to try a different tactic.

Ten minutes later, Rose managed to turn onto her back.

Initially the plan was for her to lie like this and wiggle her way down the bed and out of his hold. Plans changed, however, so instead of squeezing away from him, she shifted her body to the right until her face was kissing distance from the most exquisite masterpiece she'd ever seen—his chest. *Picasso who?* A work of art—his ripples, cuts and the mysterious trail of dark hair leading down to his happy place epitomized the strength and beauty of the male figure.

Wrong maybe, but Rose decided her new plan was to savor however many minutes she had left of him sleeping in order to marvel. And marvel she did.

With feathered touches, she examined his chest.

Aided by the daylight, the tattoos adorning his skin were visible for her inspection. An enchanting phoenix, drawn in a sort of yellow-orange graffiti design, was surrounded by a blazing fire and covered his torso, extending around his back, running up the side of his neck. Over his heart there were words. *Earn Your Trident Every Day.* She outlined each letter, electric heat below her fingertip.

Her exploration was cut short when a sudden movement from Shane hitched his leg farther up her waist. Rose swallowed a sigh as his erection pressed into her center.

Pure thoughts. Pure thoughts. Pure thoughts.

She tried to get out of his grip again, needing some

distance. She raised his leg to pull him off, but he moved, shoving his limb between her thighs. It connected with a powerful pulse right to her vagina and...goodbye to her panties. Sirens wailed through her system—a flooding alert.

Rotating her hips, she shivered as delicious spikes of arousal traveled from her high nipples to the tuft of hyper-aware nerves at her center. There was a moment of clarity— *what in God's name am I doing?* —before her body went all *'Et tu, Brute?'* on her. She did it again, grinding her clit to his leg. This time the pleasure was so robust she had to bite her lip to keep from crying out. The moaning noise interrupted Shane's light snoring, and Rose became still. As if on cue, his cock twitched against her, proving that she wasn't the only one suffering.

"Hmmm." He rumbled in his throat.

Opening his eyes, Shane stared down at his chest where her hands were splayed. Like she'd been shocked by electricity, she jolted back.

A masculine chuckle followed.

"What are you doing up so early, beautiful?" he asked lazily.

Her panties coated with evidence, Rose held on to his leg like it was her new Enrique. There was no way he *didn't* know what she was doing. She shimmed her hips to try to remove his leg then commence running away because *ohmyfreakinggod* she was more humiliated than she'd ever been in her life, but it only served to stimulate her more. "I..."

"What was that, sugar?" he whispered.

Assuring she wouldn't be able to respond, Shane pulled his leg back before bringing it forward to massage her parts. His named spilled out in a provocative sigh.

The pulse below her underwear shot down to her toes. Shane watched her squirm through lowered eyes. The last thing she wanted to do was moan. Uncontrollable pleasure flowed past her lips as he repeated the movement. She shuddered when he leaned forward and brushed his lips across hers. He brought his hand up the back of her thigh, hauling her closer to his source of heat. His cock was stone on her body. How easily could he slip aside her panties and thrust inside her? With one shove, he'd give her everything, every delicious inch stretching and pumping through her. She was that wet and he was that rock-hard.

"Tell me what you need," he murmured over her lips.

Looking at her with dilated pupils, Shane was magnificent, out of this world stunning. So was her ability to screw up every employee relationship she'd ever had. Rose closed her eyes.

Shame and frustration painted her thoughts. "Shane."

Releasing her before she could tell him they couldn't continue, Shane rolled to his back. "How'd you sleep?"

What? That's it? Were they not going to talk about what had just happened?

"Good," she answered in hesitance. It was an understatement. Remembering the last time she'd been so refreshed after a night's rest was impossible. "How about you? You look tired."

"Me?"

She thawed over his sleepy smile.

"I slept better than ever."

"I"—she sat up, fumbling with her clothes—"have to meet my brother for breakfast."

Silence passed between them. She thought he was going to bring up what had happened, but he didn't address it and her heart relaxed. Around him, she forgot about rules and responsibilities. Shane was a man who made her forget *everything*—her past, her present, her failures and future. And the fact that she was his boss and he her employee...

Malcolm's warning came to mind. *'I'd hate to see her go.'*

Rose was a professional. She needed to start acting like one.

"Let me take a shower first. I'll drop you off," he said. "Is that okay?"

"Okay." Caught dead in the act, there was no hiding

the fact that she had been feeling him up. To take it a step further, Shane had continued where she had left off.

Probably knowing bringing it up would do nothing but upset or embarrass her, he hadn't.

Shane had taken all the confusing emotions she was throwing his way. It was confirmation. Underneath his bad-boy exterior, he wasn't the think-only-of-myself player he made himself out to be. Shane Williams was a good man.

While she waited for Shane to finish, she dressed in her get-up from the previous night, her mind a spindle of worry. With all that she had gotten off her chest, there was still so much she had to figure out.

However, there was no denying that a weight had been lifted from Rose like gray clouds rising after a thunderstorm to expose a crystal-clear sky. She raised her fingers to her lips, heat in her cheeks. The bedroom door opened, and Rose jumped, dropping her hand.

"You ready?" He was dressed in black jeans and a fitted shirt.

Rose gathered her purse from the nightstand, making sure to keep her eyes off him. The door swung lightly as Shane let go of it and entered the room. His hand on her shoulder made her still and forced her eyes up.

"Rose?" he said, softer, more tenderly.

His hair was wet and disheveled from running a towel through it. She caught whiffs of soap coming from him. Desire danced through her stomach.

She cleared her throat. "I'm ready."

"Let's get you home then." His brown eyes were calmer than she probably deserved after her stunt this morning or yesterday's exhibition in his car. She allowed Shane to grab her hand and tuck it softly in his. They headed outside.

The sun shone above them as they rode down the highway. Country music came out of the radio, but the silence between them was deafening. Rose didn't try to fill it with useless small talk. She had no words to express how grateful she was to him or how confused she felt being in his presence. Sneaking a look across the dashboard, she wrapped her fingers around the seat belt covering her chest. He made her heart do funny and foreign things.

When Shane pulled into her apartment complex and parked, she asked him to walk with her because she was nervous to see Holton, but as soon as he came into view, acknowledging her with his boyish half-smile, she rushed into her brother's arms. "I'm sorry I was never here for you. I'm sorry I wasn't good to you. I love you." The waterworks came mid-speech.

"Me too, Cookie Monster." He squeezed her tighter. "I love you, too."

"Rose," Shane said from behind her, "I'm going to leave."

After introductions had passed, Rose escorted Shane to his car, but before he could load into the driver's side, she stopped him. "Do you want to eat with us?"

"It's okay. You two need some time together." Turning his head from her, he yawned behind his hand.

Did he really sleep all that well?

"Anyway, I've got to catch up on some work." Lips breaking into a smile, Shane teased, "My boss is this mean ole lady who'll have my ass if I come in Monday morning empty-handed."

His laugh pursued her own. "Shane, thank you." She twisted her fingers together. "Thank you for listening and —"

Leaning forward, Shane surprised her with a kiss to her forehead. Soft. Sweet. His lips were like a ray of sunshine, caressing her with their warmth.

She leaned into the embrace, breathing in the smell of his body wash and something that was just his alone, masculine and welcoming. "You're stronger than you think, pretty Rose."

With him saying so, she almost believed it was true.

* * * *

Across from her, Holton sliced through a chunk of pecan pie. Shoving it into his mouth, he chewed, giving Rose some much-needed time to do her own sort of digesting.

After the coffee and French toast — thank God, he'd waited until after she'd been sated — her brother had laid it all out on the table.

Holton was in love with her best friend.

There was nothing Rose could do about it.

One day, Olive Wayward would be his wife.

"I'm…" The food was unsettled in her stomach. "I'm confused about what you're asking me."

Her jokester brother had disappeared after the entrée. In his place sat a man with serious eyes and an unyielding goal ahead of him, determination notching between his eyebrows. Holton set his fork beside his plate. "I'm asking for your blessing."

"Shouldn't you be asking — ?" Rose caught herself before she could say 'Olive's father or mother.' Olive's family wasn't as tight-knit as Rose's was. Living all the way in Myrtle Beach, her family never visited her and she seldom visited them. Therefore, Rose really was the perfect person to ask. With a friendship that had lasted from the awkward prepubescent years, the self-righteous days of their addled youth and all the way to them being fully functioning adults, Rose considered Olive a sister. But… "What exactly happened between you two?"

Holton looked to the distance as if his answer were there. Resting his green gaze, greener and deeper in color than hers, on Rose's face, he answered with a defeated shake of his head, "Because we missed you, we'd see each other a lot. One thing led to another and…"

He shoveled his hands through his hair.

"It was like that about a year after you'd gone, and when she visited you out in Texas, she came back all different, said she couldn't do it anymore. She left. We talked still and became friends again, but I don't want to be her friend." Her brother pleaded, "Rosey. I can't."

Teary-eyed, Rose buried her face into her hands. Unless she had been short of hearing, Rose was certain Holton had said that he'd been with Olive for a year—an entire year.

Yet she couldn't be angry at him because he'd had the confidence to do what she never could. Holton did the scariest thing in the world. He'd fallen in love. Rose wouldn't punish him for it, either.

Her heart broke into shards with the thought of putting her brother and best friend in a situation where they felt like they couldn't love without consequences. Rose might not know what it was like to throw her full heart into anything but work, but she loved them both.

"What if it ends badly?"

"At least I'll know I tried."

"You have my blessing." Her voice wavered. "Holt, about leaving—"

"Rosey, I'm happy. I got a job that keeps me fulfilled. A house. A family that loves each other. I'm alive and healthy. I'm happy. You be happy too, okay?"

She nodded, wishing she could be, but she couldn't and she wouldn't be able to, not until she got as far away from this place as possible.

Chapter Thirteen

Shane's sister had canceled on him.

Granted, it wasn't her fault, but it was still sucked that he wouldn't be seeing Heath, Eric or Sam any time in the distant future. Eric was coming down with something, and it threw Sam's schedule off track. All the vacation days she had planned to use to visit Shane, she'd had to use to take care of her little man. Shane had told her he'd wire her money for a sitter, but his sister didn't trust her baby boy in anyone's arms but her own, understandably. Shane wasn't mad, but he couldn't deny that he was sad.

He'd been looking forward to their visit, and with all the Moreno & Blu Associates business happening, he didn't know when he could make it to Atlanta.

As he browsed over his designs, Shane realized he wasn't personally clued into what Matthew Moreno liked. He'd worked with the man for six years, but he knew him about as well as…

Well, he'd just sum it up as him not knowing Matthew Moreno all that much.

In his defense, few people did. Regardless, there was no way Matthew would look at what he and Rose had created and think it was anything short of perfection.

They'd done two years of work in a couple of short months.

They'd fabricated an entire company. Years of projections, fringe campaigns, holiday mockups and more had been run by study group after study group. On top of that, they'd created a timeline for the company's banquets and many clients, so Matthew and his team would see the past, present and future working with Lambda Digital, comparing and contrasting some of Moreno & Blu's real-life campaigns and specialties. They wouldn't stop there, though.

Reaching out to hundreds of hospitality businesses in the nation, Rose was working to create a database of potential partners to target every type of Moreno & Blu Associates' client. Shane had some insights on the competition and he'd bet his life that they were going to win.

With so much work down and more to go, Shane felt like he was going off to the coal mines every day. The work was tedious. Relentless. Winter was almost over, but he was stuck in Lambda. A cave. Working...then working some more. He needed a break.

Twirling his stencil in his hand, he was drawing a blank on deciding which motion graphic and persona he wanted to utilize to build the fifth landing page. He lowered his eyes to fight the exhaustion, sitting back against the smooth leather upholstery.

High stress levels made it harder to control what he saw in the darkness.

That's why he liked the outdoors so much. It took the edge off. But Shane hadn't been outdoors all afternoon, and his stress was off the charts, so it didn't surprise him to find an image of blood behind his closed eyes, waiting for him.

Blood and screaming. Dust and guns popping in the distance. Yellow plains of sand laid out in every direction. Shane tasted the heat on his dry, swollen tongue.

He was shouting. Sweat was dripping into his eyes, blinding him. Lennon was unconscious on his back, much heavier than the hundred-and-fifty-pound sacks they'd made him heft for miles during training. Knees giving out, Shane fell. His face smashed into the sand. He swallowed some.

Lennon crashed down on him. Muscles screaming for release, Shane locked his jaw, crunching dirt between his teeth. He didn't think he would make it. A bullet whizzed past his head.

Opening his eyes, Shane exhaled deeply, pain swarming his temples as he surveyed the graffiti-covered walls of his office. He tossed his stencil on the desk, unlikely to be working any time soon. Exiting his office, he wondered if his pretty boss would be up for a distraction.

* * * *

"That's it, sugar. Squeeze it like that." He wet his lips, loving the way Rose's fingers poised over him. "Make sure you've got a nice, strong hold." With her bottom lip caught between her teeth, she grasped him harder. Shane winced. "Not too hard or you're going to hurt me."

"Sorry." She unraveled her fingers from around him, only a bit. Shane sighed, his pulse gushing like white rapids in his veins as her erratic breathing washed over his mouth and nose.

"You remember how to ride it?" he whispered, afraid someone would hear him. He couldn't believe they were doing this here, out in the open so anyone could see. He always knew Rose had an adventurous side to her, but damn, not even he'd tread through this territory.

She blinked, her eyes beaming with sexy confidence, making him tighten underneath her. "Like I could forget." Shifting her hips, she groaned as she positioned herself on top. "I can't believe I'm doing this."

"Me either," he said hoarsely. "I didn't think you'd want to again."

Her breasts spilled toward his sight as she leaned forward, lifting her hips to realign herself. Sweat played over her collarbone and his. "Let's just do this fast. I don't want to get caught."

"No, you're gonna ride it slow." Beyond them, the sounds of people speaking closed in. "I don't care if people see. Take your time. It will feel better that way."

"It's going to be painful, slow or fast, Shane. My vagina already hurts from this angle."

With a smile on his face, he shrugged. "I can't help how hard it is, sugar."

Rose glimpsed up from her hands. "You're thinking something perverted, aren't you?"

As a matter of fact, his mind was racing with thoughts so dirty that they'd make a demon blush. She scoffed when Shane smiled. "When did you come to know me so well, sugar?"

Earlier, Shane had gone into her office and told her they needed a break from anything involving Moreno & Blu, so he would be taking her to an indoor bike range. She'd suggested they go somewhere with fewer people.

Since they were at the office already, Shane had mentioned the common room. The employees had gone on a group lunch, leaving Shane and Rose alone to work on their deadline.

He hadn't expected her to agree.

Taking out the XC trail bike that he always left in his office, Shane hadn't thought she'd be so rusty in experience until the adjusted seat post and saddle had been between her legs and she had been wobbling like hell. Shane had had to walk beside her as she rode, making sure that if she happened to tumble, he would catch her before she got hurt. But Shane didn't think she would fall. It wasn't like she had forgotten how to ride, but she'd said the last time she had ridden a bike, she'd been ten.

"I'm going to let go, okay?" Shane slid his hands out from under hers, the bike wobbling slightly after his release.

Rose gasped, her arms shaking. Was it bad that he thought she looked extra pretty, all nervous like she was?

"It's okay, sugar. I won't let anything happen to you."

Shaky maneuvers, her feet pushing the bike forward as she pumped them, took her in a squiggly circle around Lambda's layout. She laughed and rode on, her hair picking up when she gained speed, caressing the wind.

"Woot! Woot!" Shane cupped his mouth and hollered. "Lookin' good there, sugar!"

Rose lapped around the room, all nervousness vanishing from sight as she accelerated.

"Rose." Malcolm appeared at his side, correcting Shane.

"Yeah, whatever." He waved a disregarding hand. "She hasn't ridden a bike since she was ten. Ain't that somethin'?"

"You like her."

Shane looked at his friend, finding that his gaze wasn't returned. "What?"

Turning his eyes to Shane, Malcolm sported a thoughtful look. "Are you sleeping with her?"

"No." *Not anymore, at least.*

"Good. She is a valuable member of our team. I want her to continue being so."

The words didn't sit right with Shane. With or without sex involved, if Malcolm wanted to dismiss Rose from Lambda, he'd have to go through him.

"You didn't deny it, though." His friend sounded confused. "Do you like her?"

Shane didn't answer, not knowing how to.

"What about the other girl? Blondie?"

Shane wasn't worried that Malc would connect the two. Shane had mentioned the name 'Blondie' before Rose had started working for Lambda.

"Blondie?" Scratching his jaw, Shane removed his gaze from Malc, noticing Rose finishing up her final lap. The smile on his lips was automatic. Rose had finally gotten comfortable.

He couldn't wait to have her on some real trails.

"I like Blondie a lot."

It made Shane anxious, always second-guessing himself when it came to his new feelings for Rose. Most days he was resisting the urge to kiss her and others he was yelling inwardly about how he had a line of women waiting for his call. Why was he spending all his time wondering what it would be like if there were only one? Shane had made that mistake before, making one woman the center of his universe. She'd ripped him apart, and he didn't make the same mistake twice. But…

Rosemary Berkowitz wasn't like any woman he'd ever

met.

"Don't know if she feels the same." Shane lowered his voice. "Did you do what I asked?"

"Yeah, I reviewed next year's projections." Malcolm sighed. "You were right. If this deal doesn't go through, we're going to have to start looking into dismantling the business within the next a year or two. We won't have enough to pay off the loans from expansion."

"That won't happen." Shane fisted his hands, a mix of frustration and resolve tightening the muscles in his shoulders and arms.

"There are over a hundred companies in this race." A crinkle of distress caught between Malcolm's eyebrows as he passed his gaze over the employees coming back from their breaks. "I'm worried that combining yours and Rose's talents may not be enough. Maybe you should've stayed in New York. You could be in a penthouse right now, surrounded by your advertising awards and all the wealth you could ever dream of." Malcolm cut him with a sideways glance. "Ever think of going back?"

"Not for a second," Shane answered without thought.

Malcolm wasn't some random friend. He was his fellow SEALS teammate—his brother. There wasn't a day that went by where Shane regretted his decision to be a part of Malcolm's dream, building Lambda. His friend's eyes crinkled and he gave Shane a face-splitting grin that made Shane's uneasiness scale that much higher. Everyone would lose something valuable if they didn't capture this deal.

With every cent of the company's money poured into the expansion, Lambda wouldn't survive another two years without snagging a big client. The long list of businesses they worked with now had kept them afloat so far, but the workload had been staggering and wore on the employees. Malcolm had made a hard decision pouring the rest of his funds into adding onto the creative and search department and hiring Rose. He'd taken a gamble, but his best friend trusted that the Lambda team would grow stronger. They had been growing, too. Lambda had taken on three new clients. Small fish. It wasn't enough. Moreno & Blu would be enough to guarantee their company's future. *What in God's name am I doing?*

Eyes trapped on Rose, Shane was hit with guilt like a punch to the gut. It was a mistake.

Every yearning in his mind and body was a mistake.

Lambda needed Rose more than Shane wanted her.

He looked around the office, built with his own money, then to the employees, smiling and happy, seemingly oblivious that he could ruin everything they'd created by falling for one beautiful, blonde-haired distraction. Shane had never felt so conflicted in his life.

Pulling up in front of them, the *she* that had taken permanent residence in his thoughts combed her hair away from her face, giving her head a shake that brought blonde strands flying. A palate of color at her cheeks, she looked winded. She looked free.

"I'm sorry. I hope I'm not in trouble," she said to Malcolm.

"Not remotely." Malcolm returned her smile. "You haven't ridden a bike since you were ten?" It made Shane uncomfortable, the way his friend was smiling at her.

"Shane!" She jabbed his arm playfully. "I told you not to tell."

His pocket vibrated.

Pulling out his phone, he took one peek at who was calling and, jaw clenched, declined.

After Rose had spent the night at his place a month ago, he'd broken things off with every late-night girl for good. Amy, in particular, had proven herself persistent, ringing him at whatever chance she could get.

Following the night at Base when he had met Rose, Amy had ended their friends-with-benefits arrangement with some choice words about him being an arrogant bastard after he, not wanting to lie, had told her he had gone home with another woman. But once someone had slipped Amy the news about Shane's six-figure salary, she'd had a

180

miraculous change of heart.

Yeah, Shane wasn't buying it.

Joining the conversation between his best friend and Rose, he must've mistaken the discomfort in Rose's eyes when she glanced toward his phone. "Want grab lunch?" he asked.

"I've already taken mine," Malcolm said.

Shane looked at Rose, waiting for her to answer.

"Like I want to have lunch with you," she finally said.

"Nothing like friendly banter between co-workers," Malcolm said, taking his briefcase off the floor and heading back to his office. "See you two later."

"Whatever you say, *Cookie Monster*."

When he'd heard Holton calling her Cookie Monster last month, it'd been driving him crazy not knowing how she'd earned the endearment. Cornering her in the office earlier that week, he'd pleaded. It had taken a while to wear her down, but she'd given him an answer sooner, rather than later. The truth was better, and worse, than he'd ever imagined. His green-eyed friend used to be obsessed with Cookie Monster — the blue thing, whatever the hell it was — from Sesame Street, and 'obsessed' was letting her off easy. Her cherry-blossom cheeks had raged when she'd confided that she used to tell people that Cookie was, get this, her *boyfriend*. Yeah, Shane didn't stutter. *Boyfriend*.

"That explains why you keep rejecting my invitation for a date. You've got horrible taste in men." When he'd said that, she'd glared at him, the same way she was glaring at him now.

Rose said she'd had a crush on Cookie Monster because he made her laugh.

How embarrassing was it that Shane went to his office after that conversation and googled Cookie Monster, just to watch his jokes and see what she found so funny?

Pretty fucking embarrassing, particularly when Malcolm had walked in. He didn't even want to begin to explain how that conversation went down.

"Stop calling me that."

"Ah, but you're so pretty when you're angry."

Rose gave him a look that said she was seconds away from telling him just where he could shove his compliment.

"Wait." Holding on to her elbow, Shane stopped Rose from leaving. Angling toward her and away from the crowd of employees, he said, "Have lunch with me—and dinner." Maybe they could try another tactic at winning this client.

"Shane." Rose frowned.

"It won't be a date," he amended. "My friend is coming in from out of town in a couple of months, and I'd like you to join us for dinner." It didn't appear she believed him. "That is, unless you have some issue with seeing me outside of work?"

Relentless as ever, she smiled. Another thing he'd learned about Rose was that she loved a good challenge—a woman after his own heart.

She hopped off his bike and started toward their offices, he assumed, to put it away. Twisting her head around, she pinned him with a narrowed look. "You're paying. Both times."

"Fine by me, sugar." Shane hoped she liked surprises.

* * * *

Swinging her pen between her middle and index fingers, Rose eyed stacks of documents spread across the conference desk—blueprints, market research, the updated user-acquisition strategy. Rubbing her eyes, she yawned. Darkness swarmed the sky and downtown had disappeared under a haze of sleepiness. Her gleaming silver earrings reflected in the glass window covering the whole length of the wall, the hoops she'd bought herself when she and Olive had gone mall shopping last Saturday. Too bad she wouldn't be able enjoy them for their intended use.

A night out.

Like most nights, Rose was spending tonight indoors,

working. The Moreno & Blu project was cutting away at her social life, not that she had much of one, but if a workaholic was complaining about working too much, there had to be a problem. Luckily, they were down to two months.

The conference room lights blared against the glass window and she stared from across the table at herself. Her ponytail had lost enthusiasm and hung loosely down her back, strands sticking out here and there around her face. The top buttons of her blouse were open lazily.

Jesus. Were those bags under her eyes?

She stifled a moan, falling back in the chair.

Rose noticed the door opening in the reflective surface. She raised her eyes to find Shane lowering his gaze to her bared shoulders. She'd lost the business jacket. Her sleeveless blouse swooped low at the neck. He followed the dip of her shirt to her breasts, causing shivers inside her belly.

"That took a while." She pulled the hair behind her back over her shoulder, her skin hotter than it had been before he'd walked in.

His chest rippling below a midnight shirt, Shane set down a green-dotted box.

"I got there right when they turned on the *Hot Now* sign." He opened a twelve-count box of Krispy Kreme donuts and Rose almost jumped over the table and kissed him.

Does this man know me or what?

Coffee cups were scattered around the table. Shane went to the opposite side from her and set down two more between them.

The delicious smell of caffeine and sugar made her mouth water. Stomach grumbling, Rose gave him a thankful smile. She reached over the documents and plucked a plain glazed donut from the box. It melted in her fingers. "Oh my goodness." Rose moaned as the first bit of the gooey-baked mixture slammed into her taste buds, the perfect combination of crisp and sweet. The only good thing about working late was the excuse for extra sugar.

"Here, boss." Shane's face held a grin. "Black. Two sugars."

Rose grabbed the coffee from his hands, their fingers touching for a moment and releasing a hot shock of pleasure up her arm and through her chest. Her throat warmed as she washed the dessert down with the refreshing drink. She took another bite.

"Should I leave the room?" He raised a brown eyebrow, tilting his head to the side and exposing the tendril of the tattoo on his neck, after she moaned once more, deeper for dramatic effect.

"Ten minutes." Her lips curled. "Then you can come back."

"Ten minutes?" He ran his hand through his hair and blew out a sigh. "I can treat you better than these donuts can, sugar." Shane grinned before taking a chocolate-topped donut and bringing it to his lips.

Her cheeks heated. She was glad her chewing was preventing conversation.

At the corner of her eye, his phone screen illuminated white. She frowned. "So"—Rose acted casual—"you're pretty popular today. Who's been blowing up your phone?"

A flicker of surprise passed over Shane's face. "Amy," he deadpanned.

She sucked in air, and his honesty twisted her insides.

Emotions she'd no business feeling pried through the wall she'd built ever since the night in his apartment when they'd spent hours getting to know one another.

"I ended things with her. I ended everything."

She raised her eyes. Shane fostered a gentle smile. *Everything?*

That smile did funky things to Rose's heart, made it skip a couple of beats. Rose took another sip of her coffee, trying to smother her own curling lips.

"Oh." She was glad he wouldn't be able to feel the unnecessary surges of relief entering her, accompanied by questions that began with 'why' and ended with a sinking feeling of discomfort. "How did that happen?" she couldn't resist asking.

Thick cords of muscles moved in each bicep as Shane brought his arms to his chest, crossing them there. Rose had a vivid flashback of them wrapped around her. Pretty sure she was drooling, she rubbed the corner of her mouth with the back of her hand.

"There was never anything special between us to begin with," Shane assured.

Wiping her fingers on a napkin, Rose didn't want to give him any reason to think she was asking out of anything but professional curiosity, so she changed the subject.

"There are issues with Moreno & Blu, internally."

She opened her browser and the tab she'd bookmarked, a news article that explained Matthew and Brendon, his husband and co-owner of Moreno & Blu, had had some disagreement months back. It had gone public. Apparently, Brendon had promised to plan an event for one of his Hollywood friends without consulting Matthew, the business side of Moreno & Blu. Turned out their company hadn't had the time to take on the project. The plans had been a bust. The company's reputation had suffered.

Shane carried the laptop closer to him. "This explains why only Matthew will be taking part in the competition."

"Do you think the competition is at risk?"

The article said corporate stocks were affected by the disagreement. Matthew and Brendon weren't on speaking terms, either. From Rose's research, she'd learned that Matthew's parents had owned a company themselves, a successful one that had failed because of a spousal disagreement and caused his parents to get divorced. She could only imagine how Matthew was feeling now.

Shane pressed his lips together, his face thoughtful. "No. This should stay separate."

But there was a worry in his expression that made her stomach drop. Cell phone vibrations on the table's surface tore through the quiet.

Amy. Her name was still in his phone. Jealousy poked its ugly head. Turning away from the computer screen, Rose took another snack. She moved her hair behind her ear.

"You ended everything with Amy or you ended *everything*?"

Rose wasn't a fool. She'd seen the way women looked at Shane every time they went to grab coffee together or traveled downtown for a meeting or two. Did she believe for a second that he would drop all that female attention? And what did it matter?

She was supposed to be doing things, right?

There was a five-year plan with her name on it.

"I ended everything," he repeated.

Nope. That wasn't a surge of happiness she was feeling.

Still, out of nothing *but* professional curiosity, she asked, "Why did you do that?"

"There is no one I want."

The self-assurance he used to speak left no doubt in her mind that he meant it. *No one? No one at all?* What was she thinking?

Her chest ached as she repeated his words in her head. Why should she be upset?

Caring about Shane was wrong.

Everything about this whole situation was *wrong.* She'd come to Charlotte to fix the mess she'd created and had landed in a bigger mess all on her own. How could she be so stupid?

"No one." She pursed her lips. Not even...her.

"Well, there is one person," Shane added, drawing her gaze to his stubble and dark eyes she wanted to melt into. The spider tattoo moved as he rubbed his thumb against his jaw.

"One person?" Her heart beat as if it was about to break free from her chest.

Their moment of silence was heavier than the rain during a thunderstorm and the air, thick with unspoken desire, was electric. Watching him smile, she only hoped that the storm passed soon or that it would have mercy and destroy her quickly. He fixed his heady eyes on hers, eyes filled with passion that made her skin feel like fire and her insides liquid.

"One person."

Chapter Fourteen

I'm a murderer.
Lady Fate is a bitch.
Shane Williams is my archenemy.
I may or may not be in love with him.

These were all the thoughts scrambling through Rose's head while she wended her way through morning traffic.

Over four months had passed since her first day at Lambda Digital. Three months since she'd confessed — pain bolted through her fingers as she tightened her clutch on the steering wheel — to Shane about her recurring nightmares. She'd experienced a moment of weakness that night. There could be no other explanation. Her rationality had fled. After Simon showing up out of the blue, her family finding out the truth about their relationship and seeing Holton and Olive locking lips, everything had been blurred, her emotions frenzied and her logic addled to the point of extinction.

So, yeah, she'd confessed.

Like something cancerous, her assault had been eating away at her for twelve years.

Telling someone besides Holton, her mom and her best friend was somehow refreshing, or, at least it had been in that moment. She regretted it now.

Shane knowing the truth made her feel vulnerable, particularly because ever since the night she'd slept at his house, sometimes she caught him staring at her funny.

Nothing bad, but under her insistence, he'd stopped treating her like she was the egg shells he didn't want to break. There were moments when they'd be working and she'd find him staring at her with this expression like he was seeing her for the first time.

As the weeks went on, every day stretched out longer than the last. She was surprised when she looked in the mirror and found that her skin was still young, her eyes tired but vibrant and her hair not gray but a warm blonde.

How she hadn't grown into an old woman was beyond her wildest imagination because it was like years had passed since she'd begun working at Lambda, not months—or, that's what it felt like.

She loved her employees and the lively atmosphere, but she was exhausted...and sexually frustrated. As confessions went, being around Shane almost every day made her wonder if she had always had such flimsy morals or if Shane had some magic way of dissolving them.

Daydreaming? Not even close. Let's just say, if people could read minds, Rose would be fired for harassment because her sweet 'daydreams' had been dwarfed by full-blow fantasies of him sneaking into her office and finishing what they'd started on her first day aboard. She was slack lining. Her sexual tension was so sharp it was lethal...thus the murder.

Granted, the day was bound to come eventually. Guilt still curled its thorny claws into her when she ventured to think about what had happened and what *could* be happening if she weren't a cold-blooded killer. She was a criminal, deserving of punishment.

Enrique. Just thinking about him made her deprived vagina weep. Enrique, her poor six-and-a-half-inch vibrator and possible soul mate, was dead.

Two weeks before, his three-year life had come to an end.

Angry that he couldn't do the thing Shane had done when he'd gone shallow, shallow, shallow and, at the right moment, thrust so deeply that it was as if he were lodged permanently inside her, Rose had thrown Enrique against the wall.

Both Enrique and her sanity had shattered at once.

Whenever she saw her archenemy smiling, she could have sworn he knew she was a murderer, too. Like it was sketched on her face, or maybe not *Murderer*, just *Sexually Frustrated*.

Then there was the love thing, but maybe 'love' was a dramatic word.

When Simon had come and gone, she'd realized that she didn't know what it was like to be in love with someone. She'd loved Simon. She cared about him, but the feelings she had for him were more friendship than romantic. The feelings never made her breathless. *He* never made her breathless.

Shane…

Shane took her breath away every time he smiled.

She could already see her five-year plan crumbling to pieces.

Her ability to resist him was becoming harder and harder. One thing she refused to do was fall for Shane's charm, but she thought sometimes it might already be too late.

If Lambda didn't come out successful with the Moreno project, she'd have to resign. And if Lambda did win, she would work on the project, gain that fuel for a good resume and resign still.

Making up for her failure was her only hope at having a normal, nightmare-free life, right? She couldn't afford to be distracted, no matter how tempting that distraction was— no matter how wrong the idea of leaving Olive, Holton, Lambda and Shane was starting to feel.

When she arrived at home, she found Olive sitting on the couch with a jar of Nutella and pretzels, waiting for her. They hadn't spoken much since Simon, but it wasn't because Rose was upset with her.

The deadline for the Moreno & Blu project was descending. The closer it got, the longer her work shifts became and the shorter her nights. Rose never had time to do anything but sleep and work and normally she wouldn't mind, but since living in Charlotte, she'd learned that she *liked* going out on the weekends with Olive and having…well, a life outside her job. So, she was excited that tomorrow—Saturday—she was finally doing something. She was going to have dinner with Shane.

It wasn't a date. His visiting friend would be there, but she was still nervous as if it were one.

"You said dress-up, right?" Olive asked.

Rose tossed her work bag on the couch. "Yeah."

"I went through your clothes and couldn't find jack shit, so I decided on a mini shopping spree." She pointed to the bags labeled Nordstrom on the floor beside her. "You've three options, but I say go with the red."

"Why are you always spending money on me?"

"What is the point in making money if you can't spend it on sexy outfits, high heels and chocolate?" Olive grinned, proceeding to lick her fingers free of Nutella.

Rose shook her head.

Digging past the gift paper, Rose peeped inside and gasped. "Olive," she gawked at her friend, "this is too much."

"I'm sorry I never told you about Holt," Olive said abruptly.

Sadness darkened Rose's thoughts. Holton and Olive weren't speaking, and Rose had a feeling she was the reason why. Setting the bag aside, Rose sat on the floor beside Olive.

"You've nothing to be sorry about. You know that, right? I don't know what's going on"—Rose paused to swallow the ball in her throat—"between you and my—"

"There isn't anything between Holton and…" But she couldn't finish her sentence.

Rose figured it had to do with the longing on Olive's face. She took her friend's hand in hers, realizing now that all the men in Olive's life had been a distraction. Rose had never seen Olive so torn. Olive had never allowed herself to get close to anyone, but she'd gotten close to Holton, and Rose wouldn't stand in the way of someone's happiness.

"Whatever is or isn't happening, know that I love you both. Olive, you're my best friend, and as long as you're happy, I'll support whatever decision you make."

Olive's eyes, golden-brown and warm, shimmered with moisture. Reaching over to Rose, Olive hugged her. "Thank you."

Rose closed her eyes, hugging Olive back.

It reminded Rose of the hug her momma had given her the day Simon had shown up, and she imagined this was not *where* but *what* home was. Arms you could always run into if you needed strength to forgive or guidance to direct you through troubled times.

"Enough of this emotional talk. You know I can't get sappy when I don't have alcohol in hand." Olive pulled away, her smile back full-force, though her eyes were shiny. "Hop your butt in the shower, Rosey, and when you get out, we'll try makeup and hair styles for your dinner tomorrow. And paint our nails."

Oh, God. They were playing dress-up.

Rose smiled. "Will there be drinks involved in this girls' night?"

Olive looked appalled. She sorted through another bag and pulled out a bottle of tequila, wiggling it before Rose's eyes. "It's not a girls' night without drinks."

* * * *

His phone ringing splintered through his dreams.

Shane reached through the darkness and picked it up. "Hmm, hello?" Resting it on his ear and cheek, he raised his forearm over his eyes.

"I woke you?"

At the sound of her voice, he blinked and sat up. "Rose, why are you…?" Looking at his alarm, he panicked when he saw how late it was. "Sugar, it's two in the morning. Are you okay? Is something—?"

"I was thinking about you."

He lay back against his pillow, his muscles relaxing, and rubbed his eyes. "You scared me. I thought something was wrong."

"Shane?"

That was when he noticed the slur at the *S* and the lethargic way she sighed his name. She'd been drinking. He let go of a smile. "You sound like you had a fun night but shouldn't you be in bed? If I remember right, I'd say we have a dinner tomorrow you need to be well rested for."

"I had fun. Olive and I played dress-up and drank lots — lots and lots and lots." She gave a drowsy laugh.

"Where are you now? How do you feel?" He worried she might be sick.

"I feel sorry," she said breathily.

"Sorry for what?"

"Sorry for Melissa, because I don't think I can give her what she needs."

Shane was overcome with a sudden sense of despair, the pain in her voice cutting through his own foggy mind until he was fully awake. "Rose."

"Sorry for making everything hard for you. Kissing you and —"

"Sugar, you can kiss me whenever you'd like." It wasn't much of a confession since she already knew he was open to their lips making friends any day.

"So, what? I have free rein over your lips?"

"You have reign over me everywhere." He wasn't okay with conversation leading down this road when she was intoxicated.

"You'd like that, wouldn't you?" Her voice had taken on a teasing note.

As much as he'd love to tell her how much he'd like it, Shane thought it best to leave phone sex or anything resembling it for future, sober adventures. "Sugar —"

He was interrupted by her yawning. "I'm sleepy."

"Why don't you go to bed?" He wouldn't be going back to sleep any time soon, not when his body had already started responding to possibilities of her sultry remarks.

"I can't."

"Why is that? Are you not laying down?"

He imagined her lying in her bed. Saw her wearing his gym shorts and shirt like she had been when she'd slept over, or maybe she wasn't wearing anything at all. He liked that, too. Yeah, he'd picture her with nothing—blonde hair dressing her pillowcase, face relaxed, lips pressed into a sweet and sleepy line.

His cock roused, growing harder when she sighed, "Because you're not here."

Heart working overtime, Shane must not have heard her right.

"I want to sleep with you," she breathed into the phone, and though Shane didn't think she meant sex, his body wasn't so easy to convince. "You help me forget the bad things."

Shit. When she said things like that, it was difficult for Shane to do the right thing, to leave her alone, to resist for Lambda's sake. He'd spent months in hell, resisting.

"How about this," he said. "I can stay on the phone with you until you go to sleep. Does that sound good?"

"You promise?"

"Promise," Shane said, knowing it was more than his word he was giving her.

As the night progressed and he kept his promise, he thought of a quote from some lovey-dovey novel by an old fart who'd died way before Shane's time. He hadn't gotten race cars, dragon or ninjas books growing up. No, his mother would read sonnets, poems and nonsense about star-crossed lovers to him before bedtime in an attempt to give him culture. He'd memorized some of the lines. Tonight, pieces of one stuck out in particular.

'A thief in the night, love gave no warning when it came. It crept, slowly and swiftly, striking in a single blinding moment, and when that light dimmed and my vision settled, she was there, standing before me, her smile having closed but on her lips still

lingered.'

Shane's mom had been lost in the notions of soulmates, love at first sight and all other things hopeless and romantic. Unbelievable stuff. He'd never bought into that crap. But Shane had to admit, if only to himself, that if some silly things like soulmates existed then he wished Rose was his.

Chapter Fifteen

Shane had forgotten to mention that by 'friend' he meant world-famous tycoon, Matthew Moreno, who had come to North Carolina on business and who was, at that exact moment, sitting cross-legged in front of Rose, his confident eyes awaiting a response.

Say something, Rose. You've gone quiet!

"Rose?" Shane gave her side a slight nudge of encouragement.

"Oh, sorry." She turned her anxiety toward Shane. He hadn't given her the question, but she still asked him, "What was the question again?" Rose was freaking out. It wasn't every day, *or ever*, that she met someone who had been dubbed as *TIME*'s Person of the Year.

Of course, she'd have had to meet Matthew Moreno during Lambda's presentation a month from now, but that was then and this was...*today*.

No matter how well Olive had dressed her or how confident she had been walking into this dinner, she had not been prepared to meet the man she'd been doing research on for months. The man *still* staring at her, lips sealed and eyebrows positioned in a way that made Rose wonder if he were entertained by her tongue twistedness. She froze before relaxing as Shane's hand rested on her thigh. He squeezed as if to say, "It's okay. Don't be nervous."

"How are you enjoying your work at Lambda?"

Lah-mm-b-da, Matthew pronounced, accentuating the *ahhh* and *mmm* sounds. He had an Italian accent. It was sparse but as apparent as his voice was authoritative.

With Shane's hand on her leg, her courage was restored.

"Well," she began, hoping her anxiousness wouldn't snoop through the smile she managed. "It's awesome. I—" She stopped herself and frowned, feeling silly for using a word like 'awesome' to a man with an Ivy League vocabulary. "I mean, everyone" —Shane removed his hand to grab wine and she lost her train of thought—"there, um, everyone is great to work with. We have" —she twisted her fingers in her lap, wishing Shane would give her back his comfort—"a talented team."

Rose pushed her chair back, feeling her insides swirl like confetti.

"If you two will excuse me." Apparently, Matthew Moreno turned her into a blubbering fool. "I have to use the ladies' room." Rose excused herself before the heat on her cheeks could reach the rest of her body.

When Shane had told her that he and Matthew had worked together, she'd gotten that they were acquaintances, but dinner dates? She hadn't known they were *that* close. 'Flabbergasted' and 'panicked' were words that wouldn't begin to describe her state when Shane had walked her through the shut-down restaurant and to the table, surrounded by guards and kitchen staff.

The table where old money sat in a suit and with a haircut that looked more expensive than her quarterly income, giving her a smile that she'd recognized from the front cover of *TIME*.

Traveling through the building, inhabited only by their dinner party and staff members—because millionaires couldn't eat with the common folk—Rose made it to the restroom in no time at all, but she didn't need to relieve herself of anything save the tremendous amount of uneasiness gathering in her bones. Taking a tissue, she began patting her moist palms.

What is my deal?

Relying on Shane to get her through dinner because she was too intimidated by Matthew Moreno to formulate an educated sentence was not how she wanted to spend the night.

Rose had to gather her wits because if she couldn't hold a conversation with Matthew now, she wouldn't be able to when it mattered the most.

At first, the idea of her sharing a meal with the man who led the largest work project of her career was terrifying, but as quickly as she had been caught off guard, she'd realized this opportunity wasn't one she could waste.

The competition had fifteen minutes to impress Matthew. Rose had that, plus an evening of fine dining. She blew out a breath, nodding.

I've got this. I've totally got this.

Stepping in front of the restroom mirror, Rose smoothed down her gown. The dress Olive had chosen for her was gorgeous. Fitting Rose's precise measurements, its elegant material hugged her breasts and flowed down her body to pool around her feet. There was a slit in the gown that stopped mid-thigh and flaunted her leg and the shiny gold heels with straps that came to circle her ankles. With her makeup subtle, her hair stacked in an intricate bun and rubies dangling from each ear, she was pretty dang hot. Like she'd thought countless times, she wasn't unattractive, but in a dress like this, it was easy to mistake herself for someone beautiful.

'Gorgeous.' She remembered how the words had left Shane's mouth and ended in a breath against her cheek. The blush Rose had been running away from attacked her skin, and her neck and ears broke out in warmth. Placing her fingertips on her cheekbone, the spot Shane had kissed, she smiled, recalling how the world had dissolved under his touch. She started as someone pushed the restroom door open.

The subject of her wayward thoughts slipped inside. Incapable of helping herself, she toured her admiring gaze over his figure. Shane was mouthwatering—a man who wore sexual appeal like the finest cologne—but tonight? Tonight, Shane was dressed to kill, and he was killing…her inhibitions.

"What are you doing in here, Shane?" It came out breathy-sounding.

"With you watchin' me like that, sugar, I may assume that you're thinking about how good I look in a suit."

"I don't... I don't know what you're talking about." It was a lie, but she didn't need to tell him that. Shane was fully aware of how attractive he was.

Instead of replying, he started forward.

"I think you know what I'm talking about." His gaze lowered to her mouth as he came to a stop in front of her.

Matthew Moreno may have had everything women and men wanted — power and money and appearance so out-of-this-world it was like he had stepped out of a fresh photo shoot that had used Adobe Photoshop — but he wasn't Shane Williams. Shane Williams looked like the type of man who enjoyed starting fights and finishing them. He was a bad boy, toughened more by three years overseas. Unlike Matthew's flawless skin, he had calloused knuckles and scars and a slight bump on his nose from having been broken in the past. His swirling tattoos met with his posh black suit were a dangerous combination capable of making women everywhere swoon. Part brute. Part gentlemen. All badass.

He smiled, and his lips, full and wet from having been licked, caught Rose's attention.

"I could be wrong," he said in a tone that suggested he wasn't, "but I get the feeling you're thinking about kissing me. What do you say, sugar?" He lifted her chin. "Am I wrong?"

She tore her gaze from his mouth. Need threaded in her belly.

"Dinner with Matthew Moreno, huh?" Rose tried switching topics, not sure if she could handle Shane's flirtatious side tonight. "I would have loved it if you'd warned me."

Shane's lips jerk in amusement. "Why are you ignoring

my question?"

"Shane," she cautioned him.

"I'm beginning to regret it," he whispered, lifting his hand to her hair and placing a lock of blonde behind her ear. "The way you look in that dress makes me want to drag you out of here and lock us in my bedroom forever." Dropping his hand from her ear, he outlined her jaw. His eyes flickered to her lips. Heat swirled around her body.

Again, the restroom door opened, letting in a cool draft that refreshed her high temperature. Waking up from his touch, she stepped back.

"Sorry." The waitress who had entered pointed to the stalls. "I need to use the bathroom."

"It's fine. We were just speaking privately." It was a bad excuse, and she didn't stay for the waitress or Shane to confirm that. Without peering back, she exited the room.

She only noticed Shane hadn't followed her out when she sat down at the table, alone.

She spared a moment to take a relaxing breath and reminded herself that she was a capable adult who *could* create proper sentences. However, it was hard to focus on her pep talk when Matthew's demanding presence was pulling up her chin, as if to tell her that, when he was in the room, he'd have her attention. Did all rich people give off the same overpowering energy?

"Mr. Moreno..." she started, holding her chin high.

Matthew was friendlier than ever as he made conversation with her almost like he could tell how nervous she was and he wanted to calm her. But no matter how easy exchanging dialogue became, there was a part of her put off by his *everything*.

Without being rude or inconsiderate, Matthew Moreno made her feel small.

He always kept the conversation on her, about her, even when she tried to stray to his life and career, a clear sign that the power dynamics leaned in his favor.

Most of the time, Rose could gauge people well. Knowing

a lot from his biography and numerous interviews, she assumed that she had an advantage at reading him.

He was blank, giving nothing away.

She got the feeling that, despite all her research, she didn't know Matthew at all. How was she going to present to him when she couldn't pin him down for a second?

"Will it be only you that we present to?" Rose allowed herself to sneak a quick look to the back of the restaurant where Shane was. What was taking him such a long time?

"Myself and others."

Myself and others? Could he be vaguer?

"It would work in your favor, having Moreno & Blu as a client?"

"It would be great for Lambda." Consternation ticked away at her.

His eyes were as unfathomable as they had been on the magazine's pages. "Yes, I suppose it would be an advantage for them, as well."

Rose studied his calm expression, then she realized the distinction he had made.

It would be a great advantage for them, *as well*? Which meant he was aware that winning Moreno & Blu as a client would benefit Rose as an individual.

That had to mean... She went cold. "You know what happened?" Her fear ballooned and her throat tightened, breathing becoming thin. "That's not why I'm doing this," Rose immediately defended. Twining her fingers together, she worried if she'd already put Lambda in jeopardy. She shouldn't have come here. She'd never be able to forgive herself if she ruined this opportunity for Shane. How did Matthew know about her past? No...not how. *Why?*

"People act in their favor for different reasons, Miss Berkowitz." Matthew placed his wine glass on the table and a member of the wait staff rushed to fill it. He paid them no mind, only folded his hands on his postured legs. "I was not asking yours."

"I'm not going to lie. It was." Rose didn't think it possible to lie to someone like him. She played with the napkin in her lap, incapable of meeting his expression. "The advantage of winning and redeeming myself was one of the main interests for me accepting a position at Lambda, but it's not anymore. I've changed." She looked at him. "Shane…"

Shane was a freezing winter morning, like sunlight kissing her eyelids while she lay in her bed. He made her feel awake, roused her from the nightmare-like state that had been her past and her present search for perfection. What was the point in searching for a perfect life or keeping a five-year plan when…when…Rose was here, now, and she had never been so happy than when he was beside her?

"How did Shane change your direction?" Matthew wondered aloud, not sounding judgmental, despite his obvious and understandable lack of sympathy.

When had Shane changed her direction?

She thought of Shane's entitled smile, his annoying defiance, the way his nose scrunched when he laughed and how the tip of his tongue poked out from the side of his mouth when he was concentrating hard. Rose smiled. Watching him work was enchanting. But…if she left after Moreno & Blu project, she'd never watch him again, never see him again. Her heart protested. *Never see him?* Tears moistened her eyes as the realization hit.

The *may* or *may not* shifted into a definite 'yes'. At that moment, Rose knew that Shane's flaws were better than any perfection she'd find own her on. He hadn't changed her direction. He'd changed her heart.

Raising her head, it was like Matthew had helped her realize the truth. He couldn't have known Rose loved Shane before even she did, right? "I care about Lambda. I want—"

"What?" He tilted his head to the side. "I've been trying to figure out what it is you want with Lambda since I was informed of your altercation with a previous employee."

She fought to keep back tears as her regret grew. "I want to be forgiven for my actions." Her voice trembled. "I don't want Lambda to be punished for my mistake. I want to show you all the hard work we've put into this project. I want to us to be successful."

It wasn't only Shane she cared about. Everyone at Lambda—Tiffany, Jim, Malcolm and the staff, who had been so welcoming to her, all meant so much.

"And what is success?" It was like he was giving her a quiz.

He had stripped her layers in just a few words, reading her like an open book when she'd thought she was closed. There was no point in hiding when he saw right through her.

Sniffling, she straightened her shoulders. He saw her doubt and biggest regret, but she refused to show him weakness. "What is success to the great Matthew Moreno?"

Sitting back in his chair, he tilted his head, sweeping his eyes over her body, but not in a sexual way. "Success is the moment you know with absolute certainty that someone loves you as much as you love them." He glanced over her shoulder. "Isn't that right?"

Turning her head, she found Shane at her shoulder. Apprehension bit into her. How long had he been there? Had he heard their entire conversation?

Shane swapped his pensive look for a friendly smile. "That's what Grandma always told me. Still remember that old conversation?"

Matthew gave a gracious laugh. "How could I forget?"

Rose gazed between the two, her heart squeezing as she realized her selfish need to have a perfect life may have hurt yet another person.

* * * *

When the night was over and Rose was plump with savory food, expensive wine and countless thoughts on what the heck to do about her conversation with Mr. Moreno, Shane grabbed hold of her hand, keeping it close as they waited outside for a limo.

His fingers, fitted around hers, were so comfortable that she couldn't protest the inappropriateness of the gesture. Mr. Moreno was long gone. Now it was just them.

Forgetting they were co-workers, she held on to him and leaned into his side. They untangled when the limo driver pulled up.

Opening the door for Rose, Shane smiled as she dipped inside.

"Why did you get a limo?" She spread out on the comfy couch.

"I didn't." He sat down beside her and unbuttoned his suit jacket. "Matthew picked it up for us. That man loves theatrics."

"How did you two become friends? He is so different than you." Matthew was almost everything Shane disliked — wealthy beyond hope, extravagant and *intense*.

"I admire him."

"Because of his hard work?"

"More than that." He tugged off his tie. "Think I've got it bad with my family? Once we got drunk and he opened up to me some, which is about as rare as finding a pearl in the sand, and what little he told me about his family…"

Shane grimaced, running his hand through his tousled hair. "Let's just say, there is a price that comes with the amount of power he has. After everything he's been through, I respect the man."

Rose imagined it was hard growing up with divorced parents. She hadn't known her own father. He'd left when she had been a child, but at least her childhood hadn't been plastered on websites everywhere. Matthew's parents had divorced and the whole world had known.

"Then it should be easy to get his attention for the Moreno —"

"If it were easy to get his attention, we wouldn't be working our asses off like we are. He's not going to give me the upper hand because he knows me. If anything, he is going to be more critical. He is merciless when it comes to that company."

Her stomach sank. "You guys are friends, though."

"Emotions and business don't mix, especially with Matthew. Now, are we going to talk about him all night, or are we going to finish what was started in the—"

It was her time to intercept him. "This is such a huge limousine."

Moving around the stretched-out interior was a breeze. Rose could almost stand to her full five-foot, five-inch height. She'd never been in a limo before, but the ones she had seen in movies were never this big. It looked large enough to fit an entire bridal party—both the bridesmaids and groomsmen.

With a bar console, four sleek leather couches outlining every side, a big-screen television and a mirrored ceiling, that cars like this actually existed was baffling. This must have been one of the many advantages of being Matthew Moreno.

"It's so big you can play Marco Polo in here," she noted absently.

"Wanna try?" His daring smile created a shiver of pleasure up her.

He has no clue how arousing that smile is, does he?

"Try what?" Rose turned away from his eyes, glittering with playfulness, worried that her face might give her new realization away.

"Want to play Marco Polo? Bet I could win."

"No way," she scoffed. "I'm the queen of Marco Polo."

Every time she and Holton had played in the pool when they'd been younger, she'd always won. Always. No way Shane could outwit her keen sense of hearing and inherent navigation skills, even with those army-bred senses of his.

"I doubt it," Shane challenged. "I could find you in a second."

Examining the dark-lit interior, Rose was already calculating ways she could win. They were heading to her house first, so it would be a long drive and, with weekend traffic, it would be even longer. "If I win, you cannot complain about my management over you *ever* again."

"Seriously? Ever? That's a long time, sugar."

"Fine," she sighed. "A month. No complaining – *at all*."

"Okay, no complainin'." He grinned. "But if I win, you can't complain about my flirting with you for a whole month."

"I wouldn't have to complain if you didn't do it all the time."

"I can't help myself, sugar. I'm a natural-born ladies' man." Shane winked.

Oh, she was so going to win, if only to step on that mammoth-sized hubris of his. "You have to cover your eyes when you go. No peeking!"

"I don't need to peek to win." Reaching to the seat beside him, he picked up his tie and offered it to her. "Cover your eyes."

"Oh, no." Rose remembered his tie being wrapped around a woman's eyes the night they'd first met. She did not want to be reminded of Shane's risqué adventures. "You're *it*. Best two out of three."

Shane handed her the black piece. "Tie it on me, then."

Smirking, she made a mask out of his neckwear.

"If you're as good as you say you are, sugar, this could go on forever. We need to set some ground rules."

"Find me in twelve Marcos." Once she was done with his tie, she sat back and removed her heels. "If not, you lose and we start the next round."

He rubbed his chin, which looked funny with his eyes covered. "Okay, deal."

As Shane started his countdown from ten, Rose scrambled through the limo, her heart beating with excitement as she climbed over the leather seats.

She stopped before she could reach the farthest end, knowing it'd likely be the first place Shane tried searching. Her face hurt with how much she was grinning. To silence her laugh, she clamped her lips closed, not wanting to give away her position.

Eventually, he ceased counting and called into the quiet, "Marco!"

Taking the smile out of her voice was nearly impossible. "Polo!"

"Oh, I'm definitely gonna win." Shane moved in her direction.

Before he could get too close, Rose tiptoed to the middle of the car. Marco Polo wasn't supposed to be played in a limo, but that fact didn't discount the fun.

Shane's hands swiped over the seat she had abandoned. When he found it was empty, he began again, his smile widening to match her own. "Marco!"

"Polo."

It was like that twelve times, Shane shouting Marco and her reciting in response.

She'd had to contain her laughter throughout the entire event, which wasn't an easy feat. Shane looked hilarious on his knees, blindly searching the car for her.

Rose never thought she had any kinks before, but seeing a hot guy with a blindfold around his head responding to the sound of her voice was definitely her new fetish.

It was a good thing Shane had covered his eyes, too. He wouldn't be able to see how aroused she was. It had to be the alcohol making her flushed, or a combination of that and his scent spiking her bloodstream and pumping her with adrenaline.

The first round went to Rose.

She hadn't been fibbing when she'd told him she'd named herself the queen of Marco Polo. Shane didn't seem to like that he was down one match. He swore that next time he'd be on his A-game.

Rose bounced on the edge of her seat and her bare feet flat on the carpet. Flattening her palm against her eyelashes, she obscured her view. "Ready?"

"Mmm," Shane responded in the distance.

"Ten," she began. "Nine. Eight. Seven. Six. Five. Four.

Three. Two. One."

She paused to give him a moment to make his final arrangements. Straining her ears to see if she could catch him moving, she heard nothing.

"Marco."

The sound of wheels against cement and distant honking as the car moved with traffic was all that responded.

"Oh, what? You're scared now that I'm going to kick your butt or something?" She laughed, holding her hand tightly over her face. "Marco!"

Chills surged up her skin as the sides of her dress lifted, and his large hands followed behind, curving over her thighs. He pressed his lips beside her knee—warm lips, and wet.

"Polo."

It was rough sounding, and the hot exhale after it might as well have been blown right above her clit. The activity in her nether regions was instant. She was already becoming wet and expectant. Her nipples were perched high, ready to be sucked into his mouth.

Every nerve in her body seemed to end where his touch began. Removing his lips, Shane ended the kiss. Her legs shivered in objection. Keeping her eyes sealed behind her hand, she moistened her lips and tried concentrating, but her thoughts were strained by the rugged breath blasting on her skin. Shane didn't move from his position but stayed still and waited.

"Marco." The word was said as lightly as he'd kissed her.

Her legs spread—on their own, she told herself—as her dress was balled up and pulled to her waist, leaving her exposed. Shane, too, escalated, dragging his mouth along her limbs, which shuddered under his careful pursuit. She began breathing faster. His voice was tight and low, like the drumming under her skin. "Polo."

"Marco."

He burrowed his fingers into her thighs as the warm wetness of his mouth spread along her flesh. He kissed her goosebumps. Every slow suck and slower lick seemed intentional, as if he were showing her what he wanted to do, how he'd use his tongue to take her over the edge again and again. The central nerves between her folds pinched and pulsed as desire hooked into her skin and spread against his dedicated mouth. There was something sexy about his hushed voice, like he'd only just wakened from sleeping. "Polo."

"Marco."

With her panties soaked through, Rose was glad to have worn black ones so he wouldn't be able to tell how wet she was. Shane hadn't even touched her private parts and she was coming undone. He closed his fingers over her ankle, and while he worked his mouth higher up her thigh, the hard scruff over his jaw abrading her skin, he pulled her leg farther until they were opened wider in front of him. The car moved. Honks sounded. She heaved a sigh.

"Polo."

"M-Marco." She was saying it quicker now, desperate to feel what would come next. The hand she'd appointed to cover her eyes was beginning to sweat, but she didn't remove it. Rose didn't want this to end, and she feared that if she dropped her hand, it would.

Moaning, she bowed her back as his teeth bore into her skin, biting hard.

An animal-like growl emitted from the back of his throat. "Polo."

"*Shane.*" Her high-pitched call was laced with exigency.

The straps of her garter belt unsnapping sounded louder with her eyes closed.

They jumped on her skin as they came undone. He went back to cup her thighs. She could hardly believe his mouth was on her. The coolness of air conditioning contrasting the heat of his tongue. He began skimming his fingers up her legs. When he hit the thin strand of fabric at the sides of her waist, he curled them in his hands. Shane didn't need to tell Rose to lift. Rose lifted for him, and he drew her panties down slowly, the lace scratching her sensitized skin.

When her underwear was removed, embarrassment came hurtling like rocks in the pit of her stomach. Rose removed her hand but didn't open her eyes. She clawed her nails against the leather seats as he resumed his wet massages on the high inside of her thigh. It was amazing how in the moments when she should be focusing her whole attention on something — in this case, Shane driving her wild, bathing her leg with kisses — she couldn't stop thinking about other things. Other things being...

He is eye level with my vagina.

What if she weren't attractive down there? *Oh, Christ.* What if she smelled?

Rose kept her goodies thoroughly pampered, but the conversation she'd had with Matthew had been a sweat-inducing one. Two at a time insecurities batted her mind, making Rose question herself and what Shane would do when his kisses reached their final destination.

Though aware it wouldn't have been the first time his face had been all up in her goodie basket, she had been tipsy that night and his house had been dark. The limo was dark, a little.

God, no. This was not what she wanted to be thinking —

Circling his arms around her thighs, Shane dragged her forward so that she was barely hanging on to the edge of her seat. Rose tensed when he kissed where she would have had pubic hair had Olive not convinced her to get a Brazilian. *Thank you, Olive!*

His raspy voice came from below her, "Don't be nervous, sugar. I'm going to take good care of you."

Then there was another kiss but lower, on her outermost labia, and she couldn't have stopped the moan that spewed from her, even if she'd wanted to.

How had he known she was nervous?

Oh yeah, her legs were shaking like two maracas during Mardi Gras.

Silencing her thoughts, Shane repeated himself, soaking

her folds with a determined stroke of his tongue. Hot pleasure expanded. His breath lashed against her. She tensed as he paused.

"Sha—" The word melted into a head-tossing moan as Shane gave her lips a full-mouthed kiss that prickled all over her body, in every cell and every nerve ending. She pushed her pelvis forward on impulse, her clit twitching below his swirling tongue. *"Oh, God."*

He lifted his head. "Amazing."

"I agree wholeheartedly."

Shane laughed. "You like my mouth like that, sugar?"

He lowered his lips back to her flesh where they started doing something Rose couldn't describe as anything less than miraculous, making it impossible for her to answer him.

And the medal for most talented mouth goes to...

"Open your eyes," he demanded, his voice muffled. "Watch me taste you." Squeezing her thighs, Shane trailed his tongue between her folds, flicking up and past her nub. "Watch me eat every inch of this sweet pussy," he whispered before leaning in for slower kiss.

It took Rose a couple of blinks, but she managed to clear the fuzz from her eyes.

Her vision focused, settling on Shane's gaze, staring into hers while he kneeled between her legs. His jaw, spread wide over her intimate area, ticked each instant he lashed his tongue over her center. Unfurling her nails from the couch, she reached through his hair. It spread like silk between her fingers. Her legs vibrated as Shane flattened his tongue to lap.

"Holy shit."

Thinking it wasn't an attractive quality in a person, Rose tried not to curse too much, but there were some moments in life, she admitted, where cursing was the only way to express the gravity of a certain situation—like right then, Shane's tongue thrusting inside her before pulling out, only to be replaced by his fingers. Tipping her head back, she curled her toes into the carpet. A moan broke from her throat. Her legs tingled.

This was most definitely one of those *holy shit* moments. Peeling open her eyes that had closed again involuntarily, Rose was breathless watching Shane's expert mouth and his rapacious fingers pumping inside her.

Like she was the center of his universe, Shane's full attention remained on her. He never let his eyes or mouth stray. He took good care of her, just as he'd said he would, and Rose was now certain that everyone should play Marco Polo in a limo if given the opportunity.

Then thinking was as useless as trying to stop his name from leaving her mouth. Rose had never experienced the sensations he was creating. It was so good—sharp and hot in the most fantastic way possible that she couldn't narrow it down to words, only moans and begging for more. Everything disappeared but his touch. Air rushed through her lungs, she tensed and electrical pulses ping-ponged against her walls when two fingers became three. *Holy...*

"Oh, Shane. *Shane.*"

He drew back. "You gonna come in my mouth, sugar?"

Whimpering, actually freaking whimpering, Rose bounced her head, tightening her fingers in his hair.

"I want you to, pretty Rose. Give me everything, and watch. Watch the only man who is ever going to touch this pussy again taste what his."

Before she could register his words, he rolled his tongue against her center like it was a barreling wave against the shore and, at once, he quickened his fingers until they were punching deliciously inside her. Rose only had time to hear his groaning then she closed her eyes and was tossed into oblivion.

Chapter Sixteen

The moment Shane had seen her, he'd known he had to have her.

It wasn't the first time he'd thought those words, but it'd be the last, because to him now *have* meant *keep*. He'd given up on resisting. No way would he allow another man to make Rose moan like she'd done for him earlier.

A virile growl came to rest low in his throat as he envisioned the look of bewilderment on her face when he'd driven his fingers inside her, like she'd never known fingers could feel so good.

Tonight, he'd show her everything he could about fingers and feeling good, and from now on, the only name on her lips when she came would be his.

Placing the bottle of wine on his kitchen counter, Shane never let her out of his sight. He curled his fingers around each glass stem and took the two half-filled drinks to where she stood on his terrace, reviewing the city. Downtown was alive, brilliant with color, but his gaze had only one destination. The gown she wore complimented her body like it'd been made for her, squeezing her ass and waist. A massive heat brewed inside him when he imagined his hands and lips imitating the satiny fabric, outlining every beautiful curve. Darting his tongue over his lips, Shane salivated when he realized the taste of her lingered there. Once hadn't been enough. He wanted to be crouched between her legs again, kneading his tongue against the delicate bulb at her middle until she screamed for him, begging for more.

Before dinner, when Rose had stepped out of her

apartment as the limo pulled up and Shane had gotten his first glimpse of her in that dress, he'd been tempted to call the whole thing off. He'd wanted to drag her back to his place and have his way with her.

However, the opportunity to meet Matthew was one Rose would appreciate — even if she'd have to work through her nervousness — so, with reluctance and multiple adjustments to his hard-on, he'd set aside his will to possess her. It was another sign his feelings for her were out of his control. Acting on his own behalf came easily to Shane — his life, his rules and whatnot. With Rose, he didn't want to be inconsiderate or self-interested. She deserved someone better than that.

"Do you know how good you look in that dress?" Like red velvet. Her back, exposed by a deep plunge of fabric, disappeared as she came to face him.

Raising his eyes, Shane let them hover over her mouth, which boosted at the edges in friendly reception. The best feeling in the world was seeing her smile, akin to seeing snow for the first time or reaching the highest point of a mountain by foot. It was indescribable. She was stunning, inside and out. Shane offered her the wine. She drank it down in gentle sips.

"You look pretty handsome yourself," Rose confessed, and he brushed his eyes over her body again. "What do you want from me, Shane?"

His attention stilled at the sound of her frustration.

Chalky sky above them, silver cityscape at their sides, the surrounding darkness clashed with artificial light. In the mayhem, her green irises had turned dimmer, yet they still managed to shine with radiant clarity. Holding her gaze with his, Shane told Rose what he wanted in a guttural tone that he hoped would tempt her to indulge. "I want to take you to my bedroom."

Rose had started to taste more wine, but she paused before the glass could reach her lips. Shaking her head, she set the drink on the patio table.

He went on, not wanting to be stopped by any objection, "I'll slip your dress off your shoulders while kissing your neck, nibbling the spot you like underneath your ear. When you're naked, I want to take my time exploring your body. You have an amazing body." He took a moment to run his eyes down her hypnotizing form. "I'd like to taste it.

"Once I've done that, I want to make love to you. All night I've been hard with the idea of being inside you again. Do you know how difficult it is to hold a conversation when all you can think about is fucking someone until they can't stand properly?" Noticing her ruddy cheeks and her large eyes, he paused. He wondered, briefly, if he'd gone too far. "Do you want to me stop?"

Twirling, she faced the city again, looping her fingers on the balcony's railing as if needing to steady herself. At this angle, Shane could see her chest rise and fall in quick succession.

Her mouth released rocky breaths. "There's *more*?"

"There's a lot more." *Hours more. Months more. Years, even.*

"I meant"—she exhaled a lungful, as if she were having trouble wrapping her head around what he was saying, let alone responding to it all—"what do you want from me long-term? You're used to having women around, but I can't give you a sex partner. I have plans. *Life* goals—"

"You're not like other women, Rose." Cliché as it sounded, it was the truth.

Perhaps he'd never allowed any woman enough time for him to find out if they were different or not. Now, he didn't care to. Rose had become an unyielding force, sneaking into his life and his daily routine. His boss. His friend. To him, she *was* different.

"I'm so confused, Shane." Blonde curled around her temples.

He yearned to reach out and spiral the strands in his fingers, but his feet stayed adhered to the ground. He didn't want to give her any reason to stop speaking.

"There is always this *tension* between us, and it's

exhausting fighting it. But we're co-workers! We can't. I..."
Her sigh of defeat pained him. "I want to know what you
want from me, not tonight or tomorrow but in general.
Maybe it will help me figure out what the heck is going
on. I hate not knowing..." She lowered her hands and her
voice. Her eyes were moist with tears.

Unease slithered over him. It killed him to see her
like this. Her confidence had shed in the midst of their
confusing relationship, but Shane couldn't discount his
relief because...she was saying she cared for him, too.

He swallowed, his throat feeling like it could use
something to drink, so he brought the glass of wine to his
mouth and gulped until it was empty. *Here goes nothing*.

"I want to buy you a picket-fenced house, if that's what
will make you happy." Once they came out, he'd never be
able to take the words back. He had to keep going, whether
heartbreak followed or not. Shane had to tell Rose the
truth that had been building inside him, and confessing to
someone was an all or nothing deal. He had one chance to
convince her that he was good enough to hold on to the
most precious thing she had to offer — her heart. So, if Shane
was going to tell her what he wanted, besides stripping her
gown off and fucking her senseless, he might as well do it
right. Fuck, he was nervous he would scare her off again.

Nervous of opening his heart for the first time in years.

Screw wine. He needed a straight shot of whiskey.

His gaze came to meet the woman who'd racked his
thoughts and dreams for months. Strength. Beauty. Deep-
rooted pain. Restless curiosity. *Does she have any idea how
unbelievable she is?*

"I want to take horseback riding lessons if it means
becoming the type of man you want." With a step toward
her, the space between them vanished. "I'm not counting
on you abandoning your five-year plan, Rose." He caught
a stray lock of hair between his fingers. "Make *me* part of
your plan. I want to be the person you're looking for — the
person who keeps your nightmares at bay, who makes

216

you come every night." The rightness behind each word made him speak faster. "I want to be yours, Rose. Partner. Employee. Who cares? No one —"

Shane had seen the whole kiss-to-silence thing in shitty chick flicks his sister used to force him to watch when he'd been no higher than her knees. To him, it was overused as hell.

Women really fell for that?

When Rose pushed her breasts to his chest and those soft-as-pillow lips on his, Shane shut the hell up in a second. He didn't just shut up, though. He dropped his wine to wrap his arms around her, pulling her against him. The glass crashed on the ground, shattering in fragments at his feet. He smiled when Rose muttered a preoccupied apology. Was he worried? Fuck, no. *What glass?* There was a sexy woman with her fingers in his hair and her mouth on top of his. The only thing he was thinking about was how good Rose felt. Perfect in every way.

Shane gave a silent shout out to whatever karma, fate, coincidence or chaotic randomness had dictated their meeting. It was amazing how one accidental encounter could turn his life upside down. Wasn't that the moral of their story, though? One day, someone just strolls into your life and you have no clue they're going to change it forever. *Back to the kissing.*

Rose was a fantastic kisser. The way her lips could be soft but unrelenting made his knees weak and his cock harder than he thought possible. And her tongue? A fucking blessing.

Before he could do something inappropriate like pull her dress up and take her on his balcony, moonlight so bright that his neighbors would thank him for the movie tomorrow morning, he hooked an arm under her knees and lifted. She flung her hands around his neck with a smile and a cute squeal that tugged at his lips.

"Now the sex part?" Shane teased.

He delighted in knowing that he would be making her

laugh a lot more in the future.

"Now the sex part," she agreed.

Once she was on his bed where she belonged, Shane proceeded to peel her dress off. Stripping her was a slow tease. He'd been serious about what he'd said earlier. He was going to take care of her—always.

Running his fingers down her shoulders, he pushed her dress straps low. He fell to the sensitive area under her ear, kissed her there and his heartbeat blasted off in his chest. Moving his hands across Rose's decadent body, the rich fabric of her dress sliding under his callouses—smooth, but nothing compared to his lips on her skin—he was in Heaven. Their lips moved in unison while he unclothed her, and his muscles tensed as her dress disappeared on the floor. Along with thanking the man who made skirts, Shane wanted to high-five the shit out of whoever thought of garter belts. How the hell did that idea come about? Who cared? It was pure genius. Thank fuck he had masturbated before dinner because the image of her alone—clothed in nothing but tiny panties and lacy stockings, held up by seductive straps that settled on the front and back of her thighs—was enough to make him come.

Aware of little but her soft breathing, Shane moved his open mouth up her body. He was in love with how she quivered and the helpless way she said his name like it were a symptom for *please*.

He slipped his fingers behind her neck. He lifted her toward him, taking her lips slowly at first, then harder. Tonguing the dip at their middle, Shane coaxed her to open for him. He thrust his tongue inside, exploring, absolutely intoxicated by how responsive she was. Between kisses, Rose helped him out of his shirt. With her hips, she rubbed against his cock every time their bodies connected, her womanly softness fitting against his contrasts.

Sinking, he brought his mouth down her neck. Her chin. Chest. Breasts.

Jesus. She had the sexiest tits ever.

He took a moment to appreciate the beauties. They were a perfect fit for her body and his palms. Hard, jutted-out points, surrounded by coral areolae and, beneath that, expansive swoops that left plenty for Shane to lick and nip. The appreciation sunk to his already-hard cock, making his erection uncomfortable as it pushed into his bottoms. Unbuttoning his pants and shoving them to his knees, he sighed as some of his stress melted away.

"You make me so fucking hard." He kissed her breast.

She moaned in response, eyes closing as he let his lips follow their slopes and arches, circling her areola. He moved around and licked over everything but her saluting buds. Pushing her breasts out, Rose told him, without words, what she'd like him to do. Too bad Shane wanted to hear it out loud.

"Let me hear it, sugar."

For motivation, he let his tongue dash over one stiff nipple while he pinched the other, not wanting to abandon it, before sealing his lips around the one he'd hurt and sucking it all better.

Damn, her moans. There was nothing like her moans or the taste of her skin, slightly salty from sweat. When he pulled back, breathing hard, he smiled, seeing her eyes warm with craving.

"Is that what you want?"

"Yes." Her stomach heaved. "Again."

Close to exploding with desire, he widened his lips over her breast, which was already wet and glistening from his mouth. From where he was sitting, it could be soaked even more. Lowering his mouth to the flowery bud, Shane showed Rose how much he appreciated her perky beauties, and she showed him how thankful she was—moaning his name like it was a prayer—to finally have his mouth's full attention. Every so often he would switch between breasts so one wouldn't get too sore. It wasn't long before they were both red and covered by hickeys.

Rolling his hips between her thighs, Shane groaned as

wetness touched his boxers. Knowing that he'd already made her so drenched did him in. Need waved through his system.

Giving her nipple one last tug, he released it. Rose let go a goading plea for him to keep going, but his determination had grown singular. Falling more, he traveled her abdomen and hip bones with his mouth, everywhere, slowly closing in on her center.

She shouted, jerking her body when he reached her hairless mound. "Shane!" Rose sprang up. "Stop. Let me. You've already done this once today. I get that you want to be selfless, but I want to touch you, too."

She thought he was being selfless? "Trust me, sugar. This is all selfishness."

His elbows pushed harder into the mattress as he hooked his arms under her legs. Vision wandering to the luscious lips at her junction, he wet his mouth with her juices, placing a light kiss on her vulva and making her jolt again. "I have to taste you some more. I want my tongue inside you again." Their gazes joined. "Lay back down so I can make you come."

It took a couple of seconds, but Rose lowered to the bed sheets.

Tightening his arms around her thighs, he yanked her closer. A pulse of heat shot through his cock as he sunk his head. Intent on making her come so hard she'd never question her attraction to him again, Shane spread her feminine slit with his fingers and her clitoral hood rose, exposing the swollen bud that he bent toward. His flesh touched hers, detonating a moan from them both. *Selfless? No.* He was planning to assail her. Shane eased the tip of his tongue across her nerves, enjoying her jerks and her fingers holding on to his shoulders.

Taking her harder, he began to swirl and flick his tongue over her clit with relentless pressure, steadily increasing his pace before opening his mouth to plaster it over her entire pussy. He grinned at the sounds she was releasing, inhaling her womanly scent deep into his lungs. *Fucking perfect*. Her vocal encouragement made him feel like a king.

Her sunny hair billowed against her breasts and tossed over her skin as she arched her back off the mattress. Shane raised his hands up her chest. Hard nipples pressed into his palms.

He ravaged her, tasting every ounce of her sweet arousal, like he'd wanted to for so long. He grazed his tongue along her textured flesh in ways he'd never forget—lapping, quick and slow and often somewhere in between. Droning his pleasure, a groan, into her honeysuckle flesh, he smiled when the vibration made her giggle and moan.

Shane lifted his head enough to speak. "You like that, sugar?"

"Hmmm, so much. You're so good at that."

"I like it, too. Love it."

To prove this, Shane continued licking and loving her with worshipping lips. Her clit was soft on his mouth, sensitive. Rose reached through his hair with more enthusiasm and tucked whole locks of it between her fingers, holding him where his tongue excited the most. She gyrated her hips, waving her pussy to his tongue. Her inner thighs touching his cheeks as he worked her toward the cliff. In time, she neared her orgasm. He felt it in her trembling legs, and Shane stopped so the moment for release would escape her. Handing her frustrated look a knowing smile, he dipped his head to her middle again, starting all over. He was depriving her of her orgasms—one, two and going on the third. But, if he weren't so distracted with eating her pussy, he'd tell her that when she did come, it would be well worth it.

Burrowing two of his fingers into her, Shane was glad to now be holding down her legs because she tried to snap them closed, where they'd locked at his cheeks. He chuckled again. She was what he'd been waiting for and more than he could have ever imagined. Rose was so snug—he couldn't wait to be inside her—that as her walls began to spasm, it forced his fingers out of her channel. Rearranging them, he let quick pumps of his hand push against her squeezing constrictions. Shane sucked her clit with greater fervor, bringing her up and down until she was quaking and screaming. Incapable of robbing Rose any longer, he created a brisk pattern in and out of her, repeating the fast strokes of his tongue over the rigid roof inside her. Slapping the inside of her thigh hard, he squeezed the spot he'd hit and groaned. She writhed, her eyebrows tightening and eyes closing as she uttered her pleasure. He didn't stop or slow down, even when her shouts of release rushed up his back and her arousal flooded his mouth. Grunting with satisfaction, he opened his lips as far as they could go, wanting everything she could give him.

"You have such a talented tongue," she mused after she'd caught her breath.

He laid a strand of kisses along her leg. "The better to eat you with."

Her breasts bounced as she propped herself up on her elbows, her bright smile reaching out to Shane and further warming him. "What are you, the big bad wolf?"

"Woof," he growled, biting her inner thigh.

"Fuck me."

He laughed at her response.

"No, really, please fuck me." Urgency braided through her words. "Like...right now."

Damn, did he love hearing those words. "Want my cock inside you, sugar?"

Her body hummed under the effect of his statement, dousing him with a craving that flowed down his chest and joined the raging heartbeat that seemed to gather at his thighs. Already dizzy from the smell and taste of her, Shane couldn't hold back. Regardless of whether he wanted to continue teasing Rose or not, he wouldn't be able to. The throbbing in his cock was bordering on painful. Pre-cum already dripped down his thigh. He needed her, needed to feel the heated stretch of her skin as she molded around him, to see her professional mask slip.

Condoms were in his nightstand. He fetched one then undressed.

He went toward the bed. Rose's eyesight was glued to his erection. Her shameless ogling did wonders for his self-esteem.

"Like what you see?"

"Yeah." She snatched the foil packet from his hand. "I *love* what I see."

Shane chuckled, remembering when they'd first met she'd been hesitant about putting on his condom. It was like she was different—freer and more open—but still the same Rose that had crashed into his life.

"What are you laughing at?" She tore the package in her fingers.

"Just think you're pretty, is all."

Shane gritted his teeth to keep from wincing, more tender than usual, as she rolled on his condom. Falling back on the mattress with a thump, she motioned for him to follow. He moved above her, snuggling his nose and mouth into the curve of her neck.

She gave off a girlish laugh of her own.

Shane's lips curled. "What are *you* laughin' at?"

She raised her hands to the sides of his cheeks, brushing the stubble there.

Dropping his eyelids, Shane relished the feeling.

"You don't have to take riding lessons."

He looked at her, speechless.

Her cheeks, laden with rosy warmth, plumped. She smiled for him. "Don't buy me a house with a big fence, either."

His heart swelled. He understood what she was saying. It was okay not to fit into her plan. She didn't want him to. Shane, as he was, sufficed.

His only response? *Kiss her*. Kiss her like hell and never stop.

While Rose's lips shifted under his, she reached between

their bodies. Grasping his member in her hand, sending shockwaves like electrical currents down his chest and straight to the tip of his erection, she guided him to her. Taking charge, Shane grabbed himself.

Below the pads of his fingers, blood pumped through his shaft. He slid forward.

His muscles tensed at the first penetration. Leaning his forehead on hers, he pushed farther into her body. The spicy scent of red wine washed over his lips when Rose blew out a gasp. He was only able to fit a few inches of himself inside her before having to withdraw.

"Open for me, sugar." His voice was strained and his breath came out heavy. Combing his fingers through her hair, he kissed her lightly. "Relax your muscles so I can get inside you."

Reaching backward and finding her leg, Shane elevated it to his hip. He circled her thigh behind him, her foot digging into the back of his glute.

She caused pain to his biceps with her sharp fingernails as Shane eased his cock inside her again, grunting the instant her taut heat wrapped and contoured around his flesh.

"That's right, sugar." The pressure against his cock gave way. "You're doing good."

Gilding deeper, he slammed his hips into hers, forcing her body and breasts to jump as he planted the last of himself inside her. Wetness. Warmth. Nirvana. Shane rotated his hips, and she tilted back then she expelled another moan. He wanted to laugh. How long had he dreamed of being inside her like this? Now that he was there, Shane never wanted to leave. The blissful squeeze of her silken folds soared up his cock and through his muscles, firing off every pleasure signal in Shane's head until the so-snug suction around him eclipsed all else.

Unpacking every inch save the tip of him, Shane began entering her with gradual pace, each time activating a series of her cries that exploded on his mouth.

Was now a bad time to brag about what great taste he

had? Looking at her, all flushed with puffy lips and half-lidded eyes, he couldn't have picked a better woman.

As he'd noted the morning after he'd first met her, Rose was beautiful from her perfect pussy to those now-red-painted toes, though she wasn't a no-named girl anymore.

This was *his* girl, trembling below his exertion, her vocal cords ringing out his name. He thrust forward, plunging through the soft depths of her pussy. Sensation raged through his body with each empty and fill. Rising to his knees, he brought her along with him. Without exiting her, he wrapped her arms around his back. She hugged his waist with her legs. He kissed every part of her face. Then, gripping her ass, he moved her to a new angle.

"*Shane.*" She didn't stop at saying it once. No, his girl repeated it the same way his cock beat into her body at second intervals, releasing all his tension and all of hers.

Months of coveting, anger and frustration quickened his movements, warping them into an aggressive onslaught that had him clenching his teeth and his body tensing everywhere. Sweat rolling down his back, he sealed their mouths. He wanted to finish with her, but holding back had never been so hard, probably because Shane had never had this type of pleasure.

It was more than their skin striking together like a wooden match to concrete — fast, hard, burning. It was everything Shane had never known he wanted. It was passion. It was claiming.

She was perfect. She was his.

'Don't take riding lessons.'

Lowering his hand, he rubbed her clit with his thumb and delved his tongue into her waiting mouth, never wanting this moment to end.

It was all he could think to do when his heart was so full. He kept it up, kissing and fucking her with everything he had, until the very moment she released his lips to arch her head back.

"Right there. Don't stop that." Rose groaned, her nails and

nipples and legs riding his sweat-drizzled skin. "Please. Oh, God, Shane. I'm about—" A cry pierced through her sentence.

"Look at me." Bringing her face to him, Shane fisted his fingers into her hair, and he let out a groan. Her tight contractions pushed against his upward thrusts. Her impending climax devoured his senses. "I want to see your face." He held her ass cheek in one hand, wrapping his tongue with hers as the pressure on his cock tightened and her legs shook around his hips. Damn it, he wasn't going to—

Shane couldn't even finish the thought, though, because the moment her pussy began convulsing, his brain emptied and his settings blurred. An inferno of all-consuming bliss erupted up his spine and through his cock, spurting out in milky jets. She fell backward to the bed. He fell with her, kissing and pumping. He would never get enough. Everything faded into the background—everything except her clear jade eyes.

* * * *

Waking up to Rose was a surreal feeling.

Shane could get used to it and not just because she was cuddling his chest like he was an oversized teddy bear and naked as the day she was born. Though, that was a perk.

It was seven in the morning and despite staying up all night to indulge in multiple rounds of lovemaking—*sometimes* lovemaking, other times they did what couldn't have been considered anything but straight, animalistic fucking—he wasn't remotely tired.

Refreshed. Rejuvenated. Relieved that when he split open his eyes, the bedroom lit with the gray-blue of early dawn, he didn't see a note at his side but her long hair surrounding her sleeping face. He was experiencing many things, but not exhaustion.

Because he wanted to let her sleep—tangled in his bed

sheets she looked far too cute to wake up—Shane decided to slip out of bed and get some work done before going for his daily run.

When he got back, he'd wake her up with…yup, breakfast in bed.

That's right. Shane was choosing breakfast in bed with his girl instead of going out with the guys like he did every Sunday. It was official, Shane Williams had it bad.

Snorting, he could practically hear Usher's *U Got it Bad* looping in his head. And, no, Shane was not a fan of 'sensual' R & B music. It was another thing, besides awful rom coms, his older sister had subjected him to. He'd even had to go to one of the guy's concerts when he'd been younger because she hadn't had anyone else to go with her. So, he had some Usher songs memorized by heart. Sue him.

After finishing up some designs, he changed into his workout clothes. He took the elevator downstairs. The chilly air blasted into his lungs as he charged down his normal running trail through the city park. A pleasant burn invaded his chest and nostrils.

Gaining speed, he smacked his feet into the sidewalk in time with his drubbing heart. Five miles, sometimes six, would be enough for him to satisfy himself.

Eager to get back to his house, to Rose, today, he made it three. By the time he arrived back at his condo, his skin was soaked with sweat. Droplets of it that had clung to his hair, dripped down his forehead and the nape of his neck. Raking his fingers through the wet strands, he pushed them out of his eyes, attempting to catch his breath.

"Mr. Williams," someone addressed him as he approached the valet of his condominium.

Pivoting on his heel, he turned to the sound. In an instant, he recognized Matthew's security guard from the previous night, unable to recall his name.

The guy couldn't have been more than five foot seven in height. There was a drastic difference in their sizes. Shane was a boulder compared to him. But Matthew had hired him for security, which meant that regardless of how tall he wasn't, he had a specialty that could benefit someone whose income fit him into the one percent. Knowing that, Shane was automatically on edge.

Discomfort moved over Shane when he trailed behind the guard to a nearby coffee shop. He speculated as to what Lucas—he'd gotten his name before agreeing to follow him—had meant when he had said, "Matthew wants to have word with you."

Shane didn't fear anyone—not God, not Satan and not men like Matthew Moreno, who were powerful enough to play both. That didn't stop the nervousness he was feeling.

Why? Shane was confident he knew what was about to come down on him.

Overhearing Matthew repeat the saying Shane had told him a long time back, he realized that Matthew hadn't been talking to Rose. Success being measured in love? Shane believed that with every fiber of his being. The issue was that Matthew didn't.

Instead of answering Rose's question about the definition of success, Matthew had, knowing Shane was listening, given him a warning. Shaking it off, Shane had put it all in the back of his head. Now it was real—a few feet away. As he walked into the shop, the smell of baked bread and coffee hitting him instantly, he couldn't rid himself of the gutting feeling that he'd just sealed Lambda's fate.

* * * *

Italian flowed smoothly from Matthew's lips as he spoke into the cell phone. He lifted his hand in acknowledgment, his face showing an apology.

Shane tapped at the edge of his seat, waiting for Matthew to finish his call. Shane assumed he was doing business. Something Rose and Matthew had in common—the only thing—was that they both loved to work.

Work. Work. Shoot me. Work. Shane loved his job and was

passionate about it, but he loved being outside of work, experiencing nature, more. Matthew had chosen to sit in the back of the coffee shop, away from the other guests. Slow jazz played above them. Lucas was standing at the side of their table, blocking their view of the rest of the coffee shop. Shane couldn't remove his worry as he watched Matthew conduct his phone call. *Is this it?*

"My apologies." Matthew ended his call. "Business per usual." With a silver butter knife and fork, Matthew sliced through a sugary pastry and plopped it in his mouth without peering to Shane.

Shane's jaw ticked, his patience wearing thin.

"Now" — Matthew sat back in his chair once he'd placed his silverware down — "I don't think I need to tell you why I've invited you here, Shane."

The confirmation in Matthew's words sunk into his skin like daggers. His hands tightened into balls below the table.

"I have a good idea," Shane said, "but I'd like you to elaborate." Maybe Shane was wrong. He prayed he was, but as Matthew began speaking, Shane knew he wasn't.

"I make it a habit to steer clear of partnering with companies that could be considered" — he tilted his head, looking off for a moment, like contemplating how to say it — "unstable. Relationships among employees would not be considered stable, Shane. Quite the contrary. I would describe them as being capricious and easily prone to causing complications within the work environment, which may affect employee performances and, in turn, business profits."

Fuck. Shane's heart seemed to climb to his temples. He had been right. Matthew knew, but how? What had given him away? "I don't know what you're talking about."

Matthew's face was serious. "Let's not do this, Shane."

Panic grasping him, Shane clenched his teeth. There had to be a way to convince Matthew to give Lambda a chance, to show him that Rose could never be a threat to this project. Shane grappled with all these things, sweat lining his forehead as anger and fear pummeled him.

"How did you find out?"

Thoughts frenzied, Shane wondered where he had gone wrong the previous night. How would he fix this mess? Fuck the money. Like Malcolm had done his, Shane would take out money from his own savings, his own pay check, if he had to in order to push Lambda further until they fished a big client. All the hard work Rose and the team had put into the Moreno & Blu project so far would be a waste if he couldn't convince Matthew to keep them in the process. That was what made him most upset. Not Lambda's debt from the expansion, but that they all trusted him. Rose. Malc. *Everyone* trusted him.

And Shane had failed them.

Reaching forward, Matthew picked up the coffee mug from the table.

After bringing it to his lips, sipping and asking Shane if he would like his own — *do I look like I want a fucking cup of coffee right now?* — he set it down and resumed, "I'm right, aren't I? You care for her. How long has it been going on, Shane?"

Rage sloshed in his ears as his carefree friend leaned back into his chair like he didn't have a worry in the world.

Shane burned with the need to break something or shout at the top of his lungs. All night he'd tried to conceal his feelings. He'd even stayed in the bathroom for fifteen minutes after his flirtation with Rose, just so that his hard-on would go away, afraid he wouldn't have been able to hide it. He'd made sure not to be obvious, keeping his distant from Rose until Matthew was gone, but no matter how he cut it, Shane was responsible. Helpless strangled him.

Shit. *What did I do?*

He'd put Lambda and the woman he loved at risk…

He loosened his fingers from their fists.

Loved?

The word was unintentional but fit as perfectly as Rose fit in his arms. He loved her? Heart beating faster in response,

Shane said the words out loud.

"I love her."

She was the woman who drove him crazy, the woman who bossed him around and pissed him off more than anyone in the world, and he loved her. Covering his eyes with his hands, he proceeded to drag them over his nose and mouth then, letting them fall, limp, into his lap. "She deserves a chance. Lambda does. I'll do whatever it takes."

How could he explain this to Rose? She would be devastated. All she wanted was a chance to redeem herself and Shane had taken that from her, snatched it away by his selfish need to have her beside him. His body trembled with anger toward himself and his *friend* in front of him.

"Businessman to businessman, I can't allow my company to work with Lambda, given that its founder is romantically involved with an executive. Friend to friend, drop out of the competition, because if you present to the board, you will be rejected."

"I can't." He'd ruined it for Rose. His love for her had stomped her only chance at happiness. What if she didn't forgive him? What if he couldn't find a client large enough to save Lambda in the next two years? He'd lose it all.

"For her sake, you will."

Shane bit the inside of his cheek, but that couldn't keep him for voicing his opinion. "This is bullshit. We have dedicated months to Moreno & Blu. Rose's proposal would impress even your high standards." His hands shook, his words came out hard and aggressive. "Your audacity is astounding." Shane narrowed his eyes. "Who are you to preach about relationships in the workplace? You, more than anyone, should understand—"

"I'm doing this *because* I understand." The shop seemed to quiet, voices hushing as Matthew raised his tone, his coffee mug shaking in his hand. His eyes were wide and dark. Shane felt the café walls closing in on him. "I understand more than anyone the damages relationships can do to business, Shane, which is why I can't allow this.

Now, because of our history, I'll give you one chance. One. If you want a place in this competition, if you want to give Lambda a fighting chance—" Malcolm quieted and a chill crept up Shane's back. "Fire her."

Chapter Seventeen

Vagina ache. We meet again.

Rose gathered the bed sheets above her breasts, and when she sat up from the bed, a whimper ejected from her. Her second night with Shane had been no different than the first in the sense that Rose needed some Advil and a steaming hot shower to relax her muscles.

Her whole body was brutally sore.

Smiling, she ran fingers through her hair. Sore in the best way possible, that was. Being that the bed was empty, Rose browsed around the room. Where had Shane had gone? Tucked underneath the blinking alarm clock that read half past eleven a.m. was a sticky note.

She picked it up.

Went out for a run. Be back soon.
P.S. You're cute when you're sleeping

Was Rose supposed to find it creepy that Shane had checked her out in her sleep? Because she didn't. I had the opposite effect. Rose was flattered by the compliment.

He though I looked cute? She found herself cheesing to the empty room.

Since she was starving and Shane would probably be hungry when he came back from his run, she decided it'd be nice to have breakfast ready for him.

In the corner of the room, her clothing was stacked in a sitting chair.

Spending the night at Shane's hadn't been planned, so she hadn't brought any alternative clothing. She'd have to wear her gown home. Already preparing herself to be bombarded with a hoard of questions from Olive, Rose changed into a pair of Shane's boxers and a Nike shirt she found in his dresser, hoping when he saw her wearing his clothing, he wouldn't mind.

Journeying through his apartment, she stretched her arms out while she walked because she was stiff. Actually, she was a lot of things—warm, achy, happy.

That last one being the most intense.

Everything that had happened the previous day came back to her in a surge of giddiness, though it was followed by doubt and equal worry. She didn't want to focus on what would happen next right now, so she pushed it aside with memories of last night.

Shane's words. His actions. The way he'd pampered and assured her with each gentle kiss and touch. Rose was so terrified to dilute the memories that she forced them out of her head because each time she relived them, her subconscious change tiny details until the story was muddled and misrepresentative.

Instead of focusing on what had happened, she decided to focus on how she had felt—cherished, worshiped, adored. Shane had treated her like a goddess. Again, she smiled.

What does this mean for us?

What are we now?

The questions she tried to displace came back full throttle.

Rose wanted to stay at Lambda. She wanted to be with Shane, but what would Malcolm do if he found out the truth? There was also the issue of her conversation with Matthew. Should she reach out to Mr. Moreno and assure him that her past wouldn't be an issue? What if he wouldn't accept that? There so much doubt and confusion swimming through Rose's mind that she almost didn't notice the sound of keys jingling as she passed through the living room.

Front door opening, Shane entered his condo. Her mouth dropped open and not because of the frustrated curses that followed him inside.

Having taken off his shirt, he'd balled the red cloth in his hand and was wiping the back of his neck with it. Sweat trickled from his hair to his face. The chiseled muscles in his chest and arms gleamed like he'd been oiled for a photo op. Gym shorts hung low on his hips, exposing the dark trail at the center of his abdomen, which was neighbored by defined v-shaped cuts at both sides. It should be illegal for him to look so good.

Noticing her open adoration, Shane smiled. The smile exuded natural confidence, which sent butterflies through her belly.

"Mornin', beautiful. You look nice."

With no other thoughts in her mind except those of lust, Rose traversed the space that separated them with a few short strides. "Sugar, I've got to talk to you about…"

Listening to what he was saying, concentrating in general, was a tremendous task when they were standing this close together—him shirtless, her extremely horny.

She touched his chest, and whatever he was saying died on his lips. Shane was on fire, his skin blazing and slick against her palms. Vagina ache or not, she wanted him again—sweaty, sloppy and right here in the foyer. A rousing frenzy brewed inside her.

Last night he'd treated her so well, showing her his passion in a way that made it unquestionable. She wanted to do the same. A light bulb went off in her head. She'd thought about doing it many times but never had the chance to… until now.

She tugged at his gym shorts.

"Rose, you don't have to. I'm sweat—"

Lowering his bottoms, shorts and briefs, Rose sunk to her knees, and Shane's words were cut off by a sigh. He was already erect but seemed to elongate more when she took his cock in her palm. Shane wheezed before discharging another curse, and she flickered her eyes to his face, finding his eyebrows knitted and lips shiny and wet. She moved her attention back to the hard pole of flesh she was grasping. How the heck had he fit that thing inside her?

In the daylight, he looked bigger. *Huge,* she observed with a sense of satisfaction, not to mention heavy. Weighting down her hand, she had to wrap all ten digits around his girth to feel like her grip was secure. She had never been one to find penises attractive, but Shane had a good-looking one. Veiny and pale with a fuchsia-domed top. Rose wanted to see what he tasted like. So, she did. Peeking it out from between her lips, she let her tongue dash over the head, lapping up a tiny pool of semen that had oozed through the thin slice of flesh there. Shane's hands, which had been cupped over his face, fell into her hair.

Spreading his fingers, he gripped her roots.

She did it again, this time allowing her tongue to slide patiently over the creamy accumulation, and she was rewarded with his enormous groan that raced up her body.

Encouraged by his language, Rose took the entire bulbous head into her mouth, sucking on it. Shane tasted sweet and salty, and it made her cheeks and body enliven with heat.

Squeezing her fingers around him, she proceeded to slide them down to the far base of his cock and bring them back up until the side of her fist touched her lips. She kept doing this, pushing more and more of his tangy liquid in between her siphoning cheeks.

Shane was making a lot of pleasant noises, every one of them affecting Rose in a different way. Part of her wanted to stop and ask him to take her right then. Part of her wanted to suck him harder until he spurted his gooey liquids down her throat. All of her wanted to give him satisfaction in whatever form it came. Since she'd moved her hands so they now rested on the sides of his muscular thighs and he had started his own unique rhythm, forcing his cock deeper into her mouth, Rose decided the 'suck him harder' form was best.

Digging her nails into his skin, she took him down with enthusiastic swallows, shivering when the tip of his cock rubbed the back of her throat, and he wasn't even halfway in. He retracted from her mouth, his shaft covered with enough saliva that it shined like the rest of his body, before pushing her lips wide open again. The rock hardness stroking the inside of her mouth was an erotic contrast to her soft cheeks and tongue. Shane jerked his hips when she wrapped her fist around him once more and cupped his testicles. She loved how the bulging veins in his cock protruded beneath her fingers. She began coasting her hand back and forth, the way he seemed to move his hips. Losing herself in the feeling and taste of him, Rose demonstrated how much she appreciated everything he'd done the previous night.

"Whoa. Slow." His contrasting tone fought with his words. "Slow down, sugar. I'm gonna come if you keep that up. I don't want to come in your mouth. Sugar—"

His speech was replaced by a groan. She lightly nibbled on the head of his cock. Pacing her fingers to match his quick breaths, she stroked him hard. His legs were shaking like the building was moving beneath his feet. Her own body ached for his touch.

"Rose. Oh— Stop." He tightened his hand in her hair. "Now." Lethal undertones made her quit what she was doing and glance up at him.

As fear—not fear *of* him but from fear of the idea of upsetting him—buzzed through her, she dropped Shane's penis from her mouth, running her tongue over her lips, tasting his premature ejaculation there. Shaking his head, he bent. He hooked his strong hands underneath her armpits, and he elevated Rose so that she was standing in front of him.

"Not in your mouth," he chastised. "Your pussy." Letting his hand plummet, he clutched her right at the center of her thighs.

Her insides hailed with delight and arousal.

"*This* is where I finish. Always." His steamy brown eyes were intent and his tone level. "You got that, pretty Rose? As long as this is mine—and that will be an indefinite

237

amount of time — I'll come here."

She didn't get to answer him or relish in his possessive words — or contemplate why she found them so sexy, domineering had never been her thing — because she was being turned around. Bringing up fond memories of their first encounter, he pinned her against the wall. Who knew it would become her favorite pastime?

His boxers — the ones *she* was wearing — were pushed off and were falling down her legs. Shane lifted her shirt over her head. The second she was naked he brought her feet off the ground. Soon, she was in his arms with her shoulder blades flat on the wall, moaning because he was kissing her mouth and breasts like crazy. Circling her legs around his waist, she gasped when Shane dragged his cock through the fissure at her middle.

He circled around her opening, and Rose pushed her pelvis upward, moaning higher as the move placed the cockhead she'd just been sucking on right inside her, nestled among her flexing corridors. It was so hard compared to its surroundings. She rotated her hips, desperate for more of him.

"Condom," he reminded in a growl on her lips, but like she'd been doing since he'd walked in from his run, she decided not to pay attention.

Pleasure was a powerful thing. It could make even the smartest people act without thinking. A habit-forming drug, the *idea* of pleasure alone was enough to have one groveling. The *idea* of being connected to Shane in the most intimate way, without barriers, was as powerful as her imagining how phenomenal it would feel to have his bare flesh setting hers ablaze. It was enough to make Rose want to behave with reckless abandon. Squeezing her legs around his waist and shifting herself, she pushed him farther inside her. It was just an inch, or maybe two, but it was enough.

Both released sounds of ecstasy. They were shaking and frantic with the urge to continue, but Shane didn't move like she wanted him to. Hair, dark and silky, cut off pieces of her vision as his forehead touched hers. Their breath mingled.

"You're killing me, sugar."

"I'm on birth control." When she had been in the relationship with Simon, he'd wanted her to get the Depo-Provera shot. For years, she'd been getting it. Moving to North Carolina hadn't changed the habit.

Shane looked at her, unresponsive. His face flushed.

"Have you ever —?" she began.

Rose had gone without a condom with Simon before, but they had both been tested numerous times, and after she found out he was cheating, she had gotten tested again.

"Only once with my ex. Since then, no. I get tested —"

"Every six months." She remembered a conversation they'd had on the matter at work once. Yes, they'd had conversations — initiated by Shane — about sex and protection and all that jazz.

"Are you sure you want this, sugar?"

He pressed his face to her cheek. His breaths were coming hard. It seemed like he was trying to control himself from moving without permission.

"With you?" Running her hands up the muscles in his upper arms, she answered by nodding. Angling her lips to his sweat-coated face, she brushed their mouths. "Yes."

He brought his mouth to her jaw, withdrawing his erection.

Clutching harder on to the back of her thighs, his kisses started on her cheek and ended at her lips. Opening her mouth for him, she received the kiss, and as he pushed his tongue inside, his hips came barreling forward, crushing her against the wall and shoving his cock, with toe-curling force, through every crevasse of her narrow canal. She sobbed, wrestling with the pain she attributed to his girth, and when Rose thought she was so stuffed that she was going to shatter, Shane retreated.

"Rose." His throaty voice became faint as he plunged into her once more, intense pleasure following every movement.

"Jesus, Rose, you're the best thing I've ever felt."

There was no delicate easing inward like there had been last night.

Shane thrust his lower half to hers again, not stopping until his whole cock was swallowed inside her. He stayed like that long enough for her to feel their heartbeats unite where they joined, before drawing his thick erection out, slow enough to torture her.

Rose shook, every molecule in her body attuned to a single sensation—pleasure—as Shane moved her up and down, his fingers squeezing the back of her thighs. Each time his steel mass delved through her tissues, it rubbed the place inside her that tightened her muscles, blurred her vision and pushed her one step closer to the starry-eyed brink. Bodies colliding, they were hot, flaming with desire, and when he kissed her, it was like two stars imploding.

She incinerated, feeling as if her entire being would splinter with the way he pumped forward, filling her with heat that expanded through her limbs and formed into an endless ripple up her flesh. She struggled to keep her moans quiet as his rhythm quickened into a zealous pounding, but he gave her one of his husky growls and told her to be loud. He loved her loud, he told her. Loved hearing her yell his name, he went on. Between all the noises they were making, neither of them heard the working of the lock or the door opening.

"Shane, what the hell?" Bub started.

"Fuck," Shane hissed, and his arms came to circle Rose's head. Still inside her, he lowered her face to his shoulder so Bub wouldn't see her. "Close the fuckin' door!"

"Rose?" Behind Bub came a second voice, one that Rose recognized.

"Don't." But it was already too late for Shane's warning.

Rose had already lifted her head, and just as the door was being closed, her vision connected with the voice she recognized.

Malcolm.

Rose had been in more humiliating situations.

Actually...no, she hadn't.

This was by far the most humiliating situation she had ever found herself in—more humiliating than the #teamrose and #teamjessica texts that had gone around her office, more humiliating than getting fired in front of her entire team for assaulting her co-worker or having her ex-fiancé shout out how he'd stopped loving her after their third fuck...in front of her mother and brother during their final conversation. That scene had beaten the world record for embarrassing scenarios, and Rose had never imagined it could be outperformed. She was wrong.

Worried because Shane hadn't shown up to their normal Sunday breakfast outing, Bub and Malcolm had decided to stop by his apartment. Too preoccupied plowing his boss into senselessness, Shane hadn't answered their phone calls when they'd gotten there, so Bub—his cousin *would* have a key to his apartment—decided to let himself and Malcom in, and the two men had gotten a front row seat for the most humiliating moment in her life. They should have brought popcorn.

"If it's any consolation, I didn't see anything." Bub shuffled on his feet.

He rubbed the back of his neck, something Shane also did when he was uncomfortable, before reaching out to hand Rose the beer he'd gotten for her from the kitchen.

It wasn't, but rather than say so, she applied the glass rim to her lips and tilted her head back. Needing alcohol more than her composure, she gulped the whole bottle of Yuengling down in a single, harsh take, in preparation to deal with the repercussions of her actions. Malcolm had warned Shane not to sleep with her or she'd be let go. It was safe to say that Rose now considered herself jobless. Bottle drained, she set it on the living room table.

Glancing up at Shane's cousin so she could thank him

for fetching her something to drink, Rose found his mouth was wide open and his eyes were stretched in a dramatic way that displayed his disbelief. Her face flushed, its temperature rising.

He has to have seen a woman chug a beer before. He owns a bar, for Christ's sake.

Nevertheless, she turned away, embarrassed by the unwanted attention and still reeling over the fact that he'd seen her getting screwed like a nail into the wall by his relative.

When Malcolm and Shane came out of his home office — *what is taking them such a long time, anyway?* — the first thing she wanted to do was offer the CEO an apology.

Not for sleeping with Shane but for breaking Malcolm's trust.

As a professional, Rose couldn't forgive herself for caving into Shane, especially because Malcolm had taken a huge risk hiring her as marketing director in the first place. Second, she wanted to peacefully resign. Rose wouldn't be able to take it if she were fired twice in one year.

Could she be any more of a screw-up?

There was no way she was going to get another chance to fix her reputation that'd been left in pieces when she'd moved from Texas. Finding Lambda? It had been the needle of hope in the haystack that had been her destroyed career. On top of that, Shane had invited her to dinner with Mr. Moreno so she could have an advantage in the project, and she'd screwed everything up, not just for herself, but for everyone at Lambda. Disgust knotted in her stomach.

Tiffany had been spot on when she'd said Rose would fall for Lambda. Over the months, she'd grown to love working there. The atmosphere was fresh and fun. The employees weren't employees but good friends. A team of trusted confidants, Lambda was a family that had welcomed her with open arms. Rose had even come to like that they all referred to her as 'boss'. The thought of their disappointed faces after finding out what happened and, because of it, there was no longer a marketing director to spearhead the project that could take their company off the ground, made Rose queasy.

The third thing she had to do was beg Shane for his forgiveness because, regardless of Malcolm being his friend, Rose didn't know how he would get out of this situation with his job unscathed. Fired or not, Shane would still be put into a compromising situation because of her. It wasn't bad enough ruining her own career. She had to jeopardize the careers of the people she loved.

Moisture rolled down her cheek, but she refused to burst into sobs. There would be no more crying and no more feeling sorry for herself. She was going to take responsibility for what she'd created. Rose couldn't allow the rest of the team to suffer at her expense. She'd have to find a way to coax Malcolm to let her work on the Moreno & Blu presentation until completion. Even if she didn't reap the benefits of signing the account as a client, given that they won, or, maybe, if there was no way Malcolm would let her stay on board, she could convince Shane to step up his game and take the role of leader for the project. Behind closed doors, she would help him work on it.

"You want me to get you something, Rose?" Bub asked. "A napkin?"

"No thanks, Bub. I'm going to see what's holding them up." Standing from the couch, Rose swallowed back her rising fear. She started toward Shane's office.

The door was cracked open when she got there. She would have walked in. She wanted to. Though her insides were all shook up and her heart was zooming at a rate way too fast to be healthy, she planned to fake confidence when proposing her idea to the CEO.

But instead of joining them, Rose paused.

Right at the door she stopped, incapable of pushing it open.

"It must be so easy to be you," Malcolm said. "Not caring about the consequences of your actions seems so much

funnier than being the one to pick up after your messes."
Messes? Was that what she was considered now? "Yet even when you put your company in these situations, you still get to prance around Lambda without consequence. You don't deserve to be founder."

Founder? What was Malcolm talking about? Shane, the founder?

"You don't think I know how much of a mistake last night was? But what do you want me to do, Malc? Tell her we're done? This is *my* fault. She thinks we have a chance. I'm sorry, Malcolm. I'll fix this, but we can't fire her—" Their conversation going silent, the men turned toward the office door as it opened.

Mistake? Feeling unsteady, she pushed the door wider.

Last night was a mistake?

"Rose."

"A mistake?" She repeated his words, and Shane's face turned pale, ghost white.

'She thinks we have a chance.'

"Rose," he croaked. "That's not—"

Ignoring him, Rose turned from the room.

Clutching her stomach, she paced down the hallway, sickness building up in her throat.

The memories of that *mistake* and the mistake she'd made again this morning, thinking that last night *meant* something for them, that they *were* something, seized her mind, close to paralyzing her with pain, but she pushed through it. Rose forced herself through his apartment, trying to keep his poisonous words out of her head as shame and regret slammed through her body.

She needed to get away. *Founder? Mistake?* He'd lied to her. He'd said he didn't lie, but that was what all lairs said, and she'd believed him. She loved him. Wiping her tear-stricken face, Rose didn't care that she was bawling or that she was wearing a pair of gym shorts, a pajama shirt with no bra and no shoes. *Away* was all that she could think about, hear or feel—the furious need to get as far away from this place as possible — until someone caught her arm.

"Rose." Shane held onto her upper arm.

"Let me go." Tears rolling down her face, she was too weak to shout, and she wouldn't have if she could. Rose wasn't going to waste another ounce of her energy on Shane Williams.

"Sugar —"

"I never want to see you again."

Rose yanked her arm out of his hand, wanting nothing more than to run. If she ran, maybe she wouldn't feel them anymore — his words bulldozing against her heart, pounding her into nothing. She'd trusted him and he'd lied right to her face. He'd promised her he would be honest. Promises weren't worth a damn thing. Hadn't Simon taught her that? Looking up to the man she thought she loved, Rose brushed the tears away and held her chin up. Meeting his eyes hurt, but she stayed strong. She had to. "I'm leaving."

'She thinks we have a chance.'

Shane held on to the sides of her shoulders. "Let me explain."

"Let me leave, Shane." Fresh tears clouded her vision.

"No!"

Even stretched with anger, his features were handsome, and she hated it. She *hated* herself for falling for his charm, for making herself vulnerable.

"Damn it, Rose, this isn't the part where you overhear something that could be misunderstood then get pissed and leave. No, that *isn't* what's happening here." The spark of fury in his eyes grew into a flare.

Rose tried to loosen from him, but it was impossible.

"You are going to stay, and you're going to let me explain, because I love you, God damn it, and I'm not going to let you leave without knowing how much."

She held her breath, her heart speeding through the pain. *What did he say?*

"We're gonna head out," Malcolm interrupted.

Rose shielded her face as they passed, too ashamed to meet their eyes.

When Malcolm and Bub had gone, Shane resumed. "I spoke to Matthew this morning. He told me... He found out, Rose. He told me Lambda needed to drop out of the competition, because if we entered, we would be rejected. Either that or"—he shook his head, dropping his hands from her—"something that wasn't an option. Rose, stay. Let's talk about this. I—"

"Rejected?" Matthew had *rejected* Lambda already? He hadn't even seen the presentation. "What exactly did he find out?"

Was this because of her talk with him?

Did Matthew reject Lambda because he knew Rose was using him? Using Shane?

Stepping closer, Shane brought his hands to her face, his eyes searching hers. "He saw it clearly. He saw what I couldn't hide, that I'm in love with you, and he was right."

It was the lowest she'd ever heard his voice.

"I love you, Rose. I love you, even though I shouldn't, but all I want is for you to love me, too."

Her fingers itched to comfort him, to run through his hair, up his arms, tell him she loved him back. Sealing her emotions, Rose tried to keep a clear head.

Shane loved her? How could she believe him? Stories floated around the office of how good he was at making women fall head over heels for his *bad-boy* charm. Almost as good as he was at ending it with those girls when he got bored. Rose wouldn't fall for it. No matter how genuine he seemed, Rose couldn't trust him. He said he'd never lie. How could she trust anything that came out of his mouth when he'd been lying from the beginning?

"Say something."

Her pain reflected on his expression.

"Please say something to me, sugar."

"You're the founder of Lambda?" she asked, hoping she was wrong, that she had misheard Malcolm earlier. How

246

could he keep something that big from her?

"Sort of," Shane said, and her heart seemed to sink into her stomach. "That's doesn't matter, Rose. I only had connections and money. Lambda —"

"But, it *does* matter." Shane was supposed to be the one honest person in her life.

Yet here she was chewing him out, but hadn't she been dishonest, too? Rose had used him, used all of them. Didn't she deserve this? A lie for a lie. "I have to go. I can't be here."

"I care about you. Rose, I love you." The determination on his face was replaced with despair. "Rose?"

Rose's heart broke as his eyes watered over. It was too confusing. Rose didn't know what was true anymore or if the truth even mattered.

Even if she weren't getting fired by Malcolm, Matthew had rejected Lambda. Everything was shattered. Her hopes of having a nightmare-free life were gone. Melissa and that man would haunt her forever. This would never have happened if she'd stuck to her plan. She should never have strayed from it, never fallen in love.

"I was going to leave if Moreno & Blu won," she said, and Shane's face fell. "I enjoyed the sex between us, but you and Lambda were just a stepping-stone for me to get ahead in my career. Nothing else."

He dropped his hands from her cheeks. "What?"

"I'm sorry, but there was nothing special between us and there never will be." Turning her back, she left him with the look of a man who'd had his heart ripped out of his chest, who'd been destroyed.

Chapter Eighteen

"Tell me a story." Rose lifted her head from the couch to where Olive was sitting on the living room floor, painting her toenails.

From her position, Olive pouted. "A story? Oh, I've got one!" Olive cleared her throat. "There once was a woman named Paddy. She liked to call her boyfriend Daddy. She sat on his cock and gave it a rock —"

"Olivia Wayward!" Holton shouted from the kitchen, and Olive snapped her lips closed, ending story time with a smile. "I'll tell you later."

Her brother came out of the kitchen with three cans of beer and handed one to Rose. "You will tell her no such thing, dirty girl." Olive's beer came with a kiss.

Rose scrunched her nose. "Gross." Seeing Olive kiss the guy version of her was weird. "Does dating my twin brother mean that you're like sexually attracted to me or something?" Rose asked, and that her curiosity was genuine made her concerned.

"You have a nice ass," Olive replied, matter-of-factly.

Holton coughed up his beer.

"This conversation is so out of the scope of what I can handle. Let's reel it in, ladies. We've got a movie to watch. The sooner it's over, the better."

Rose laughed, maybe the first real one in weeks. Her brother's distaste for chick flicks reminded her of... "Or I could not watch a movie and drown my sorrow in vodka," she murmured, forcing the image of Shane away.

Holton and Olive looked at each other.

Rose noticed, as had everyone else around her, that

her attitude had been sour for two weeks…ever since her incident with Shane, Malcolm and, let's not forget, Bub Fowler. Along with her mouth hardly opening to do anything but complain, her body was exhausted, lips chapped and hair like a bird's nest atop her head. Not going into work meant not having to wear pretty skirts and high heels — the good life.

Complacency. Unemployment. Actually… not unemployment, per se.

For reasons unknown to her, Malcolm had told Rose she could take all the time she needed to decide if working at Lambda Digital was what she wanted to do. She had sat down with him earlier that week, and he'd listened to her profuse apologies with his normal calm persona before inserting his two cents.

Rose *had* misunderstood his conversation with Shane. They hadn't been talking about *her* but about losing Moreno & Blu as a client. Malcolm was willing to bring her back on board and risk her relationship with Shane because of one important thing. Lambda was losing money. Malcolm had confessed this with a sullen expression, explaining that Moreno & Blu was their ticket out of debt. Rose had screwed it up for everyone, though he hadn't added that part. Malcolm was willing to allow her to stay because they needed her and Shane both, he'd said, but most importantly, he'd called them family. Lambda was a family and Rose, according to Malcolm, had become a part of that, which still made her want to go into full-blown tear mode.

Family.

Then Malcolm had told her something else, something that wasn't CEO-to-employee professional, but rather advice from a person who cared about both her and Shane. *Blondie.* That was the name, outside of *Peeping Tom* — she shivered, recalling how she'd gotten it — that Shane had dubbed her before he had been aware of her actual name. Shane and he had had frequent conversations about this mysterious 'Blondie'. Malcolm had never seen his close friend so enamored. Was that another reason he had decided to forgive them both?

Plucking a tissue out of its paper box, Rose blew her nose. Crying sucked. Outside of making her feel like a child, her tears had come so frequently that her cheeks were raw from having been scrubbed with tissue paper so often.

Contemplating every angle and scenario, Rose still had no idea what to do or what next move was the right one. Two weeks of ignored voicemails sat in her phone, and two weeks of trying to figure out what she *actually* wanted discombobulated her thoughts. Rose was being pulled like a tug of war between two lives—the one she always thought she would lead far away from this place and the one with Shane. But hadn't she already decided that Shane was worth forsaking her five-year plan? More than perfect, Shane was flawed.

He was in love with her? Since when?

He was the *founder* of Lambda Digital?

How could she have missed so much?

For months, he'd taken her whipping him into shape. He could have stopped her any time, but he hadn't? Why not? Why hadn't he told her the truth? These thoughts shook in her head like dice in the palm before a big roll to determine if she would win or lose.

Again, she found herself mad at fate for bringing *him*.

At the insistence of Holton and Olive, who were 'trying things out', Rose was watching a romantic comedy with them because the cure to heartbreaks was seeing Ryan Gosling shirtless—or that was what Olive had told her. To be more specific, she'd said, "A shirtless Ryan Gosling can make any woman forget about her man." Rose prayed Olive was right because Shane, his agonizing face as she'd walked away from him, was all she was able to think about.

With her legs thrown across Holton's lap, she fell into the movie. Sometime before her heartache had been cured by Ryan Gosling's abs, Holton tapped on her leg. He reached over the couch and dug Rose's phone out from between the cushions.

"Your phone's vibrating," he said.

"Ignore it," Rose answered too fast.

"Are you ever going to talk to him, Rosey?"

If *him* meant Shane, then —

"It doesn't say 'Shane'." Holton stared at her screen. "It's a New York number. It says —"

"New York?" She craned her neck to see her phone. Confirming that it was a Manhattan area code, she reached across her brother's lap and snatched it from his hand.

"Hello?" Moving into the hallway, she answered, hoping it was the call she'd been expecting for weeks. "Hello, Mr. Moreno? Is this Matthew — ?"

"Miss Berkowitz." Matthew's casual voice spoke over her.

"Matthew." *Holy* — He'd returned her call. He'd really returned her call. She was on the phone with Matthew Moreno — the millionaire philanthropist, the event planning tycoon, the *asshole* who'd taken away Lambda's right to run in the project they'd been working on for months. "You got my messages." Her voice was packed with heat.

"My assistant says you have been rather persistent about getting a hold of me."

Matthew had to have a smirk on his face. She just knew it.

"If this is regarding my decision to —"

"How could you tell Shane you saw some *feelings* between us, therefore screw all the work that I've done and Lambda's team has done?" It was like a geyser exploded the second she opened her mouth. "We both know this isn't about Shane and me. We did nothing to persuade you we were more than friends." Unless Matthew had the ability to read minds, there was no way he could have known that Shane and Rose cared for one another. Which meant —

"This is about my past, isn't it?" Matthew had to have been covering himself, blaming it on a relationship he couldn't possibly have known existed. "You're punishing everyone for *my* mistake?" Rose took a deep breath. Yelling at a millionaire was kind of exhilarating, but if she suspected

251

she'd get a rise out of Matthew Moreno, she was wrong.

"Are you finished?" he inquired.

"Um." Caught off guard by the boredom in his tone, like he hadn't gotten an earful from her – or didn't care – she didn't know how to respond. "Yes?"

"Let's get to the real reason you called."

She scoffed. The world thought this guy was a nice person? "And, pray tell, what is that, Mr. Moreno? Tell *me* why I've been calling *you*."

"I did nothing but confront Shane with a suspicion."

Rose curled her fingers around her phone *hard*.

"Of his own doing, his feelings were made clear."

"What suspicion?" That night there had been nothing too suspicious happening. Rose and Shane had barely spoken at the dinner. "No, you told him you knew the truth."

She could imagine Mr. Moreno's face as he spoke, cold, his eyes lacking empathy, sitting at his desk with his rich-kid posture – legs crossed, shoulders straight, chin high and entitled.

"Why would I tell him something like that, Miss Berkowitz?"

"You're saying that you didn't actually know about his feelings for me?"

Her fury rose. Thinking Matthew had learned about his feelings for Rose, Shane had confessed? It made sense, perfect sense. Matthew was a businessman, a high-stakes gambler. Confronting Shane with what he suspected could be true couldn't have been difficult. It had been a huge risk, but it had been one worth taking for his company. He'd do anything for Moreno & Blu – lie, manipulate, betray.

"You did it on purpose, didn't you? How could you do this to your friend?"

How could she do this to Shane? Lie to him. Manipulate him. Betray Lambda.

"I don't believe the most important thing to our friend is the Moreno & Blu partnership," he asserted with the same conviction he must have used to manipulate Shane.

"Relationships like yours and Shane's don't work out in the end. I won't bring that into my company."

"You—" You *what*? *You asshole? You liar?*

Matthew had done what was best for Moreno & Blu as Rose had tried to do what was best for herself by coming to Lambda and playing Shane when she'd found out that he and Matthew were friends. Tears dripped down her face. "Goodbye, Mr. Moreno." She had nothing more to say to a person like him.

"Miss Berkowitz?"

"What?" What did he want now? To tell her how pathetic she was?

"Success, in whatever definition it's assigned, is meaningless without love."

Success is…? "Well then, you're the most unsuccessful person I've ever met." Rose gripped the phone tightly. "You don't think I can see the real reason you're doing this?"

"Excuse me?"

"I grew up without a father, too." She overlooked his intake of air and the crack in her voice as she continued her rant. "I never went through the same things you did. I can't begin to think of how much pain comes along with having your life publicized, but you persevered. You did something I could never do. You didn't let your past define you. You married the man you loved, dared to pursue things others wouldn't dream of doing and created a company outside of your family."

"Miss Berkowitz, this is not appropriate."

"Everyone knows you and Brendon aren't together, but I know something other people don't." Mr. Moreno's decision hadn't been about her working with Shane at all, or her past. He'd seen his family in Shane and Rose. Had seen his relationship with Brendon, and he'd resented it because it was what he didn't have. "You love him still. Even if you're scared the same thing that happened with your parents will happen to you and Brendon, you miss him. And I'll tell you something, Mr. Moreno. I love Shane.

He and I made a great team, just like you and Brendon have for so long. I'm not going to let you take that away. You took Lambda from me when I finally thought I'd found a home, but I will not let your bitterness stand in the way of loving that man. At one point, I admired you. Now all I think is that you need to grow up. I'm sorry for your pain, I really am, Mr. Moreno, but you're *not* your mother and father, and you never will be."

And Rose wasn't the same woman she had been when she'd moved to North Carolina.

It was time for her to fight for what she cared about instead of running from her past.

"Is that all you wanted, Miss Berkowitz?" His voice was laced with tension.

"One last thing." She gritted her teeth. "You'll see Lambda Digital at that competition. I may not be a part of their team anymore, but they'll be there. That, I promise."

Then silence. She had hung up on Matthew Moreno.

Staring at her home screen, she tried to understand what had happened. Energy rushed through her system, pumping her heart faster. Words had overcome her. She bit her bottom lip, not believing she'd just had that conversation. What had he said? *'Success is meaningless without love.'*

He was right. In Texas, she'd been successful, on her way to the top, but she and Simon hadn't been in love. She had been miserable. Her nightmares had still racked her brain.

No matter how good she'd been at her job or how comfortable she'd been there, on track with her five-year plan, she had been so unhappy. She thought if she could just succeed more, if she could just make up for her past — then she'd be content, but the happiest she'd ever felt had been in Shane's embrace.

Tears coated her fingers as she brought them to her face, wanting to be in his arms again, to hear his voice. Was it too late? There was only one way to find out. Clearing her eyes with her hand, she sniffled and began to dial Mr. Fletcher.

Rose knew what she had to do.

Chapter Nineteen

Rose stepped into Lambda Digital for the very last time.

She remembered when she had first seen the graffiti on the walls. She'd found it so nerve-racking and *different*. It was the exact feeling she'd had when she'd laid eyes on *him* – beautiful and everything unattainable in her perfectly planned-out life. Now Rose knew the history of the colorful, geometric designs. She knew the hands that had drawn them – daring hands, intimate and passionate. Her throat closed. It was Shane Williams, all right.

Resignation letter in hand, she headed to Malcolm's office, but when she got there, she found the lights were off. Malcolm wasn't in his office. Rose frowned. She checked the time. It was ten in the morning. Where could he have gone? She chanced a peek at Shane's office, disappointed that his lights were off, too.

Figuring they were both in meetings, Rose followed the hallways. She'd have to come back another time to clear her office, wanting to wait to give Malcolm the letter herself.

For the first time in forever, Rose didn't have a plan. There was something freeing about the idea of her walking out of the building and not having a clue as to where she'd go next.

Visiting Melissa's family was on her list. Rose wanted to see Melissa's grave, to say goodbye to her and the memories that had shaken Rose day and night for years. She wanted to move on. She only had one life. It was time she started living it. There was so much she wanted to experience, too – skydiving, mountain biking, driving across the country.

As she traveled through the cozy walkway in the place

that had become her second home, Rose tried to keep the good memories out of her head. She couldn't handle them. But all she saw when she passed the conference room was *him* – every after-hours meeting and every flirtatious joke she'd hated in the daytime but had loved at night. The lobby was filled with recollections of group lunches and laughter, her riding a bike for the first time in ages. Lord, she had been so embarrassed when Shane had tried to teach her.

Employees waved to her as she passed. Some came to her and struck up conversation, wondering where she'd been for two weeks. It seemed they didn't know what had happened. They probably wouldn't look at her the same way once they found out. She gave them hugs, extra hard. Tears filled her eyes but she made herself strong, trying to contain them until she reached her car. The metallic sound of the elevator opening greeted her at the front entrance. Malcolm and Tiffany entered the floor, Malcolm's head turned toward his companion as they spoke business.

Rose paused. "Mr. Fletcher."

They stopped and looked up, a lively energy surrounding them. "Rose," Malcolm said.

Tiffany dropped her eyes to the envelope. "You don't have to go."

"I…" Rose's stomach turned. It looked like some people *did* know what had happened. Despite the nausea gushing through her, she managed to walk forward to meet them. "Thank you, Tiffany. I'll miss you all, but I have to do this."

She handed Malcolm the envelope.

Instead of taking it, he explained, "What Tiffany is saying is that you don't need to go, Rose. I would like you to stay with us at Lambda Digital and spearhead the Moreno & Blu project. We have one month left to perfect our proposal."

"I'm sorry?" She shook her head, looking between them in confusion. "I don't understand what you're saying." Rose had heard from Malcolm that Matthew had specifically asked for her to leave Lambda for the company to continue in the competition, which was why she was resigning. "Mr.

Fletcher, Tiffany, I know you want me to stay, but Lambda needs this client and—"

Malcolm stopped her. "I received an interesting phone call this morning from Matthew Moreno."

Rose's heart froze. *What did Matthew say to him? Does Malcolm know about our phone call?*

"He has decided to allow Lambda Digital to participate in this campaign, as is."

As is. She was certain her eyes were bulging out of her head. Malcolm's smile brightened and he began nodding to confirm she'd heard him correctly.

"Something made him have a change of heart," Malcolm said as Rose stared at him and Tiffany, speechless with disbelief. "Mr. Moreno wants you on this, Rose. As a matter of fact, he said he was enthusiastic about seeing what you and Shane have put together."

"Me?" Rose pointed to herself.

"You and Shane—together," Tiffany added, and the way she said it made Rose blush.

Excitement coursed through her. Rose could hardly believe it. What had made Matthew change his mind? She didn't want to jinx fate by asking him herself, but she couldn't shake the idea that it had something to do with their conversation. "Does Shane know?"

"No, but as lead on the Moreno project, you should be the one to tell him. I'll send you the address where he is." Malcolm took out his cell phone. "We'll need you both back ASAP."

Tiffany stepped forward. "You'll stay?"

Yes. Of course. Rose nodded, tears spilling over her cheeks as Tiffany wrapped her arms around Rose's neck and squealed.

"Good"—Malcolm nodded beside them—"because we've got a competition to win."

* * * *

Shane's lungs burned like they'd been dipped in hellfire. His legs screamed in pain as he rode his mountain bike up the forest's trail.

When Rose had left—cold, hard pain rolled up his chest and it was difficult inhaling, a recent sensation that had come along with the mention of her name—he had called Malcolm to explain that he needed some time off. Malc had given him two weeks, so Shane had gone to his cabin near Dupont State Forest. He had to clear his mind and Eight Ball wouldn't cut it this time. No, he needed away from everything. Shane wanted to use his trip to figure out alternative ways to getting Lambda out of debt and getting one green-eyed boss back. There was no way he'd allow her to quit. She had to stay. Would she even want to stay? He thought back to their last conversation.

Shane wasn't an idiot. He realized that Rose had come into her position knowing that the Moreno project would be her big break. Back then, he had seen on her face that she'd wanted to run...until she'd found out who he really was. Anyone in her situation would have done the same thing. Did the confirmation hurt him? A little. Did he blame her? Never. At one point, he'd wanted to use her, too, but for something much worse—for sex. He wasn't one to compare, but he guaranteed the vote for whose intention was worse would lean in his favor.

His body jolted with each rocky bump of tires on dirt. The smell of nature, woods and soil slammed into him faster than the wind against his face. When his muscles, pained and sore from overuse, couldn't take the trail anymore, he headed back to his cabin. Leaves shattered below his pursuit. Spring was here, but it wasn't as beautiful as he remembered it being last year. It didn't ease the ache in his chest. For so long he had thought that by living without rules he would never feel as helpless as he had when his pop had been alive or when Lennon had died. He was wrong, *so* damn wrong. Nothing—not even being helpless—was as bad as her walking away from him, but not for long. Shane was winning her back. He had to. He loved her. Who was he kidding? Shane had likely fallen in love with her the second she'd told him off in his office. He'd take a page from her book — be stubborn as hell until she was in his arms again, because there was one thing Shane wasn't wrong about and that was you didn't give up on the people you loved.

When he pulled up, he had no breath left.

Shane removed his sweaty helmet and shook his wet hair out. Eyes closed, he took as much air into his lungs as possible. *How* was the big question. How would he win — ?

Someone cleared their throat.

The harsh sun stung his eyes. With his hand, he wiped the sweat from them to make sure he wasn't seeing things. A mirage. Golden light streamed through the trees and bathed her in warmth, brightening her skin so she glowed, radiant, or maybe that was what love looked like. Her hair hung in a braid over her shoulder. Shane wanted to kiss the exposed skin of her neck where a low-hanging shirt teased his imagination. With his entire body yearning to rush over to take her in his arms, he had to use every muscle to stay where he was, to speak in an even tone.

"Rose?" *What is she doing here?*

"Hey," she said then chewed on her bottom lip.

Shane had missed her voice and her eyes, soft and innocent, and her button nose that he wanted right next to his. How had she found him? Was she making good on her promise and coming to say goodbye? *No.*

"I went to see Malcolm today. He gave me your address."

Worry mounted his shoulders. "And…are you staying?"

It was difficult for her, he got that. After her assault, she'd wanted perfection to make up for the murder of a young girl she had blamed on herself. Perfection wasn't something Shane could offer her, but if she'd let him he would offer her his best each day.

It wasn't what she had planned for all her life, but it was everything he could give.

He almost didn't believe his eyes when Rose nodded, her

cheeks blushing the way he loved, and if he hadn't had a favorite moment or memory in his life before, he did now. His heart swelled as a brave smile covered her face. She met his eyes with new confidence. He was so still, afraid to breathe, afraid this moment would vanish, *she* would vanish, if he moved.

"I'll continue my work at Lambda Monday morning. We've got a lot of work to do. Mr. Moreno has decided the Lambda Digital will participate in the competition as is."

He tightened his hands on the bike handles. When had *that* happened?

"I will be marketing director and head this project. As the head of creative, you'll be under my authority." Her hair ruffled in the wind. "Do you understand what that means, Mr. Williams?"

His tone was defiant. "You sure that's what you want, sugar?" *Him? His flaws?* Because if she said yes, Shane planned on never letting her go.

Her lips raised. "I'm certain."

The sunlight had broken into his bloodstream now. Happiness made him dizzy. He didn't know why Matthew had done what he'd done, but he was thankful.

Shane dropped his bike. "I'm gonna disobey you," he challenged.

Rose lifted her chin. "Disobey me."

"I'm gonna piss you off." He trod closer.

She held his stare. "Piss me off."

Closing the gap between them, Shane reached for her, and she laughed as he brought her off her feet and tugged her to his chest. Shane sighed at the eagerness with which she returned the gesture, the warmth of the new season embracing him at last. The blinding light had hit him, struck him right in the heart. One day he had been walking, oblivious that a woman like Rosemary existed, and the next day he'd been lost. He'd never seen it coming. Had never seen *her* coming. He'd do anything for the strong, capable woman in his arms.

"I'm going to try to be everything you deserve," he murmured in her hair, squeezing her. She fit just right.

"Shane." She raised her hands to his shoulders and her lips above his, an apology and so much more in her beautiful green eyes. Leaning down, she breathed sunshine. "You're already so much more than I could ever wish for." Wrapping her fingers in his hair, she pulled his head against hers and crushed her lips to his.

Epilogue

One month later

"Wait." Rose stopped before they could enter the hotel.
She rubbed her hands together, palms sweaty.

She hadn't expected New York to be so hot, but mid-May, the city was as scorching as it was alive and active. Shane peered at her, a question on his face. White light washed his cheeks and the bridge of his nose. The screens plastered to the sides of buildings shone down on them. He was gorgeous in a fitted tuxedo, blending right into the city life.

Rose was out of place, however.

Charlotte was a descent size, but it was nothing compared to the intimidating skyscrapers and loud colors that were Manhattan. But right now, Rose couldn't focus on that. She was going crazy with worry. Her heart had dropped all the way to the triangular tips of her red-bottomed heels. In one hour, they'd find out if the exhausting months of hard work had paid off. New York City wasn't brighter than the flash of panic detonating inside her. Heck, she was more nervous than she'd been on her first day at Lambda Digital. Her confidence was somewhere back home, maybe hiding under her bed and wondering where she'd run off to.

Everything was on the line. Lambda's future would be determined tonight, and Rose wasn't prepared to face the fact that all the work she and her team had done could soon come to a screeching halt. A draft of air gusted across her, escorting drops of perspiration farther down her back, exposed in an emerald evening gown.

"Don't be nervous." Shane's voice brought her gaze up.

The smile softening his features was enough to take away some of the jitteriness she was feeling. Shane was so cool and calm.

Too calm, if you asked her.

Isn't he worried about the results, too?

Twisting her waist, Shane brought her to face him. His expression was light with understanding as he pulled her hair from behind her ear. Lush sensations clenched her belly when he dropped his hand to hold the side of her throat and leaned forward, his scent tempting her to raise her nose to his chest and breathe deeper. Shane was her employee — almost officially, since he'd decided that following the competition he would put any rights he had to Lambda in the hands of Malcolm Fletcher — but he was also her lover and friend, and his display of affection warmed her soul.

"Whatever happens tonight, we're gonna make it through." He rubbed her neck with his thumb, making Rose's stomach flutter with more than nervousness. Shane brought his head to hers, his forehead laying on top of her own. "You know how I know, sugar?"

Bustling sounds encompassed them — people talking, shoes clicking on the sidewalk, horns blaring as cars tried to own the roads, doors opening and closing, music blasting. Rose was so absorbed by the man in front of her, staring at her with intense brown eyes, that she didn't care about anything else. "How *do* you know?" Rose wanted to kiss the raising corners of his lips.

"'Cause we already got through the hardest part."

Shane's voice dripped over her like sugar, and she wondered how she'd ever resisted him. He planted his lips on her hairline, and she sighed, pleasure following the touch.

He was right. They'd gotten through the hardest parts by finding each other, and now that they were together, Rose was holding on strong, come hell or high water.

"Okay." She smiled with him, determination bringing her chin up. "I'm ready."

"Well then, let's go, boss."

He quirked his eyebrow, and she giggled. Shane took his hand into hers, fingers locking. They walked through the pristine hotel lobby and to the private event.

If Shane had changed her, she couldn't say. But she could say that she'd learned a lot from him. Rose had learned trail tricks like how to tune her lateral balance by shifting her weight certain ways, depending on whether she was going up an incline or down a steep rock. North Carolina was home to some of the top biking trails in the nation. She'd learned that mountains were their most captivating at dawn when you saw the sun peeking through their dips and curves. Work and fun could be balanced. Strength came in all shape and sizes. Shane had opened her eyes to the potential that had been buried under years of pain and plans.

Rose hadn't wanted a man to change her, truth be told. She'd wanted a man who could make her *better*. She wanted Shane, forever.

He moved the tip of his finger to the sparkling diamond on her left hand. "I won't ever get over you wearing this," he said, squeezing her hand.

She looked up to him and smiled, filled with so much love and happiness that, for a moment, it was difficult to breathe.

When they'd landed in New York two nights prior and Shane had shown her to their penthouse suite, there'd been a surprise waiting for her. Opening the door, she'd gasped at the roses and romantic decor designing the elegant space. It had been stunning and had brought tears to her eyes. No one had ever done something so sweet for her. After she'd showered and changed into something more comfortable, Shane had guided her to the gigantic balcony. Rose had never seen something so beautiful than the candlelit table, painting a stunning portrait of Manhattan. Her heart soared when she'd turned around from admiring the beautiful skyline to see Shane Williams, the once bad-boy player, on one knee.

Her cheeks went hot, remembering the whole night.

It had been the best night of her life.

The engagement would be a long one. They both wanted everything sorted with Lambda before the wedding, but she was looking forward to spending the rest of her years standing and working beside him. At the end of the day, the most important thing she'd learned from Shane was that love wasn't perfect. It was messy. Love was sloppy. It was human.

While they searched for their seats, someone called to them both. "Rose. Shane."

They stopped. Rose's skin pricked. She hadn't spoken to Matthew Moreno since their phone conversation a month before. She didn't imagine he was happy with her. Rose and Shane approached Mr. Moreno, who was standing with his arm around the back of a blond-haired man. Rose recognized him as the company's partner, Brendon Blu.

"Mr. Moreno, about last time —"

Matthew spoke over her as if he didn't want her apology. "There is someone I wanted to introduce you to." Matthew didn't look away from Rose when he said it. "This is the COO of Moreno & Blu Associates." Matthew's eyes went soft as he glanced at the tall man at his side. "My husband, Brendon Blu. Brendon, this is Lambda's marketing director I told you about, Rose Berkowitz, and you know her partner and co-worker Shane Williams."

"Oh, I never forget a handsome face." Brendon's voice carried an airy and fun tone that made Rose automatically like him. "How are you, Shane? It's been ages."

"It's nice to see you again, Brendon." Shane untangled his fingers from Rose to give him a handshake.

The red tendril of fire on the side of Shane's neck — his enthralling tattoo she had come to form an obsession with — stretched when he bent forward to peck Brendon's cheeks. The opposite of stiff-shouldered Matthew, Brendon didn't come off as cold at all but warm and welcoming.

His smile was playful as he exchanged greetings with Shane. It made sense. He was the one with the dazzling list connections, while Matthew was all logistics.

"Rose." Brendon turned to her. The floral-print cloth, peeking from his breast pocket, matched the natural pink flush on his cheeks. "It's beautiful to finally meet you."

Her hand warmed when he picked it up. His lopsided smile was boyish and handsome all at once. Leaning forward, he brought her into an unexpected hug. "Thank you," he whispered against her ear, low enough that likely only she could hear. Leaving behind a subtle whiff of cologne, Brendon pulled away, misty-eyed.

Her heart squeezed. She didn't know much about his relationship with Mr. Moreno but she was glad to have helped someone find their happily ever after.

Blinking the moisture from her eyes, she nodded to him. Shane raised an eyebrow.

Matthew passed Rose a look like he knew exactly what his husband had said and he might be thankful, too. "We'll be going now. Enjoy yourselves." He spoke to them in the same formal tone he seemed to always use, classical music from overhead speakers mingling with his words

"See you both *really* soon." Brendon clamped his lips shut, as if trying to stifle a grin, before carrying a flute of bubbling champagne to his mouth.

She tried not to show her surprise at his suggestive tone. Matthew frowned and whispered something into his husband's ear. Brendon's cheeks puffed as he grinned and pecked Matthew on the cheek. Red wafting to the sides of his face, Matthew shook his head but Rose saw the smile in his eyes.

"Until later," Matthew said and pulled Brendon away quicker.

"What was that about?" Rose turned to Shane when he began guiding her through a crowd of flashing cameras and finely dressed businessmen and women to their assigned table, where family waited.

Shane's sister, Sam, and her husband and his brother, Trevor, had come from Georgia. They were speaking with Malcolm. Rose had asked Holton to come along. He and Olive should arrive any moment. Shane was awfully quiet. Rose raised her suspicious gaze to him.

"Is there something you're not telling me?" Did Shane have some information he wasn't sharing with her? Pulse speeding at the thought, Rose didn't want to have false hope, but as Shane returned a wicked smile, she allowed herself to dream.

"Nothing at all." Shane shrugged, but that wasn't all and she knew it.

"What's going on, really? Do you...?"

'See you both really soon.'

Her gown tickled her ankles as she stopped mid-stride. "Shane, you don't know who they picked, do you?"

His spider tattoo raised when he pushed a casual hand through his hair, which had been combed back neatly. "I might've gotten some insider information from an old friend."

Her jaw dropped. Was that why Shane was so calm? "Tell me."

"You'll find out soon."

Anticipation raised in tremendous swells up her chest. "Tell me. Tell me who."

Locking her in his arms, Shane bent his head to her ear. "I'm not gonna name names, sugar, but I'll say I think my boss will be happy with the results."

Rose gasped. Excitement bubbled forth, and she was just about to shout from the top of her lungs before Shane brought her into a kiss, effectively silencing her.

Shane Williams had taught her many things. She'd give him that. But the most important lesson she'd learned, she'd taught herself. Life wasn't some fairy tale, where Prince Charming came galloping in on his white horse to save the day. Every once in a while, Rose still woke up crying, the malicious nightmares finding ways to sneak into her mind. She realized she'd have to fight with all she had to rid herself of those memories, to release herself from the tremendous guilt she'd held on to for years. They had challenges ahead of them, more than she could count. But with Shane by her side, she knew she'd prevail. Plus, she'd heard she had a mean right hook.

"You did it," he whispered, pulling away slightly. "You saved Lambda."

"*We* did."

Shane took her cheeks into his hands, and, with him looking at her like she was the only woman in the world, her heart had never been so satisfied.

"I love you, Rosemary Berkowitz."

"I love you, too, Shane Williams."

She smiled then his lips came down on hers, and she was too busy kissing the man of her dreams to think about lessons, life, Prince Charming and nightmares, because, when she was in Shane's arms, nothing existed but them.

Ring. Ring. Lady Fate is calling. She says you're welcome.

More books from
Totally Bound Publishing

He's determined to master her.
But she's no man's submissive.

SIERRA
CARTWRIGHT
INTERNATIONAL BESTSELLER

I M P U L S E

SHOCK
WAVE

"Cartwright's writing binds you from the very beginning and
doesn't release its hold until well after the last page."
- Erin Noelle, USA Today Bestselling Author

Book one in the Impulse series

There can only be one victor…

BREWING PASSION

TAPPED

A HOT HOOK-UP CHANGES EVERYTHING

LIZ CROWE

Book one in the Brewing Passion series

One hot entrepreneur plus a driven saleswoman and sultry brewer: simmered in the craft beer world for a unique, sexy reading experience!

WENDI ZWADUK

She's always known who she wants

MY FAVORITE
MISTAKE

She's always known who she wanted. Now she needs to find the strength to make him see they're more than a mistake.

Book one in the Strike Force series

Had he found her again only to lose her to a stalker?

About the Author

L.T. Shade

Emerging author, Lauren Shade, known by her pen L.T. Shade, lives in tropical Miami, Florida. When she's not writing, she spends her time reading, watching really cheesy romantic comedies, overdosing on Cuban coffee, and hanging out with her amazing partner and her American Cocker Spaniel, Albie.

L.T. Shade loves to hear from readers. You can find contact information, website details and an author profile page at https://www.totallybound.com/